KEEPERS OF THE SUN

Jaye Sarasin

ISBN 978-0-9957151-4-1

Cover design by Jessica Bell.

www.parfoyspress.com

'Fascinating and gripping'

Sally Hart

Author of *Out of Her Mind*

For Lewis and Darcy

Contents

RUNA – A Regional United Nations Administrative Area

Chapter 1
The Mall

A fight in the atrium? Was that what all the noise was about?

Allie didn't want to get mixed up in a fight. Not when she'd just bought all this fabulous gear.

A man raced past, jostling her back against the wall, nearly wrenching the bags from her grasp. She winced and dragged her hand away but the guard – it was a guard – wasn't interested in her or her bags as he pounded towards the crowd in the centre.

People were shouting, swivelling round, craning their necks in the direction of the atrium where all the Ministries were located. She couldn't see what was happening, blinking against the rays of the sun filtering through the great stained-glass roof of the Avila Mall. The leaves of a giant palm and the waving tendrils of a rampant liana vying with it for the light above, blocked her view.

She'd been looking for the Embassy shuttle and wondering if Alaina was back already. She certainly didn't want to get involved in some sort of scuffle.

'I see they're cleansing the area,' a voice from in front of her said.

'I hope they give them a good hammering before they chuck them out!' said another.

She needed to cross the atrium to get to the entranceway and hesitated on the edge of the Paseo Nuevo. The central plaza was thronged with shoppers loaded with their purchases from the elegant boutiques and she couldn't see if Alaina had drawn up to the main entrance or not. The lush tropical vegetation bursting from every corner and concealing even the great steel doors of the Ministry of the Interior made it even harder to work out what was happening.

Hampered by her own bags and the bunch of flowers for her mum, she tried to keep to the edge of the Paseo but another guard, rushing towards the fountain in the middle of the atrium, pushed her towards the centre.

'Someone's stolen something from the Ministry,' a large woman with unnaturally blond hair reported over her shoulder to the man behind her, her voice filled with excitement.

More guards sprinted past. Voices babbled and then a small figure clutching a slim brown briefcase sprinted across the atrium to the central reservation and disappeared into the huge clump of trees and shrubbery.

A man standing next to Allie grunted. With a jolt to the heart she realised he was one of the four-eyed and couldn't prevent the horrified start it always gave her to see one. The eye on her side was watching her, but she knew the others were busy gazing at the surrounding world. The man was nervous, skittish, like a frightened horse when it senses something unknown.

He jerked his head upwards and Allie saw the movement in the branches above. It must be the fugitive climbing up to the canopy, only visible now and then as a flash of ragged cloth or a brown outstretched hand. Each time he disappeared almost immediately into the foliage, just a swaying of the gigantic hibiscus blooms and gourd flowers showing where he'd been. The man grunted again.

The child – it could only be a child – was almost at the third level. Without doubt one of the street urchins, rogues and pickpockets mostly, who managed to get into the Mall. In theory they were barred from entry but some always found a way in, no one ever knew how. More guards were running across the atrium floor, shoving people aside in their haste.

Allie watched the child coming out of the greenery overhead, scrambling perilously along an extended branch. The guards were crashing into the shrubbery below, shouting and waving their guns, unable to see what was going on above. Her eyes went back to the little figure swinging wildly towards the third level railing. If he could get there he'd be over and away. A security guard had appeared from the lifts on the third level but he was on the other side of the gallery.

The boy was extended to his full length, ignoring the dizzying height, the terrifying drop to the atrium floor. His hand brushed the railing and then fastened tightly on it. Allie was willing him on. He was going to make it. The guard on the far side stopped, realised what was going to happen, and pointed his weapon.

The four-eyed man wheezed in, the gun barked and for a second time appeared suspended. Then the child was plunging down, arms extended, branches whipping under the pressure and then springing back as he fell. Allie hoped beyond hope they'd break his fall enough.

The body hit the mosaic floor with an ugly thud. The man flinched and her stomach contracted. It was like a punch to the solar plexus, the sight of the small body and the slowly spreading pool of red.

'They didn't need to shoot him.'

She'd spoken aloud but no one was listening to her. The four-eyed man had slipped away into the crowd.

'There were two,' someone said. 'Where's the other one?'

The crowd babbled in excitement, pressing forward, elbowing her out of the way, clustering round the little form. Police and guards were ordering everyone back.

The large woman said, 'It's not just the thieving, it's the damage they cause.'

There were murmurs of agreement.

'They're a threat. Why they don't do a better job of protecting the Mall, I don't know.'

'What more can they do?'

A thin, scrawny youth answered, his voice thick with excitement. 'I heard tell they shoot 'em at night when they find 'em in here.'

All Allie's pleasure at the shopping expedition was swept away. It was true, of course, that the thieving was a worry. Some people maintained that the older children carried knives. They were called The Undesirables, inhabitants of the *barrios de chabolas*, the campamentos, the shanty towns outside the wealthy enclaves of the Malls and the residential condos.

'They live in the sewers and come out at night to look for food in the waste bins,' Santiago in her tutorial group had said. And she was buying all this expensive gear when these children were probably starving.

She still felt sick, shaky, at the memory of the small body on the atrium floor. Catching sight of Alaina's large but elegant frame, on the far side of the atrium she was relieved to be leaving.

Her friend signalled that she was going to fetch the embassy shuttle and Allie made her way to the front causeway where diplomatic traffic was allowed to come right to the door to collect their passengers. She'd been lucky that neither she nor Alaina had had classes that day so they'd been able to come to the Mall together. Pushing past excited groups who were chattering amongst themselves about what had happened, she eventually got to the high archway and put her bags down at the edge of the entrance, away from the hurly burly of people going in and out.

As she moved her bags to avoid those passing it occurred to her what Stick would say about her shopping expedition and her heart turned a somersault.

'You're just a shopping junkie,' he'd say, laughing at her.

True, she thought, looking down at all the bags containing the wonderful clothes and a dinky little moby hidden in a large belt buckle. But none of these things could fill the space in her life where Stick should have been. Her mother had only decided to bring her to Runa Five to get her away from Stick. She still felt the internal flame of anger at her mother's attitude, her total inability to see Stick's good points, her rigid insistence on the minimal communication during their separation. Her heart twisted at the thought of him, all alone, back in Kington, in that terrible tower block. He'd have been on the child's side.

Somebody barged past and she stepped back, stopped only by the root of an enormous weeping fig. Even the entrance to the Mall was tastefully smothered in greenery. Trying to calm her jittery nerves she admired the sprays of white orchids and caught the pungent smell of gardenias, their waxen flowers and leaves shining against the bark of the tree. It was like being in a tropical jungle in here, with all this vegetation, striving for a sun which would now kill it. Since the loss of the ozone layer and most of the oxygen in the air all plants had to be grown under specially tinted glass. It was strange how humans, having destroyed the greenery of the Old World of the Blind Ages, now tried so desperately to recreate it in the New.

With a start she caught a hint of movement from within the shrubbery. The dark eyes of a cornered animal peered out at her, blinking in terror. She looked quickly away and pretended to inspect more closely one of the flowers which tumbled from the tree. When the guard on the entranceway looked in her direction she moved her bags in front of the area where the urchin was hiding. More guards were crashing about, working their way through the undergrowth. He'd never be able to get away. This was the only exit. She felt her anger rise. What was wrong with these people?

The guards' voices were louder now. She ought to do something – but what? An image flashed before her mind's eye of the handout they'd been given on leaving Runa Four, warning of the consequences of any infringement of the laws in Runa Five, the vicious punishments handed out to foreigners and locals alike. She couldn't afford to get on the wrong side of the authorities here – it was just so important that she finish her course. Her future and Stick's depended on it. But she couldn't bear to see another child killed.

Alaina pulled the shuttle into the collection bay and tooted.

How would she ever forgive herself if she did nothing?

She waved Alaina closer, pointing to all the bags, and, as the low-slung shuttle drew alongside her, flung wide the rear passenger door. She placed the largest bag on the seat between herself and the guard, looked back into the dark, haunted eyes, and gestured.

The child was clamped to the spot.

Oh come on, come on.

She was beginning to sweat. Checking that the guard was not looking in their direction, she leaned nonchalantly across the side of the shuttle, hiding even more of what was going on, and gestured again.

The boy suddenly shot from the shrubbery, scrambling forward on hands and knees like a small animal, clutching something to his chest. He hurled himself into the well of the shuttle and curled into a tight ball, while Allie threw the rest of her bags onto the back seat. Tossing her sun cloak as casually as she could over the bags and child, she threw the flowers she'd bought her mum on top of them, covering the back seat and well. Alaina was gazing ahead, apparently bored. As she climbed in next to her friend the guard waved them forward to the great gate where entrances and exits were checked. If she were caught, Allie thought, her mother, let alone Alaina's, would never forgive her. Alaina pressed the button and they pulled away, hiccupping gently up to the gate house.

'Guess they'll eventually get the eco-drive right!' said Alaina in exasperation, pressing buttons and managing a neat shimmy to bring the shuttle in line with the guard's booth man stepped down, pushing his face against the window, and Allie's stomach contracted again. The oxygen shunt on her upper arm seemed to be clicking manically, but perhaps that was just her terror.

'Could you step out of the vehicle, please?' the man said.

CHAPTER 2

The campamento

Allie felt ill. She'd lose her place at college, be sent back in disgrace to Runa Four. Her mother would be distraught. Surely the guard must hear the thudding of her heart. She made a token movement to open her door.

Alaina smiled at the man and waved the diplomatic card in his face, he backed away and they swept out of the gate onto the main corridor.

For a second Allie couldn't breathe. 'I didn't know you were allowed to use the card.' Her voice sounded high and thin, contrasting with the idiot pounding of her heart.

'I'm not.' Alaina chuckled. 'But the stupid mother leaves it in the car. I don't usually need it.' She pressed more buttons corresponding to the embassy compound and the shuttle slipped itself effortlessly into the flow of traffic on the main road.

'So who's our little pal in the back?' She swivelled round to peer into the rear of the car, seeing only the spray of flowers.

The shuttle meanwhile had pulled away from the Mall and was making its way gently towards the corridor leading to the Viejo de Avila, the mountain on which the ministerial and ambassadorial homes were based. Following the great earthquake and the destruction of most of Valparaiso and Santiago they'd all been moved to Avila, two hundred kilometres north of the Atacama Desert. The embassy compound enjoyed the most amazing views of the city and the Pacific ocean.

'Didn't you see the excitement?'

'No. I heard some people saying there were two thieves loose in the Mall but I was too busy getting the shuttle.'

'They shot one,' said Allie shortly. She thought again of the little body lying on the atrium floor and her voice shook. 'This one's trying to escape… We're helping him… They're only children.'

'Right.'

Alaina at her most laconic, Allie thought.

Her friend made some minor adjustments on the console, as the shuttle began its slow ascent, saying. 'So what are you going to do with him?'

'Let him go.'

Alaina raised an elegantly drawn eyebrow. 'You Brits are always such suckers for the underdog. I sure hope he doesn't take all our bribe money with him when he leaves us.'

Allie grinned. Her heart had finally settled into its normal rhythm.

'You're just pretending to be hardboiled.'

Alaina laughed.

'*Hé, chiquito*,' she yelled to the small figure in the back who had carefully lifted his head above the seat. 'Keep your head down. *Cabeza abajo*, okay?' And then, to Allie, 'So where are we going to let him out?'

'Well we can't let him go here because of the cameras. They're all along the corridor up to the tunnel. We'd be visible to the sky-route users, as well.'

Alaina frowned and chewed her lip, pulling at one of her long braids, the red entwined ribbon bright against her ebony skin.

'There's the bit alongside the ravine after the tunnel. The drop off to the rocks is so steep there they haven't bothered with cameras or fences. The sky-route goes round the other side of the mountain, so they won't see us either.' She laid her hand along the seat back and tapped. '*Hé, chiquito*, is it all right if we drop you near the Avila Slip?'

'*Si.*' A whisper from the back.

'What happened then? They shot his pal? Heard someone say they'd stolen a briefcase from a guy at the Ministry of the Interior. Can't see that that'll be very useful in the campamento.'

'Briefcases are the latest thing there, I hear.'

Alaina grinned and Allie smiled back affectionately. Daughter of the American ambassador, Alaina was her best friend and anchor in this strange new world. Not that the world was so very different to the one back home in Runa Four, where the division between the Haves and the Have-nots was almost as bad. She sometimes felt guilty about the comfort of her own life here, especially since knowing Alaina. Allie's mother was surgeon to the clinic serving the ambassadorial condos, and their living near the embassy compound had thrown her and Alaina together.

They were heading towards the Viejo tunnel, on a road curving round the mountainside, looking down on the Avila Valley. Where before there must have been forests and farms and green fields, now all you could see was a barren landscape – scalped earth and stone, pockmarked with clumps of the mustard-coloured weed, the only thing to grow naturally in the sun's death-dealing rays. As her gaze drifted over the view she thought how much the world had lost, registering distantly a buzzing noise but, lost in her thoughts, paying it no attention, seeing only the sun-blasted land before her.

The buzz became more insistent and spinning round in her seat she spotted, to her horror, a small traffic camera drone swooping high above their heads. Was it watching them?

'Uh oh,' said Alaina. 'Looks like we've got friends,' and yelled again without turning, 'Keep your head down. *Cabeza abajo*! Okay!'

'Actually,' she said to Allie, looking across to the flow of traffic going the other way, 'I think it's fine. They're after that bunch over there.' She nodded towards what looked like some kind of accident on the opposite carriageway. 'They're heading that way. No problemo!' She consulted the console and made a few adjustments to the music channel as they entered the tunnel.

'Have you heard from him then?' She didn't need to say who the 'he' was.

'No,' said Allie, her heart still jumping. 'We agreed to just the one email a month.' She sighed.

'So you're scared he'll forget you?'

No. That wasn't what Allie was scared of. She was scared he'd get bored, get frustrated and do something stupid, like hacking into the Pentagon for fun. That then they'd be parted for life and not just for the term of her studies.

'No,' she said. 'No, Stick won't forget me.' She wished her voice held greater conviction.

They came out of the tunnel onto the great bend above the ravine. On the one side the massive slanting rock face, huge grey slabs of slate where the corridor had been cut into the mountain side. On the other the drop into the ravine, the campamento and beyond that the sea. They were on the Avila Slip.

One of their tutors had told them that the Slip was named after the great earthquake which had splintered the Pacific coast from San Francisco down to Avila, Santiago and Valparaiso, splitting the Viejo Mountain in half in the process and sliding all the seaward land into the ocean. And with the land it had taken all those hundreds of thousands who'd lived between the mountains and the sea, down to their deaths in the Pacific. People thought they were still down there, he said, swimming against the tide, trying to get home.

Alaina pulled to a halt and Allie got out and looked over the edge, to where the ravine fell away below them. First the almost sheer drop with the odd outcrop and then the lumpy boulders and shale at the bottom of the cliff. Light glinted off the tin roofs of the hovels of the campamento and the muddy waters of the estuary beyond. Here they were reasonably safe from being observed.

'Right, *chiquito*, end of the line.'

Alaina was unfolding her tall, powerful frame from the shuttle when they both heard the far-off thrum of an engine and whup-whup of rotor blades. Allie spun round and grabbed the top of her door and Alaina stopped, frozen, halfway out. They both looked up, seeing the distant helicopter heading across the sky. They'd forgotten the Coastguards. Sitting on the bend they were perfectly visible.

They watched anxiously but the helicopter didn't deviate from its original path – probably headed for the port, way beyond Avila – and the sound gradually faded as it disappeared around the shoulder of the Viejo mountain. Drawing a ragged breath, Allie turned to Alaina and grimaced.

How could she have embarked on this crazy scheme, putting Alaina at risk as well as herself?

'So far, so good!' said Alaina cheerfully, opening the back-passenger door. The small figure slid out, shivering despite the heat, the thin, ragged shirt providing little protection against the vicious rays of the sun. He made no move, his face still pale with terror, still clutching the case to his chest.

'All right,' said Allie gently, 'you can go.' She pointed back down to the start of the Slip where a small path had been illegally cut into the hillside leading down to the campamento.

The boy made a small movement and Alaina stretched out her arm, barring his route. 'One minute,' she said, 'Not with the loot you don't.' She opened her hand flat, palm upwards. 'I'm perfectly happy for you not to be blasted but you can give me back the case.'

She was between him and the path leading to the campamento, and behind him was only the edge and the sheer drop.

'You can go by all means but I'm not going to be party to theft. And get a move on because I'm late for my mom already.'

The boy's eyes flickered and with no warning he turned away and leapt into the void.

'Holy Cow!' Alaina said.

22

Allie felt her heart plunge, her stomach turn over. No, no! They'd killed him.

Alaina was at the edge looking over.

'Gee, how lucky can you get?'

Almost in a state of suspended animation Allie joined her. He must have known that the outcrop would break his fall but he'd misjudged and had slid down from it, lying on a small ledge, hampered by the briefcase still clutched tightly to him. As he twitched small stones skittered down and he made no attempt to move further.

'He's a goner, for sure, if he doesn't drop that case.'

Light-hearted with relief Allie looked towards the path down the cliff and judged the route to the boy carefully. 'I can get across to him all right. All that rock-climbing with your brother should stand me in good stead. I'll get him to the campamento and then head for home. You'd better just go on before your mum blows a fuse. It's no distance to walk from here.'

'You sure? I'd have thought it would be kinda dangerous down there all on your lonesome, even if you do get the kid down okay.'

Allie gestured down the valley. 'Look. It's no problem. You can see the church spire from here and the clinic's apparently right next to it. Students go there regularly, you know that.'

'You haven't though, girl.'

'I'll be fine.' Allie was determined. 'Now we've got him this far.'

Alaina's brow creased and she consulted the meter built into her sleeve. 'You've had more than thirty minutes direct sunlight already so you've almost had your day's allowance.'

'I'm well creamed up.' Allie pulled the sun visor down over her forehead and grinned at Alaina. 'Chill, friend.' It wasn't like the cheerful and outgoing Alaina to be worried.

'What shall I tell your mom?'

'Tell her I'm hoping to see your brother. That should keep her happy.' Randy, son of the American ambassador and Alaina's half-brother, the young man her mum had now decided would be good for her.

'You don't have to do this, kiddo.'

Allie smiled at her. ''Oh, you know, us Brits and the underdog.'

Alaina sighed. 'I'll wait to see you get to the bottom all right.'

Allie made her way down the path until she was parallel to the child and then climbed over the rickety railing and inched her way along a little ledge in his direction. He was lying with his back against the cliff face, balanced precariously on the rock shelf below the outcrop, a sheer drop beneath him. He wasn't moving and she hoped he was conscious. The ledge she was on, no more than a few inches wide, would take her below him and just as she felt for the next place for her foot she heard the whisper of a vehicle above.

It stopped, there was a silence and then the slam of a door. The sound of boots on the road surface seemed unnaturally loud but she could see nothing from her position clamped to the cliff face. She flattened herself even more against the rock. Then she heard the voice.

'Hola, Ms Hamilton. Are you okay?'

Her muscles would have sagged in relief if she could have allowed them to. It was only Mateo, driver of one of the delivery wagons that brought supplies to the embassy compound.

'Yeah, sure, I'm fine.' Alaina sounded very relaxed. 'I just spotted a lesser spotted corncrake over there and I was waiting to see if it would come any closer.'

In the silence which followed Allie could imagine Mateo's confusion.

'It's a big bird,' said Alaina helpfully. It sounded as if she was flapping her arms, adding, 'He must be looking for fish out there.'

Allie pictured her grin. 'Don't tell my mom. I'm supposed to be revising.'

Mateo laughed. 'Surely not, Ms Hamilton. I'd better get on.' The footsteps retreated. 'Best of luck with the bird watching. See you later perhaps.'

'Thanks Mateo.'

The van door slammed and the vehicle continued on its way up to the embassy. Alaina peeked over the edge, gave Allie a thumbs-up and disappeared again.

Allie took several deep breaths and loosened her hand from the piece of rock to which it was convulsively clamped. She looked towards the boy but it didn't appear he'd registered what had happened. The pallor of the strained face, sapping the strong brown colouring, made the blue-black hair seem even darker. He tried to move and groaned, his face streaked with blood and dust.

Continuing her perilous shuffle along the ledge she put out a hand towards him, tentatively, as to a wounded animal, and saw the terror start again in his eyes. Trying not to worry about the void beneath them she edged along until she was directly below him, the ledge becoming narrower and narrower until it petered out entirely just beyond her right foot.

'You'll have to come this way,' she said, heart jumping in her chest, trying to think of the words. '*Aquí.* Here. We can only get down this way.'

She put out her hand again and grabbed his jacket as he twisted away, still keeping the briefcase clamped to him.

'Careful,' she said, pulling him gently to her, feeling the weight of his smelly, frail body against her arm. She looked into the terrified eyes. 'It's all right. I'll try to get you down but you'll have to help me.'

Eyes still wide with dread, whether at the danger they were in or at herself she didn't know, he slid slowly her way and she clamped an arm round the thin bony ribs, sweat popping out all over her as a stone rattled down the cliff face below them. She wiped a clammy hand and tried not to think about the drop. Concentrating on finding a solid purchase for each foot before moving on she shuffled along the thin line of rock, bearing most of the boy's weight and grabbing at whatever splintered outcrop she could see. Finally they came to a wider section where he could slide own next to her.

Feeling something brush her inner arm, she found a small green plant that had wedged itself in the strap of her wristcom. It even had a little root. Hidden from the sun's rays in a crack in the rock she hadn't noticed it. So rare was it to see green plants in the wild these days, except in an Enclave, that she didn't want to throw it away but stuffed it into her pocket and pressed forward. They'd reached the path which was easier but the boy was weakening and she kept her arm around his waist as they slithered down together. At least his oxygen shunt hadn't been damaged in the fall.

Once on level ground again she felt safer and looked back up the cliff to where Alaina was watching anxiously. She waved and mimed that she would make her own way back, that Alaina should just leave her.

Alaina was yelling something. It sounded like her mother and the cavalry. Allie waved cheerfully in return and they set off, she supporting the injured boy as best she could. Small dead bushes at the base of the cliff hampered their progress, the thin black branches snapping as they brushed through them. Then came taller thickets, leafless and vicious, that grabbed spitefully at their faces and hands as they passed, snagging the skin and drawing blood. But at last they stumbled out onto the narrow, rutted road that led to the campamento.

The shanty town was a dismal stinking hole, criss-crossed with foul-smelling ditches covered with green slime and filled with refuse of every description. Even in one, Allie noticed shuddering, the bloated corpse of some animal. The chaotic jumble of shacks built of driftwood, pallets and packing cases, some with corrugated iron roofs, crowded to the edge of the road and her heart began to beat faster. However, in the distance were one or two more solid buildings and the spire of the large, white-painted church so the centre was in sight.

They stumbled on, exposed to the full heat of the sun, blasting even through Allie's creams and visor and sun cloak. Where the boy's body was clamped to her side her skin burned.

The boy seemed to feel it too and stood away from her. 'I can do,' he said and then swayed, his pallor becoming even more pronounced.

Allie grabbed him. 'What's your name? Where do you live? Show me.'

The eyes that looked at her were those of a condemned man and he seemed to make a heroic decision. 'Jaime,' he whispered, gesturing in the direction of the church. 'Down there.'

They staggered forward. A small child watched them go by and scurried away. She was aware of people on the fringes of her vision watching their painful progress with incurious eyes. Some were clearly the *indigenas*, Indians, offspring of the mighty Incan civilisation of centuries ago. Others were from the lowland areas, a mixture of races, some descendants of the Spanish invaders who had pillaged much of Runa Five. Allie remembered how appalled she'd been at the treatment of the native peoples by the *conquistadores*, the murder of the reigning Lord Inca, Atahualpa, after they'd taken a huge ransom of gold to spare him.

Several of the people they passed lay, apparently lifeless, in makeshift doorways – conserving, she realised, their tiny allocation of the precious oxygen filters which they received from the government. She'd never really appreciated her own implant until that moment. One woman had the tell-tale vacant eyes and strange movements of someone suffering oxygen damage from a faulty arm pack. A man was slumped against the wall of his shack, whittling a piece of wood with a lethal looking knife. He looked up as they passed, a spike of something unpleasant in his dark eyes.

Allie's heart lurched. She'd have liked to go faster, escape this area, get to the Centre and the Clinic as soon as possible, but Jaime was weakening. At that moment, a young man came towards them from one of the myriad alleyways between the shacks and she braced herself for confrontation. To her relief he just went to Jamie's other side, supporting him, helping her hold him upright. He gestured to Jaime that he would take the briefcase but Jaime shook his head fiercely.

They must be getting close, Allie thought, as the huts and hovels began to give way to solider concrete buildings, many of the walls covered in graffiti and peeling posters. They passed some small adobe style villas, clearly houses belonging to the better off, a couple even with gardens and surrounding walls.

Allie was beginning to flag. She wondered how much longer she had before her own oxygen implant needed to be replenished. It had been at a 100% when she'd left in the morning. By the end of the day it would need a couple of hours in a piped oxygen environment to restore the levels.

They passed an official looking building on their left with *Farmacia* and *Clinica* on a small board next to the door. A man outside was hosing down the various scrawls of graffiti covering the front wall and tearing off the poster she'd seen elsewhere – *LIBJU*. It was no doubt one of the many small protest groups which, so her newspod maintained, proliferated in the campamentos. The building must be the university's outreach clinic where some of the students from her college occasionally volunteered and that would mean they were nearing the campamento's centre. She wondered if she should take Jaime inside but decided it was the first place the police would look. At least they were nearly there.

'Where now?' she said, as they came to a large square.

'The church,' said the young man, suddenly and unexpectedly smiling at her, white teeth highlighting the dirty and stained skin. She smiled back and between them they half dragged and half carried Jaime the next few metres across the square and through the big wooden doors of the church courtyard. It was cooler there in the shade of the walls and they sat Jaime down on the edge of a small fountain at the courtyard's centre.

A tall gaunt figure swept towards them from inside the Church, black vestments swinging, stopping in front of the young man and looking at him inquiringly. He'd obviously been warned of their coming and looked with pale eyes at Allie as her helper talked fluently in a local patois – Quechua, she supposed, one of the most used Indian languages in the area. It didn't sound like that of many of the embassy workers, Mapudungun speakers, Mapuche Indians who 'd mostly come from the lands south of the Atacama.

The priest nodded and turned to Allie.

'This is Padre Lamar,' said her newfound friend. 'He will look after Jaime.'

'We are most grateful that you have helped our small brother.' The man spoke in an oily and sanctimonious manner and Allie took an immediate dislike to him, wishing they didn't have to leave Jaime in his hands. He looked like the sort who'd hand him over to the police in no time if a bit of pressure was put on him.

'Rafa,' the priest said to the second boy, making no effort himself to help Jaime slumped on the fountain's edge, 'Go and tell Rosalita that Jaime is back after you have accompanied the Señorita.' He turned to Allie.

'Thank you, Señorita, a thousand times.' Once more the oily smile. 'Rafa will show you the way.' He put out his hand and Allie took it unwillingly, feeling it cold and clammy in her palm. She withdrew her hand hastily and then put it out towards Jaime, smiling an apology at Rafa, standing next to him, as she did so.

'I'm sorry, Jaime,' she said. 'I can't go without the briefcase. I'm happy to have been able to help but I'll have to hand that back.'

The priest's smile left his face. He said something sharply in Quechua to Rafa and then turned to Allie.

'We will look after the briefcase, Señorita.'

He was looking down his nose at her, trying to bring the full weight of adult authority to bear upon her. Well, he needed to think again.

'I'm sorry,' she said, her voice as even as she could manage. 'Since it was my fault, in a way, it's got here I think I ought to return it.'

The priest's brows twitched together. 'I think you do not know where you are, Señorita.'

In that moment Allie became aware of the small crowd at her back, people who'd drifted slowly in as she'd been talking, people with shabby clothes and thin starved faces like Jaime, and it struck her in full force that she was here alone. Despite the heat of the sun she felt a cold hand encircle her heart and the beginnings of terror as she saw the animosity and anger in the priest's eyes. Looking around the square she knew that no one here would protect her.

Chapter 3
Yupanqui and Dr Chavez

A patch of darkness in a corner of the courtyard thickened and swayed.

'Can I help, Señorita?'

The crowd fell silent as the figure moved out of the shadows. He was definitely an Indian, with the big bold cheekbones, the flat plane of the cheeks and the thatch of black burnished hair of the local people. But he was tall, too tall for one of the local *indigenas*. With the light glinting on the oiled skin and the soaring eyebrows you could almost believe in an antique Incan God.

'We have to thank you.'

Everybody moved back as he came forward and Allie registered with surprise that he had spoken in perfectly unaccented English. 'May we know your name?'

'My name's Allie Warrender.' Her voice shook.. 'And might I ask who you are?'

He smiled and inclined his head. 'They call me Yupanqui.'

Strange to see someone who was, by modern standards where everyone covered themselves up against the sun, semi-naked. He was clad only in cropped baggy trousers and a short-sleeved tunic. A sash went from one shoulder to a belt and leather pouch and a slip of leather encircled his left wrist.

And something else seemed strange as well. The oxygen pack clipped to the gleaming muscles of the upper arm looked different in some way, she couldn't quite work out how. Allie's mind spun. It must be okay. While it was true that the mountain Indians, more used to the rarefied air of the upper Andes, seemed to need less oxygen than those from the lowlands no ordinary person could exist in the ravaged atmosphere without any added oxygen at all.

The man swung round to look at the priest and Allie was reminded again of the ancient Incans, the Bright Ones, the sons of the Sun God.

The priest was obviously still annoyed and said something rapidly in Quechua.

The god looked down at him, raising one eyebrow.

Allie's hand was still extended, holding one side of the briefcase. She didn't know what to do. One false step and she might never get out of this place alive. Although, illogically, she knew that this Yupanqui, or whatever his name was, wouldn't let her be harmed.

He turned back to her and smiled again. 'You may safely entrust it to me, Señorita.' Instead of the rather sullen expression common to the people round them she saw the glint of humour in his eyes, not the dark eyes of the local Indians, like Jaime's or Rafa's, but an incredible blue. 'Don't worry. I'll make sure it gets to the right quarters.'

Scarcely knowing what she did Allie released the briefcase into his hand.

'I mustn't be seen.' Again the charming smile. 'Thank you again for your help…for Jaime.'

She was about to reply, wondering what she'd be able to tell Alaina, how she could justify the missing briefcase, when she heard the screaming of sirens and two police cars roared into the square outside, visible through the open doors of the courtyard.

Jaime looked up, panic plain on his face. Rafa also looked alarmed.

A large man in uniform climbed out of the first car, followed by two of his men. He strode towards them across the square and through the great church doors, the crowd shrinking back before him. Small dark eyes glittered in a round face and Allie could tell he thought himself highly important as she contemplated the narrow moustache, the thickset fleshy jowls above a bull neck and the thin strip of hair combed over a balding pate.

We have a station on Mars, she reflected, but we still don't have a satisfactory solution to male baldness. Was he Alaina's cavalry or – a sudden, heart-stopping thought – did he know what she'd done?

He barked an order to one of his men and she could see he only needed a small excuse to let them tear the campamento apart. Stopping in front of her he addressed himself to her alone, ignoring the surrounding people.

'My name is Capitan Gutierrez. Have these people been troubling you, Señorita?'

She saw the blaze in Jaime's eyes, weak as he was, and her heart began to beat uncontrollably.

'No, no, not at all.' She was surprised how unruffled her voice sounded. 'I came to see Padre Lamar.'

He obviously didn't believe her.

A man in the crowd pressed forward and one of the policemen struck him savagely with the butt end of the gun, motioning him back. The casual brutality of the blow revolted her and her heart slowed to a steady beat as she stood there, aware of the stillness and everybody waiting.

'Señorita Hamilton was concerned for you. There is a report that one of these vermin got into the Mall today. His friend did not get away so well.'

'I don't know about that.' Allie gestured to Jaime. 'This young man injured himself helping me. I'd climbed down the cliff to get this plant,' – she held up the small straggly green plant which had got caught in the strap of her wristcom – 'and I got stuck. It's so unusual to see something green growing out in the wild I was intrigued. I'm from Runa Four and we don't have such a plant.' It was actually common gorse and one of the very few plants to survive in odd parts of Runa Four but she didn't think he'd know that.

'The boy saw what happened and came to help me but he fell himself. But God is merciful.' She waved her hands in what she hoped was a pious manner. 'We both got down safely. I came to make a contribution to the church in thanks for our preservation.'

She could see his confusion and disbelief. 'No doubt Miss Hamilton told you that I was trying to get the plant.' The children were melting away into the shacks, the crowd dispersing. 'I'm afraid she must have panicked and brought you out on a false errand. I am, of course, very grateful.'

It was plain he thought she was lying although he didn't know why. And that he didn't really want to rescue her. That if the stupid little cow wanted to risk her life in the *arroyo* it was her own affair. But he must know that her friend was the daughter of an ambassador so he couldn't just leave her there.

He said in irritation, brushing the wisp of hair over his bald head, 'Well, the cameras in the Mall will tell us what happened so I won't need to trouble you about it, Señorita. Please allow me to escort you back to your parent.'

Her breath caught in her throat. She'd never thought of the cameras. But surely they wouldn't have been able to see what had happened at the exit gate? Frantically hoping her face didn't show her panic, she realised she needed to do what he said. It would serve no purpose to refuse his offer and perhaps even arouse his suspicion.

'Thank you. You're very kind.'

She turned to the priest who was watching her with patent dislike and gave him the card containing the small amount of bribe money she had on her, nodding to Jaime and his friend, seeing in the empty stillness of the churchyard corner that the Incan god had vanished along with the briefcase.

She walked straight-backed to the police car and climbed in without looking behind.

'Corncrake!' she said to Alaina, at the entrance to the common room the following morning. 'Corncrake! Fishing? Isn't the name a clue?'

Alaina chuckled. 'You see lesser spotted ones out over the ocean all the time.'

Allie laughed.

Her friend waved a hand. 'Hope it didn't cause any problem getting the Guardia out. I watched to see where you went and was a bit freaked out at the thought of you in the campamento all on your own. I mean, our little tea leaf wasn't a problem,' – Alaina had acquired some strange slang from her English literature lessons – 'but he wasn't the only one down there. So I phoned for reinforcements. Said you'd seen someone who'd fallen and gone to help.'

'I was thankful. All sorts of nasties down there, although…' Allie thought for a second and decided not to mention the god, '… although the kid seemed harmless. A priest of some kind wanted to take the briefcase. I never did discover what was in it. And I don't know if it'll get back to whoever owns it but I rather doubt it.'

That at least was true. She didn't want to share her fear over what the cameras might reveal with Alaina and fortunately her interest lay elsewhere.

'Heard from Stick?'

'Just a mail.' Allie sighed. The few words reporting his lack of success in the job search had contained nothing personal, nothing to reassure her that he still loved her and wanted her back.

Their goodbyes had been unsatisfactory to say the least of it. She remembered the stiffness of Stick's thin bony body as she'd held him for the last time, the way he had, at first, resisted her touch and then finally succumbed with a groan into her arms. She'd clasped him to her with all her force but he'd reared away in frustration.

'You don't have to go,' he said. 'You could stay.'

'But it's the chance of a lifetime.'

'And you'd rather do that than stay with me.' He was sulky, bitter, the pale blue eyes sparking in anger.

'You know that's not true, Stick. You're the one who encouraged me to become a doctor when I wanted to give up.'

'But you know your mother is just trying to part us.'

He'd rested his forehead gently against hers, holding her eventually away from him, saying heavily, 'It's no good, Allie. Your mum will never hear of you linking up with me. And anyway, do you think you'd enjoy living in the towers, surrounded by these stinking estates?'

She'd almost brought it off, she thought bitterly, until her mum's intervention. Her mother had set much store by her friendship with Jake, her great friend in their big adventure in the Enclave, and Jake's mum had almost swayed it by telling her what a vital role Stick had played in exposing the conspiracy at Ecopro and in their rescue from the blazing buildings.

But then it had all collapsed. The school's new auditors had detected Stick's hacking into the Educational Resource Centre's computer, altering a grade for a fellow pupil to enable her to get to university. And when she'd lost her place she'd swung violently against Stick, telling the auditor that it had been his idea all along, that she would never have dreamed of trying to alter the grade otherwise.

Allie's mum had been appalled. The thought that her daughter was becoming involved with Stick Michaelis from one of the lowest sink estates would signal the end of all her hopes. To say that he came from the other side of the tracks was to totally underestimate the difference in their worlds.

'How could you have been such an idiot, Stick? When I could have persuaded my mum to get you a job in the Hospital Statistics Office. You'd have been able to play with your stupid computers all day long and they'd probably have paid you to hack into the Daily Times.'

His face had been pale under the curly red hair; the blue eyes distant. 'I never gave myself higher grades – and I deserved that job – but if you choose to think that I'm a cheat...'

'I didn't say that, but you've put yourself in an impossible position since everyone else will think that you are.'

And there was this marvellous offer – a student place at the prestigious Avila Medical College in Runa Five, under the personal oversight of Dr Chavez, the world-renowned authority on biogenetics, one of Allie's chosen subjects.

He'd disengaged himself. 'You don't need to go.'

'For Pete's sake, Stick. You know I'll never get another chance like this. This woman is the tops – absolutely the tops. Mum says it's an honour to work for her and she'll give lectures at my college.'

'You don't really love me.'

The thought struck her that she would lose Stick, that his pride wouldn't let him wait for her.

Alaina was looking at her and pulling a face. Her expression must have given her away, she thought, and Alaina always did say that love affairs were really the pits. But her friend's voice was sympathetic.

'The guy'll come round,' she said lightly, and then, as they came into the common room and saw half of the students crowded to the window, looking out, 'I wonder what those idiots have been up to.'

'I think we were totally justified,' Isidora's shrill voice was saying. 'Somebody has to stand up for justice and this college is too cowardly to speak out. They think we'll be impressed by the fact that they're having a government minister come to lecture us on citizen's rights.'

'Citizen's rights!' another voice said. 'This college is just as guilty of ignoring people's rights as the government. Do you know what the cleaners are paid?'

'The college does a lot of good in the campamentos,' said the tall, lanky Randy, Alaina's half-brother.

Allie's eyes turned to where everyone was looking at the great steel and glass building visible through the common room windows and saw for the first time the banner displayed across one side of the research block in enormous letters.

LIBERTAD Y JUSTICIA.

They must have got inside two rooms at opposite ends of the block and had somehow strung the banner across. Isidora was still ranting away but Allie could see the other students were being turned off by the angry stridency.

'Is that the group that was trying to stop us getting into college today?' she asked, thinking of the commotion at the entrance. She'd been grabbed by a tall, roughly clad young man as she'd entered the college gates, holding her back while he shouted something at her about the police burning houses down. She'd been shoved about by several of the protesters and had missed her footing, only managing to regain her balance and free herself from the man's grip with difficulty. It had been quite scary.

'I don't know,' said Alaina. 'I don't know if it's the same group. I had to be here early this morning so I missed most of the demonstration. Why they're picking on the college when there's loads more on-the-mark targets I wouldn't know. Mom says there's any number of protest groups about at the moment.'

A tall young man with spiky hair made a face at Alaina's comment and thrust a leaflet into Allie's hand. 'Just read it, eh?' he said.

'Thanks, Santiago,' said Allie, sorry for him because she knew he was in love with the wealthy and passionate Isidora and, as far as she could see, didn't stand a chance of her returning the feeling.

A sharp movement flashed in the doorway and Allie turned to see Dr Chavez appear and make her way to the front, clearly rigid with anger and quelling the racket by sheer magnetic force of personality. She swept up onto the small dais at the front of the common room and looked down at them. The silence was absolute. The proud Indian lines of the cheekbones were accentuated by the hair pulled back into a kind of bun, and the dark eyes gleamed above the half glasses. She was white lipped with anger and her words were a whiplash.

'I won't bother asking who's responsible here. The idiots who've trespassed in the labs in order to promote their half-baked political opinions have succeeded in ruining the work of months. It's difficult enough trying to help the poor and suffering in this part of Runa Five, given the administration we have at the moment, without you privileged morons wrecking the small amount of good we can do. Trekking bacteria and God knows what else through the sterile areas.' She paused, still clearly enraged. 'And – for your information – the college is one of the few employers here who actually help staff with their difficulties with the authorities.'

They sat stunned; the perpetrators shame faced. Isidora pouted.

Dr Chavez looked suddenly tired. 'Well, enough said. I'll give you your work back here and you can go to your classes afterwards.'

She handed out their returned essays, everybody scanning them anxiously to see what she'd said. Dr Chavez demanded an exceptionally high standard and if your work was slack the comments were scathing. Allie wondered if she'd suffer the same fate and was relieved to see that, apart from one or two lines labelled 'sloppy reasoning' the end notes were generally favourable.

' Well shoot!' murmured Alaina, reading the comments on her own essay.

Dr Chavez caught Allie as she was going to her next classroom and stood to one side with her as the rest left. She looked at her keenly. 'This is generally excellent work, Allie. You've thought about it carefully.'

This was high praise from Chavez and Allie felt a warm glow.

'Have you thought about gene therapy as a career?'

Allie restrained a grimace. 'Gene therapy has always made me a little nervous.' Especially, she thought, after the years of abuse. 'I don't object to our trying to modify genes to remove the things that are wrong but the idea that we can create superman or woman worries me.'

One of the last great idiocies of the Blind Ages following the advent of the improved Crispr technology had been the birth of the new creatures, half animal half human, creatures with snouts and wings and sheep's brains, genetically modified for some crazy task or other. Most of the abominations, the so-called chimera embryos – named after a mythical fire-breathing monster, part goat, part lion, part snake – had been destroyed or had simply proved unable to live. The four-eyed, though, had somehow survived. They'd been bred to be soldiers before the days of the Species Integrity Protocol, one of their tutors had told them, some mad general imagining that better sight would afford a kind of military advantage.

'Didn't work though,' he'd said. 'The psychiatrists say that four eyes provide too much sensory input and it leads to brain overload. The ones who can function at all are usually just silent and,' he sought for the right word, 'sullen.'

They'd escaped the small lab where they'd been spawned and, cut off for many years by the great landslide in a small village in the mountains, they'd intermarried and produced children like themselves but rarely came to town.

'It's what can go wrong I worry about,' Allie said.

'That is sadly true – which is why we need researchers of a certain calibre to ensure that that doesn't happen.' Dr Chavez was looking out of the window at the banner then returned her gaze to Allie. '*Libertad y justicia*, freedom and justice,' she said. 'Easy words. We've lost so much that was good from the past and they imagine that they can recreate it with a few banners.'

It looked as if she would have said more but a group of lab technicians, Velasquez, Amaru and his twin, Kantuta, were passing and they stopped to ask Dr Chavez about some piece of equipment and the moment passed.

Allie looked at the three faces, puzzled, thinking that she must have seen one of the twins somewhere else, and her eyes followed them down the corridor. And then she realised it must have been Amaru she'd seen in the campamento, spotting him through the window of the police car. It hadn't really registered at the time as she hadn't recognised him without his white coat.

She turned to leave with Alaina and Randy but Dr Chavez was speaking again.

'By the way, Allie, we're having a small gathering in honour of the new UN representative for Runa Five the day after tomorrow. I've invited your mother and I hope that you'll accompany her as well.' She nodded at Alaina. 'You and your brother too, of course, since your mother will be there as the ambassador. I'll speak to her this afternoon.'

That would be exciting, Allie thought. Her mum viewed Dr Chavez with something approaching reverence and it was a real honour to be invited. It would be great to meet someone as important as the UN Representative for Runa Five. She wanted to ask what the woman's purpose was over this side of the Andes but they were interrupted yet again, this time by the secretary. The man scuttled up to Dr Chavez, clearly in a state of high alarm.

'Oh Dr Chavez! *Gracias a Dios*. I'm so glad I've caught you. The police are here again. It's about that incident in the Mall yesterday.'

CHAPTER 3

Back to the Campamento

As the bus rocked along the track to the shanty town, Allie carefully rearranged the things she'd brought in her basket. They were mostlyhigh protein, vitamin rich products, fiendishly expensive, normally used by mountain climbers as survival rations. Her mum had suggested they'd be good for starving children. There were also medicines, including various common antibiotics and pain killers, and one or two small luxuries such as the chocolate. As she reflected on her lucky escape of the day before she hoped they'd get to the right people.

All the air had been punched out of her lungs when she'd heard the secretary's voice. 'The incident in the Mall,' he'd said. 'The police were there.' She must have been spotted on the cameras, she'd thought, her heart constricting. She'd lose her place, be thrown out.

In a daze she heard Dr Chavez saying, 'Oh for God's sake, Felipe. I dealt with that yesterday and Isidora apologised to the guard on the door. Why don't these people communicate better? I spoke to the Head of Security at the Mall and she's decided not to pursue the matter. They were just trying to picket and nobody got hurt.'

Dr Chavez had turned away from the secretary who was looking deflated and pursued Amaru down the corridor but it had been some time before Allie could breathe again. It had not been her 'incident'.

The goodies in the basket came from her mum's stores. She'd told her what had happened in the campamento and described the events in the Mall and their rescue of Jaime. She'd omitted the bit about the briefcase and the Indian God though.

'His friend, the one that fell, he was stealing something, you say?'

'They were starving – the one I saved – I could feel all his bones,' she said, her face flushed. 'And the police would have taken that place apart if I'd said anything.'

'Well of course I'm glad you didn't.' Her mother looked thoughtful. 'However, try not to take sides, Allie.'

'But they're treated so unjustly, Mum.'

Her mother sighed. 'But you don't actually know these people do you, Allie – Jaime and Rafa and the boy who was shot?' She stopped and frowned. 'You're so impulsive, you know – you just rush into things. It's true that some are treated unjustly but there are often two sides to a problem. Some people lie and cheat and steal and sometimes they get what they deserve.'

'But they were only children!'

Her mother softened. 'Of course, I'm pleased you're interested in people who aren't as fortunate as we are. It's why we offer free medical sessions for the embassy maids and maintenance staff, after all.' She sighed again. 'I'll give you a hand to find the best things for Jaime and his family in the stores. Heaven knows these people are suffering. But..' she paused and looked Allie straight in the eye. 'I don't want you to get involved in local fights. I want you to concentrate on your studies. We don't know what's really going on here in Runa Five, do we?'

Allie said nothing. Just like her mum to go all po-faced about it, she thought. Surely all right-minded people should try to do something about the conditions here. Well, she was determined to help out where she could. Perhaps, thinking of the briefcase, she *had* already taken sides and she wondered what it could possibly have contained that made it worth risking a life for. Maybe if she saw Yupanqui again she'd be able to find out. He'd have made sure it got to the right people; she was certain. She didn't acknowledge to herself that she wanted to see him again because he was charming and had smiled at her despite the mistrust of the others. Perhaps he could assist her to help the local people in some way.

The bus lurched round another corner, past the hovels stacked against the side of the cliff and alongside the estuary. She hadn't asked Alaina to accompany her. For one thing the diplomatic shuttle would have been too noticeable in the campamento and Allie didn't want to stand out more than was necessary.   Alaina hadn't seemed particularly interested in her project either and had had a class that day. When she'd heard that Allie was heading back to the campamento she'd raised her hands in mock alarm.

'Gee, you're a glutton for punishment.... Make sure your wristcom is charged and tell everyone where you'll be.'

As the bus trundled towards the centre Allie wondered why she hadn't told Alaina about Yupanqui. Watching vaguely the shanty town shacks roll by and imagining Alaina's speculative eyes on Yupanqui's handsome features, she realised, guiltily, that she was hoping to keep him to herself.

It was just as hot as it had been the day before, the sun beating down on the dusty square. She lowered her visor and pulled her sun jacket down over her wrists as she got off the bus and headed towards the Church. The heat rose from the ground in a wave, a blast of shimmering air, and sweat trickled over her face and down her neck.

Reluctant as she was to have any more dealings with Padre Lamar, he was the only one she could think of who could help her contact Jaime, so she headed through the big gates again and into the tall building. In the coolness of the church she laid down the basket and looked around, seeing a small child watching her from behind one of the pillars. She smiled but the child did not move.

'Good afternoon, Señorita.'

The voice from behind her made her start. She spun round and saw the pale eyes under the domed bald head and the untrustworthy smile of Padre Lamar.

'Good afternoon, Mr Lamar.' She was not about to call this man Father. 'I'm trying to contact Jaime, the young man I came in with the other day.'

He looked at her with contempt. 'He is not well enough to receive visitors, Señorita,' Then, his eyes on the basket, 'If you have something for him you may safely leave it with me.'

She looked around the Church. There was no sign of Yupanqui. She certainly wouldn't give anything to Lamar.

'That's all right. I'll catch him another time.'

Something of what she'd thought must have shown in her face for a flash of anger appeared in his eyes.

'As you wish, Señorita. Please feel free to send for me if you need me.' He turned and swept away, his black robe whisking along the ground.

Disheartened, Allie went back out into the stifling air and looked around the square. The bus didn't leave for another hour. She sighed and looked for a patch of shade.

'*Hé*, Señorita, what are you doing here?'

It was Jaime's friend – what was it the priest had called him – Rafa, probably short for Rafael – Rafa with the dazzling white smile in the grimy face.

'*Hé* Rafa! Hi! Am I pleased to see you! I was hoping to get to see Jaime and I've no idea where he lives.'

'No problem, no problem, I take you to him.' He grabbed the basket. 'I carry that for you, Señorita.'

For a split second she wondered if her basket was about to disappear as her mother had predicted but then didn't want to offend him by refusing his help. She relinquished it into his hand and smiled back at him.

'Thanks, Rafa. And the name's Allie.'

He tried it, making the 'ee' at the end even longer. 'Allee. This American name?''

'English. I'm from Runa Four.'

'Runa Four?   We go this way.'   He was disappearing into the warren of tiny shops and huts off the main square. She followed closely, not wanting to lose him in this unfamiliar place. It was alive with ragged crowds, young men in brightly coloured shirts, old women in black bowler hats, some wearing two or three at once, one piled on top of the other. A status symbol, she'd been told. Some of the women were bare footed, walking with eyes averted or cast down, often carrying enormous loads on their backs. A small child went by holding proudly in front of him, as something most precious, a potato.

'Runa Four, like France, Russia?

'Yes, only I'm from England, a small country on the edge of Runa Four.'

He looked puzzled for a moment and then his face brightened. 'Inglaterra, I know. Keep close with me, Allee. This is dangerous place.'

He leapt over one of the slime-covered ditches.

'Not far now.' He put out a hand to help her over but she was already beside him. 'Jaime still not good. He has…' he thought about it, 'fever. Is right? Very, very hot.'

'Yes, that's right. I'm sorry. My mum has sent something which might help.'

As she spoke she had the strange sensation that the man behind them was listening to their conversation but when she looked back he'd melted into the crowd. Her heart began to beat more erratically.

'All right, Allee? We nearly there.'

He'd turned into an even narrower alley, dark and gloomy, with huts made of little more than driftwood and tarpaulin, sacking covering the entrances instead of doors. He veered aside suddenly, saying, 'Wait here, Allee,' and disappeared behind one of the grubby hangings. Allie waited, her heart giving a sudden lurch of alarm at being abandoned in such a place, feeling once again the strange sensation that she was being followed. She looked around anxiously but people were pushing their way past her in the alley and she could see no one she recognised. Her heart was beating an uneven rhythm against her ribcage.

All at once she was being jostled back against the flimsy wall of the shack, shouts and screams came from further down the dark passageway as hands grabbed her, and then someone was sprinting towards them, his face a mask of blood. She could see, even in the darkness, the man's panic. Someone was chasing him and wasn't far behind.

She'd shrunk back against the wall to allow him free passage when she caught a fleeting glance of someone opposite her in the alleyway. A young man, a teenager, his face in shadow. She had the momentary sensation that she must know him, that she recognised the curve of the cheekbone, the line of the eyebrows, but knew this was impossible.

The fleeing man was hurtling between them when the youth put out his foot. She was sure he'd done it deliberately. The man being pursued tripped over it. Stumbled – and fell sprawling at her feet. Allie could see the big gash on the side of his head, the blood still running freely.

He lay there for half a second and then twisted round and tried to rise. As she bent over to help him up her arm was grabbed from behind and she was dragged back.

It was an old woman, surprisingly strong. 'Leave,' she said.

The injured man's pursuer had reached them, wielding what, to Allie's horror, looked like a machete. The blade glinted as he raised it. But she was still, despite the old lady's efforts, between him and the man on the ground. Someone seized the arm holding the machete, bending it back, and the injured man twisted again, ducked under her arm and was off, disappearing into the jumble of shacks ahead. The man with the machete grabbed hold of her and flung her savagely aside, swearing violently. Then he too was away, chasing his quarry.

Various members of the crowd helped her upright and murmured what sounded like apologies. Heart still pounding she turned to say thank you to the old lady but she'd disappeared.

'Sorry, Señorita. Sorry.'

Hands patted her down. People smiled nervously. One of the men said, 'Just Manco, a local boy…' Then, feeling some explanation was called for, 'Drugs, I expect.'

She was trembling. The teenager too had disappeared.

'Allee?'

Her lungs expanded with a rush of relief as Rafa's face appeared from behind the sacking. The whole incident had lasted no more than a few seconds but she still felt breathless. One of the students had told her that the campamento was a hell hole but she hadn't really believed them.

'Allee, Rosalita and Jaime want to see you.'

Chapter 5
Rosalita and Jaime

It was dark in the room, only the small figure lying on the bed visible, his face lit by a Tilly lamp on the bedside table. As her eyes adjusted to the darkness she saw that it was Jaime, the bed little more than a packing case covered with a ragged cloth. His eyes were wide with fever, and beads of sweat shone on his brow, half covered with a filthy bandage over the head wound from the fall. The only other occupant of the room was a young woman, bathing his face with a damp cloth.

No one else was there. She didn't admit to herself that she was disappointed to see no Yupanqui. She didn't like to think what a strong impression he'd made on her.

Rafa introduced them, saying, 'This is Allee, and this is Rosalita.'

Rosalita smiled shyly. Another Incan face, Allie thought. The aquiline nose, the bright eyes, the proud cheek bones and almost haughty expression. The very essence of mountain beauty.

Allie smiled and said, 'I see you're looking after him. I hope he's a good patient.'

Jaime struggled up but Rafa, sitting on the bed beside him, pushed him back.

'He's a terrible patient, Allee. He always trying to get up.' Again the brilliant smile.

Rosalita stammered. 'We are very thankful, Señorita, that you help my brother.'

'It's Allie and I was glad to help.'

'She fool old Gutierrez. He's really stupid guy.' The irrepressible Rafa was laughing. 'Not so, Jaime?'

Wish I could be as certain, thought Allie, as Jaime smiled feebly. He was still clearly very weak and closed his eyes again, wincing against the folded towel he was using as a pillow. He couldn't be much more than twelve, she thought. Putting the basket down on the little table beside the bed she sat on the stool that Rosalita had pushed towards her. Now that her eyes had adjusted, she could see that the girl was heavily pregnant and felt immense pity for her. What a place to have to bring up a child.

'I'm glad to see you're a little better, Jaime,' she said, thinking that even to her untutored eyes he looked feverish still.

She began to unpack the basket gaily. 'My mum has sent some things for you. She's a doctor and I asked for something for your head and perhaps for fever. I didn't really know what was best, so she sent a bit of everything.'

As she took it all out, the bandages and painkillers, the antibiotics and the antiseptic creams, and then the high protein foods, Jaime laid his head back, exhausted, on the folded towel while Rafa and Rosalita talked amongst themselves. The language was strange to her but she thought she recognised it as the language Padre Lamar had been using. It must be Quechua, she thought, the most used language of the high Andes.

Although her Spanish was good enough, she'd had no time, with the speed of their move, to learn either Quechua or Mapudungun but she knew that Quechua had been spoken originally by a tribe who'd lived in Peru centuries ago and that it had been pronounced the official language of the empire by Inca Pachacuti. Every official in the Incan administration had had to learn it. It was spoken still by millions in the mountainous regions of the western part of Runa Five. It was, one of her tutors had said, a beautiful language – pure, liquid and flexible. In amongst the flow of unknown words Allie thought she recognised the name Kantuta several times but nothing more.

When the conversation finished Rafa slipped from the room, saying, to Allie's alarm, 'I come back, Allee.' She would have stopped him but by the time she'd realised what was happening he'd gone. She'd be left alone in the middle of this alarming place. She'd never find her way out without him.

Rosalita's eyes were shining. 'You are too good. You really help us.'

Allie tried not to show her nervousness, shifting uncomfortably on her seat, and to change the subject asked if the Kantuta they'd mentioned was the lab technician at her college.

'*Si*, Kantuta is my cousin. She works at the college. I don't know what she do but pay is very good. She live in the campamento but now she has a new house. Very nice.'

Not knowing what else to talk about Allie began to go through the little pile of goodies, explaining what her mother had said about each one, how it was to be used, what it was good for.

'These will help Jaime's fever and these, I think, might be good for the baby.'

Rosalita listened carefully to the instructions, getting Allie to repeat them if she hadn't understood something, making sure she understood what she should do with the different products, but smiled sadly at the mention of the baby. 'I hope he will be strong. They tell me at the clinic is a little boy. His daddy would have been pleased.' Her face looked even paler. 'Esteban went out one night and never came back. We never know why. Perhaps the police got him.'

Allie had heard the horror stories of police brutality, of how people suspected of opposition to the government, sometimes on nothing more than a jealous neighbour's say-so, were rounded up and imprisoned. Sometimes killed, their bodies never found. The Missing. It sounded as if there might be some truth in the rumours.

'I'm so sorry. But at least you'll have the baby.'

Again the sad smile. 'I hope. The clinic say I might have the Anderlans virus, that it might hurt the baby. Some of the other mothers have had it. Everything goes well but the baby is born dead or the women miscarry and they…' she searched for the word, 'they forget, they forget total, sometimes from just short time before but sometimes total, so it is like they have to learn their life all over again. Before none of us have help, but now with the clinics is so much better.'

'They tell me my teacher, Dr Chavez, helps at the clinics.'

'*Si.*' Rosalita was a bit doubtful. 'She used to come often but I have not seen her for long time. But is better. Before, many mothers just went away. We never knew what happened to them. I am worried about my friend Ignacia. Three of us used to go together to the clinic, Carla, Ignacia and me, but Carla lose her baby and now Ignacia is one of the Missing.'

Hands clapped as someone announced their presence through the sacking. Once again Allie's heart shrank but at Rosalita's '*Si!*', only an old lady came into the room, bringing with her a little bag which she laid on the table.

'I find some food for the boy.' She looked like the thousands of peasant woman in the campamento, old before their time, clad all in black and with the black bowler hat tilted forward over the forehead. In earlier times they'd worn brightly coloured garments and still did when they could but since the loss of the plants which provided the dyes they'd reverted to a muddy black for daily use. She removed the hat but the hand holding the little bag stilled ̃when she noticed Allie on her stool in the corner.

'You have visitor, Rosalita? The voice was deeply condemnatory. 'I will leave you.'

'No, Miramae.' Rosalita suddenly sounded very determined. 'No, Aunty. You must stop and meet our friend. She has brought good things for Jaime. She is called Allie.'

The old lady still looked very suspicious, but she nodded a greeting to Allie, saying stiffly, '*Hola*, Señorita. Welcome.'

Again the rapid Quechua, Rosalita clearly laying the law down in some way, and eventually the old lady's face softened. 'You help Jaime. You fool Gutierrez. Pah! He is a pig, that one. We must thank you, Señorita.'

'I only tried to help.'

The old lady had dragged up another small stool and settled herself down. 'All the pigs will go in the end. We will defeat them.'

With her mother's words ringing in her ears Allie turned to Rosalita.

'Rosalita was just telling me about her friend, Ignacia. I was going to ask if the clinic had said anything.'

'They did not know.' Rosalita's beautiful face was downcast again. 'They did not know what had happened to Ignacia. They did some tests for me but I do not know what my results are. The last time I went they did not tell me and now I cannot leave Jaime.'

She grabbed Allie's hand in an impulsive gesture. 'Can you find out, Señorita? Here… here…' She thrust a piece of paper into Allie's hand, some kind of prescription or doctor's note, Allie thought, with her name on the top. 'They will not tell me so I fear that the baby is perhaps damaged. Yupanqui says he is sure it will be fine, but I worry still.'

'Yupanqui?'

'He is wonderful.' She smiled shyly, settling back down after her burst of activity. 'He helps the boys. He finds them work. You have met him?'

'Yes.' It sounded a little bald. 'Yes, he was very kind.'

'He is a miracle worker. He can be in more than one place at once.'

The mention of Yupanqui's name brought a flow of Quechua from the old lady. Allie was startled by Rosalita's comment. That Yupanqui was something special she'd gathered but he hadn't struck her as some kind of magician. If Rosalita thought he'd been in two places at once it was probably only a hologram.

Miramae's eyes glittered in the light of the lamp. 'No, Señorita, it is true. He is a miracle worker. One day he will lead us and we will live in the houses of the Presidio. We know something is going to happen soon although we do not know what. We will overthrow them.' She spat. 'We will live in the houses of the rich.'

A movement came from behind her and Allie saw a hand touch the old lady's shoulder. '*Hé*, Aunty, what are you telling our friend? You are dreaming.' He smiled down at her to show that he meant no insult. 'You've been listening to that Hakan again.'

She turned and grabbed his hand. 'Eh, Yupanqui, you have come.'

His eyes took in the basket and the money lying on the side table as he moved forward into the room, the sun shield cloak swinging from his shoulders. Nodding to Allie, he said, 'Welcome, Señorita Warrender,' then to the old lady, 'Of course I have come, Miramae, I must see how Jaime is. I have brought some medicine but I see that someone is before me.'

He touched Rosalita's head – like a king to a loyal subject thought Allie – and came across to the bed, putting a hand to Jaime's brow. 'Still the fever?' I have brought you something but I think what the Señorita has given you will be more effective.'

Jaime seemed to rouse from his delirious state and looked at him in anguish, grabbing his hand. 'Yupanqui, Raoul?'

Yupanqui's eyes darkened. 'We don't know yet. He's very badly hurt but he's a strong boy, so we must hope.' He paused. 'You both did a fine job.'

Jaime did not appear to hear. 'Raoul,' he whispered. 'Raoul.'

Rosalita stood up and went to a corner of the room from which she fetched a glass into which she poured a small amount of what looked like wine, offering it, like a libation to the gods, to Yupanqui.

He thanked her graciously and drank. It was difficult to tell how old he was. She was aware once more of the charm, the intelligence in the eyes which smiled at her over the rim of the glass, the wonderful body.

For one treacherous moment she thought of Stick's skinny frame.

It was Rafa, she realised, who'd fetched Yupanqui and who'd returned with him, waiting at the door.

She stood in haste. 'I think I must go now.' She smiled apologetically at Rosalita. 'Rafa can show me the way.'

But she was too late. Someone else had come, was entering the room without the courtesy of the traditional clapped hands. It was Padre Lamar. He eyed Allie speculatively but addressed himself solely to Yupanqui.

'Your brothers have sent word. You are needed in the Great Chamber.'

'Thank you, Padre.' Yupanqui's voice was cool. Allie didn't think he liked Padre Lamar any more than she did.

Lamar nodded at Jaime and Rosalita without a great deal of interest.

'I'm glad to see Jaime is improving. I must get back.'

Lamar left and Allie collected her basket, overriding the expressions of gratitude from Rosalita and Jaime, who had roused himself to thank her.

'Thank you, thank you, *gracias*, Señorita.'

Rosalita smiled shyly.

'*Muchas gracias*, Señorita. It kind of you to think of us.' She hesitated, and then said in a rush, 'Please, *por favor*, be careful. Must not risk coming to see us if you get in danger. We very grateful.'

Allie smiled in reply, surprised that the girl should be worried about her safety rather than the other way round. She touched her arm. 'It was nothing, Rosalita. I'll come again, in a couple of days. Don't worry about me.'

Turning to say goodbye to Yupanqui she saw that he too had turned and was heading for the doorway, the swinging cloak still hiding the oxygen shunt. She remembered she'd wanted to check to see what was different about it, but now that seemed unimportant.

To her surprise, he said to Rafa, 'It's all right, Rafa. I'll accompany the Señorita.'

She was tongue-tied, stammering. 'It's all right. Please don't bother. I'll be all right.'

'It's no trouble, Señorita.' He smiled. 'Shall we go?'

Out in the sunlight again, he steered her quickly back to the square, hardly saying anything on the way, his light touch cool on her arm.

She couldn't help continuously checking behind her, however.

'Is all well, Señorita Warrender?'

Allie laughed and tried to sound unconcerned. 'Allie, please. It's nothing. Just my imagination I expect. I keep thinking someone's following me.'

He looked grave and frowned. 'These are dangerous times, Allee.' He gave it the long 'ee' like Rafa. 'And I hear you had trouble with Manco.'

'The young man who was being chased?'

He smiled a little grimly. 'Yes, the young man who was being chased. Probably deservedly so. We may have to do something about that.'

He looked down at her, the blue eyes intent. 'It was very kind of you to help Jaime, Allee.' He paused, '…and brave.' For a moment It looked as if he might have said more and she wanted to protest but he was frowning, 'Do your family know you are here, Allee? A beautiful young lady in the campamento on her own? Perhaps you should bring a brother or a boyfriend when you come.'

'My boyfriend's back in Runa Four and I'm just here with my mother'. She didn't know why but felt the need to explain. 'I'm at the college with Dr Chavez and it was an opportunity I couldn't miss so I had to leave Stick behind. But I was fine. Rafa was looking after me.'

His forehead was still creased, the soaring black brows meeting. He felt in the small leather pouch on his belt and handed something to her.

'Please, take this.'

She put out her hand, puzzled, and he placed a small, golden half-disc into it.

'If you ever need help of any kind, if you are amongst my people, show this and they will help you.'

She wanted to refuse it, to say that she was in no danger, that her mother was surgeon to the ambassadors and, as such, they were protected. But she didn't want to upset him.

'Thank you,' she stammered.

Once again he smiled gravely, saying, 'I will see you again, Allee.' Then he was gone and she was alone in the square, wondering what role he played in the politics of Runa Five and what was the likelihood of an uprising as the old lady had implied. And why he and Rosalita seemed so convinced she was in danger.

On her way to the bus she stopped at the clinic to ask for Rosalita's results. The thin- faced girl on the desk was friendly and dictated the name to the computer. While the machine whirred Allie asked her about the Anderlans virus.

'Oh yes,' she said. 'I've heard of that but they don't get it now. They have a vaccine I think.'

The machine stopped and she frowned, looking back at the piece of paper. 'That's funny,' she said and then stroked the screen and pressed another button.

She smiled an apology at Allie and tried again but after running through several screens she became silent and frowned, then stood up and went through to the small office at the rear. Allie could see her talking to a woman behind a frosted glass partition, her face animated. There appeared to be a little argument going on.

The girl came back out looking rather sullen. 'I'm sorry,' she said. 'The results are not through yet.'

Allie decided there was little point in trying to get more out of her and was making her way out of the clinic when, to her surprise, she ran into Velasquez, the lab technician, coming up the steps into the building. He looked surprised as well.

'Hi, Allie. I didn't know you were helping here.'

'I'm not, although I would like to at some point. No, I was just making a few enquiries for a friend'. She sighed. 'Not very successfully I'm afraid.'

'Can I help?'

She was about to tell him, to ask if he could find out something for her but felt a sudden nervousness. Presumably, Rosalita's results were confidential but the reaction at the clinic had been odd.

'Oh, I don't think so, thanks all the same. Just the usual bureaucratic muddle, I expect.' She laughed and he smiled back.

'See you in the lab, then,' he said and continued up into the clinic.

As she looked back she saw him talking to the woman behind the frosted glass.

Stick was hunched over his computer, his eyes fixed on the information scrolling past on the screen. He frowned.

The information on Chavez had been relatively easy to find. The idyllic childhood in the high Andes as adopted Indian daughter of a Nobel-prize-winning father, Dr Lieberhart, and his Indian wife. Later helping her father in his clinic and obtaining a first-class honours degree at Santiago Medical School for her work on treatments for sun intolerance. Marriage to a fellow student, Jose Chavez, shortly after qualifying. He'd been killed in a skiing accident two years later and it wasn't clear what had happened after that. Had she had some sort of breakdown? The next report was when she took up a teaching post in a University in Runa Two a year later but by that time the mother had died and Lieberhart himself seemed to have disappeared. It was strange that someone so famous should have just dropped off the map, though it was rumoured that the death of his wife had affected him greatly. A variety of teaching posts for Chavez at universities in Runas Two and Three followed the first. She'd become the acknowledged leader in her field of clinical genetics, successfully working on solutions to a variety of previously untreatable diseases, giving lectures all over the world.

She was also renowned for her humanitarian work, having, on her return to Runa Five several years later, set up outreach clinics in several of the campamentos around Santiago and Avila, much apparently paid for out of her own pocket. No wonder Allie had wanted to study under her.

How could he compete with someone who was both clever and good? Stick banged the screen in frustration. He should never have agreed to this half-hearted form of communication with Allie. Just the monthly email, not even holographic exchange. It was driving him mad not being able to talk to her properly, hear her voice, see the beautiful blond hair falling across her face, see her smile. Of course, holographic exchange at this distance was unfeasibly expensive.

And, he reminded himself, she'd accepted her mother's rules, had gone along with them. Eventually he'd agreed with her since he felt that to accept the college scholarship had been the most sensible thing for her to do. The most sensible thing for both of them really since they both wanted her to be a doctor. They'd just have to wait out the duration of her studies. At the end of her course she'd come home and they'd be together. That was the plan.

But would she still love him? Would she come back to him? It still seemed a miracle to him that she'd ever fancied him at all. But he wouldn't abase himself, write pleading emails begging her to remember him. If she did, she did. He wouldn't ask.

Chapter 6
The Invitation

Allie couldn't help feeling pleased at the invitation. It was an honour to be chosen amongst all the students. It was quite a coup for Chavez to get the chief UN Representative for Runa Five to a reception and half the government ministers would be there. Allie knew her mother would use the occasion to network like crazy. Of course she'd have Randy and Alaina to talk to and it would also be, she decided, an opportunity to find out more about what had happened in the Mall.

It was an imposing house, built in the old Spanish style with a fine pillared portico, the rooms beyond the entranceway encircling a central courtyard. In the middle was an ornamental pool with a small fountain at the end. A formally dressed servant took their cloaks in the hallway and while Allie waited for her mother and one or two others who'd arrived at the same time she studied the photos on the wall.

She recognised the first one as Dr Lieberhart, Dr Chavez's father, the Nobel prize winner, a man with a handlebar moustache in the old style and a rather stern expression. According to the dates underneath the photograph he'd died some years before. A similar photo stood on the table in Chavez's study at the college, next to a big, framed map of the ancient Incan Empire. The second photo was of a younger man, labelled Martin Carvajal, also, according to the dates beneath, now dead. He had thick wavy hair, even features and was clean-shaven and smiling. By the figures he must have died in middle age.

Dr Chavez appeared from what was presumably the kitchen area on her way back to the long drawing room, where it was plain from the hubbub of voices the reception was going well. She stopped when she saw that more guests had arrived and that Allie was looking at the picture. She smiled at her.

'Martin was my father's right-hand man for several years. Very talented. But a little too given to politics, my father thought. He died suddenly when he was quite young. I don't suppose there's anyone here now who knew him. However, I'm sure there are lots of interesting people you will know, as well as those from college. Do enjoy!'

It was rare to see Chavez looking truly animated.

In the reception room Allie looked around at the assembled throng, wondering idly if Chavez had been keen on the handsome Carvajal since she'd kept the photo of him. But by the dates he was long gone. And it was clear that she was now enjoying the opportunity to badger those in power about help for her clinics and Carvajal was far from her thoughts. She was now talking earnestly in a corner to a tall, elegant woman with a patrician profile, her hand on the guest's arm. Allie couldn't place the woman but thought that she looked somehow uncomfortable, her thin neck bent towards Dr Chavez jerking as she talked.

Finally she spotted Alaina on the far side of the room, instantly recognisable because of the afro braids and her height, standing out against the much smaller locals. She was clad in a green silk sheath dress, a gold necklace and arm band shining against her dark skin. Absolutely stunning. Randy was standing with her next to their mother, the Ambassador. Quite a few from the faculty were there, including Velasquez and Amaru and the College Director, a woman who was perfectly happy to be the administrator and leave oversight of the teaching and research to Chavez. Allie identified a man from the Ministry of the Interior, a Senor Guevara, having seen him on the newsapp, a thin-faced man with full lips and a sharp nose, who looked young until you saw the lines around his mouth.

But the entire assembly was dominated by the tall gracious woman standing at their centre, the Chief UN Representative to Runa Five. She was usually based on the Eastern side of the continent and so it was a double coup for Chavez to have her come, given the relatively small amount of time she spent on the Chilean side. Her face was alive with interest as she talked to the Minister for Enclaves.

'Note the natural fibre,' said Alaina as Allie joined her, and then sighing, 'Beautiful hang.'

The UN Rep was dressed in an extremely fashionable trouser suit which, as Alaina's expert eye had deduced, was certainly made from natural fibre.

'Yes,' said Allie, also sighing. 'No more linen or cotton for us.'

'So we not only lost all our food but most of our clothes as well. Those guys in the Blind Ages have much to answer for. Guess sheep need millions of miles of grass to eat before they make wool.'

'Mm. You can get yarn from smaller animals, though, like Angora rabbits.'

'And alpacas and camels,' said Alaina, betraying rather more knowledge than one might have expected. 'And vicuñas.'

'Still fiendishly expensive though.'

But expense was not a factor for the most powerful woman on the continent and her clothes were exquisite.

'Don't be misled by the gear and the designer handbag,' said Alaina. 'Mom says the woman has a razor mind.'

'Mmm. Food for my blog,' Allie said. But she wasn't really interested in the Chief UN Representative's razor mind or the minor official in the Ministry of Health who was bearing down on them. No doubt they'd provide material for her diary, to which she confided edited versions of what was happening, but she really wanted to talk to Dr Chavez at greater length and ask her about the Anderlans virus.

She was careful what she said, of course, in the blog and wrote under her avatar's name. She hadn't even told Alaina the full story of what had happened in the campamento nor about the uneasy sensation she had of being followed all the time. Even at college she sometimes got the impression that someone was standing just within earshot, not moving, waiting, moving only when she moved. But if she looked there was no one there. She remembered Stick's remark about blogs.

'Only fools blab their life to the world,' he'd said, 'and once they know all about you you're in their hands. Most blogs aren't worth reading anyway.'

But he would read hers.

She said as much to Alaina who looked at her with sympathy. Who'd be in love?

'Nil desperandum, eh?'

Allie managed to dredge up a smile.

Alaina's brother came over to stand next to them and at that moment a small dark-haired woman swept into the room, boring her way through the crowd to get to the Minister of Enclaves. It was Jake's mother with Jake himself, Allie's old friend from Runa Four, following her. Allie laughed delightedly and grabbed the arm of the young man as he went past.

'Jake, by all that's wonderful. What are you doing in Runa Five?'

His face blazed with good-natured enjoyment. 'Allie! How marvellous. They said you might be here.'

They hugged affectionately.

'Are you on Enclave work?'

He gestured. 'I'm with my mother.' A hint of pride in his voice. 'I'm only a very junior scientific assistant – still a student really. Most of the time I just make the tea.'

'So what's brought you?'

'Well, we've had reports of vegetation beginning to grow again in the wild over here. Rumours keep reaching us that in parts of the Andes there are small pockets of green on the sides of the valleys. We need to find out more about them so we know what the variables are. Maybe it would be more productive to have more Enclaves here than in other Runas.'

The Enclaves, government sponsored forests where anti-sun technology was used to protect the vegetation, were constantly monitored. Allie thought of her sprig of gorse.

'Since the Eastern part of Runa Five was the worst hit – you know, losing all the forests of the Amazon basin – they think the Western side has the greatest prospects for renewal.'

His eyes twinkled. 'Something to do with the Andes and thermals. The news has been really encouraging and Mum's here to check it out.'

His glow of enthusiasm was infectious. Allie thought that nothing Jake became involved in would be done half-heartedly. He was passionate for the Enclaves.

She wondered for a fraction of a moment if her mother had accepted the invitation that evening because she'd known Jake and his mother would be there. She'd never really given up hope that Allie and Jake would make a pair.

'How's Ginny?' she asked. Ginny had helped them in the enclave fire in Runa Four.

His eyes softened. 'Her old Threskay – you know, the pastor guy – put her forward for a scholarship and she got it so she's at Uni. Mum's sponsored her so we hope she'll be classed as a worker when she's finished.'

His voice was full of pride. Allie couldn't help feeling a pinch of the heart. She could see no sign of Jake's previous adoration. He'd been her most faithful suitor back in Runa Four but now he thought only of Ginny.

'How's your course going?' he asked.

'Awesome. Dr Chavez is first class. The research they're doing is great.' She wondered if she should mention her concerns about the clinic. 'I'm incredibly lucky to have got a place.'

He looked at her in a questioning way, as if about to say something, but she interrupted him.

'How's Stick?' She strove to keep her voice casual. 'He emailed me that he'd applied for a job at the Statistics Office.'

That was some weeks ago she thought.

Jake hesitated. She could see that he didn't want to tell her that there was not the remotest possibility that Stick would get the job. His reputation, as a troublemaker and arsonist compounded by the row over the falsified grade, would make him unemployable in any IT department where security

79

was important. It was plain that Jake felt a bit guilty about it when things were going so well for himself.

'He's fine.' He stopped. 'Just fine. Mum's working on getting him a job at Enclave Control but you know how it is' – he halted again – 'it takes ages getting through the official channels.'

Especially, thought Allie bitterly, when his file will have 'Fraud Suspect' stamped all over it.

Jake was about to say something more when his mother grabbed his arm. 'Hello, Allie dear, I'll catch up with you later. Just now I'd like Jake to meet the Minister for Enclaves, so I'm going to steal him away from you.'

Jake grinned broadly as his mother, like a small snowplough, began to cleave her way through the throng, towing him in her wake. Allie caught his arm.

'Give my love to Stick.'

'I'll see you before I go.' He smiled at her again and was led away.

She was frustrated. Jake's response had been guarded. It was what he had *not* said about Stick that worried her. She would have followed him but got caught by Velasquez who wanted to ask her about her trip to the clinic.

'I was talking to the head administrator and she told me that they couldn't find your friend's – Rosalita was it? Rosalita's results. She said it looks like they've lost them so she may have to have them done again. If you can tell me her surname I'll check if they've called her in.' He gave her his rather lopsided smile.

It was like Velasquez to be helpful. He'd spent an entire afternoon rebuilding Isidora's experiment which she'd somehow managed to foul up, and had made no mention of it to Dr Chavez, to Isidora's deep relief. He'd have been handsome were it not for the lack of mobility in his face. Rumour had it that he'd been seriously burnt in a kitchen fire in his youth and although they'd been able to grow his own skin from stem cells the years of surgery must have affected the nerves on one side.

She saw that Jake had left the Minister and was talking to Alaina, who'd thrown her head back in sunny peals of mirth. It was funny to see them together, the small, slight Jake with the tall and elegant but undeniably well-built Alaina.

'I'm sorry,' she said, turning back to Velasquez. 'I don't know her name. It was on a piece of paper and I gave that to the receptionist at the clinic. It might have been…' she sought for the memory but found nothing, '…Placido or something like that.'

He'd taken out a little notebook and was writing the name in it. Since this was her opportunity to find out what was going on she would put it to good use.

'I was in the Mall the other day when they shot that boy.' She tried to make it sound as if it was just a passing thought. 'Did you hear about that? They said he'd taken a briefcase. Must have contained something important for him to have risked his life for it.'

Velasquez looked up, closing the notebook.

'Mmm. I heard that too and then somebody told me it only contained old planning files.' He gave her his crooked smile. 'Mark you, they would say that, wouldn't they?'

Allie smiled. 'I suppose we'll never know. Can't understand them shooting children, though.'

Velasquez' eyes darkened. 'The present regime doesn't seem to value human life very highly, especially not the *indigenas*.'

Then, seemingly aware that he'd slipped into indiscretion, he put the notebook swiftly into his breast pocket and turned away, murmuring something about seeing one of the college's sponsors. Looking after him she wondered if he was part Indian himself as he stopped and buttonholed the slender, patrician woman she'd seen talking to Dr Chavez. She'd just remembered that she was the Undersecretary in the Ministry for Business and Agriculture, only because she'd been on the news recently complaining about being passed over for the job of Head of Department. She was waving a thin hand adorned with a magnificent ruby ring as she talked to Velasquez, and still seemed to have a look of dissatisfaction on her face.

Allie turned away as Alaina came sloping back, her face bearing a broad smile.

'Very dishy, your Jake. I could tell you weren't going to introduce us. He told me all about you and Stick and the fire in the Enclave. You guys must have had a real exciting time. Saving the forests of the future, eh? No wonder you and Stick have this thing going. Though I'd have picked your little Jake, myself.' Alaina's eyes twinkled. 'Fancy him going to the lunar module for three weeks. Jammy devil.'

'Well, he never told me that.'

'It's my natural charm. People tell me things all the time.' Alaina grinned. 'Anyway, we don't need to worry about his trip to the moon. We've got something almost as good. A gang from the embassy has booked some cabins up at the Lago Noche crater. There's an Enclave there now, so the public's not allowed in, but ambassador's privilege, you know.' Alaina waggled her eyebrows. 'It's got real trees and a lake with black ducks, set in a huge volcano. Extinct, I'm happy to say, and pretty bare and inhospitable, but you'd be able to go rock climbing with Randy.'

Randy was a very fit young man if a bit full of himself.

'Sounds irresistible. I'd have to square it with my mum.'

'Sure. Look I'd better go and do my duty.' Alaina flashed the charming smile. 'Butter up all the old men at the Ministry.'

Allie looked again for Jake but couldn't see him. She was beginning to worry that she shouldn't have given Rosalita's name to Velasquez, even though what she'd remembered was probably nothing like the one on the prescription. And she'd made plain her interest in the boy who'd been shot. Perhaps she was being paranoid but she worried about what was going on in the campamento, and the feeling she'd had of being followed. It was hot in the room despite the air conditioning and she began to feel hemmed in. Pushing her way through the crowd and keeping a wary eye out for Jake, she went outside.

In the courtyard garden she wandered between the borders of exotic blooms, shaded by towering eucalyptus and a high cactus hedge, and listened to the fountain trickling happily. It was in the centre of an ornamental pond crossed by a wooden footbridge. On one of the little rocky islets was a tiny hacienda style house for ducks. Previously the courtyard would have been open to the sky but was now covered with the specially tinted glass. The outer wall was also of glass and beyond, in contrast to the green plants within, a bare reddish landscape stretched away to the blue-grey rock-face of the Viejo de Avila.

She still felt faint from the heat and sat on the cold stone of the pool's edge, breathing in the heavy scent of the gardenias. It was dusk and no longer possible to see the far side of the courtyard.

She was just deciding to go back and find Jake when Dr Chavez' secretary ran quickly to a side door and opened it. A man slipped through and stood waiting for the secretary to close it behind him. He was wearing a dark cloak against the cold Andean night air and the wonderful carved features were shaded by the gathering gloom, but there was no mistaking the noble profile, the soaring eyebrows. He strode across the courtyard towards her, the cloak swinging, his head held high. She wondered what he would say at seeing her there and remembered his smile.

She was just about to say hello, to enquire after Jaime, Rafa and Rosalita, when she saw that he was looking straight at her, a slight frown on his brow, the eyes cold and unseeing. She stood up and made as if to go towards him but as he came forward she saw no hint of recognition on his face, no word of greeting. He was looking straight through her.

A servant who had come out of the house was bowing obsequiously, coming between her and the hard, unsmiling face.

'My Lord,' he was saying, 'Dr Chavez awaits you.'

It was like a blow to the stomach. She could feel the hot flush of embarrassment sweep over her, glad only that the gloom concealed her discomfiture. For a second she wondered if she should run after him, make him look at her properly. After he'd been so helpful in the campamento. He'd even given her the half disc. But then – the thought slammed into her consciousness – he'd wanted to make sure that she wouldn't betray them. She was pretty certain the briefcase hadn't gone back to the Ministry. He'd just used her good nature to get what he wanted by being charming.

Dr Chavez had followed the servant out into the courtyard. She kissed Yupanqui on both cheeks like a relative or close family friend and led him back into the house – not towards the party, Allie noticed, but round towards the private quarters at the back. A few seconds later Velasquez and Amaru came out of the salon and followed them round.

Going back to the reception she found that Jake was just leaving.

'Have to be up early to get to the valley we're checking out.' His eyes sparkled. 'We'll catch up when I get back.'

She'd lost her opportunity to find out more about Stick.

'That was fun, wasn't it?' said her mother on the way home.

'Yes, yes, great fun,' Allie said, stealing another look at the dirty, crumpled piece of paper which Amaru had shoved surreptitiously into her hand as they were leaving.

'*Allie, please come.*' The scribble was not easy to decipher. '*I need help. Rosalita.*'

'She wants to see you,' Amaru had said.

Stick was quite pleased with himself. Huddled in his great coat against the cold, he and the computer were as one, his fingers floating over the screen, his murmured instructions bringing up information and sending it away again in complicated patterns. Previously he would have connected himself to some rich person's heating supply but since knowing Allie he'd felt obliged to heat his room honestly, which generally meant not at all. Jake had told him once that when some of his former illegal actions had come to light Allie had stood up for him saying that he, Jake, shouldn't sit in judgement on one who suffered such disadvantages, who'd had such a terrible life, that she would love Stick whatever he'd done. And somehow that had made it impossible for him to continue any unlawful activity and so in winter he froze.

He was entertaining himself with tracking down the League of the Dead to take his mind off the temperature in the room. Since the people at Ecopro, when charged with damage to the Enclave, had tried to blame it on The League he'd kept a weather-eye out for them, even though it was well known they were just a myth.

He wondered if someone was piggybacking on the name, since he kept coming across it in odd corners of the web. And he'd found a game site which had the League of the Dead listed as one of the players. He'd joined one or two of the games and was surprised to find himself beaten in the third round, although he hadn't been trying very hard. He could hardly remember what the game was about or the names of the players, although one of them was called Aleister, he recalled. What he ought to do was play more seriously, one of these games for money, perhaps, and – idle dreaming – earn enough to fly out to see Allie.

His present researches were really just to distract himself from worrying about her.

Almost unconsciously he went back to the previous set of screens. He could find no trace of this Rosalita at the clinic other than a patient number. He'd checked all their files. The clinic itself seemed to be quite genuine, of charitable status, funded largely, as far as he could see, by Dr Chavez and one or two worthy locals.

What was Allie getting into? He'd read her latest private blog notes with alarm. What did the old lady, Miramae, mean by saying that they would live in the houses of the Presidio? Some sort of uprising? The regional government in that part of Runa Five was well known to be corrupt and there were any number of protest groups which the authorities were constantly trying to suppress. One called *LIBJU* seemed to be a little more organised than the others but none of them stood a chance against government weaponry.

He hoped Allie wasn't going to get into trouble. She'd used a very secure encryption on this part of her blog – he'd set the program up for her himself before she left – and he doubted very much if anyone else could get into it. But what if she'd said anything about these people to someone outside?

And he had a further major worry.

She sounded entirely too keen on this Yupanqui.

CHAPTER 7
The fire

Allie mentioned the proposed trip to the crater to her mother the following day.

'There's a group going from the diplomatic set. Alaina's mum and dad are going to come up when they can, and it's a wonderful area. There's a forest enclave and a big lake with black ducks.'

Her mother was not so keen. 'You're only just into the second trimester. It would be better if you used the break to revise.'

Allie was touched with a stroke of genius. 'Randy's going, of course. We'll be able to go rock climbing.'

Her mother sighed.

Allie had decided to say nothing about Rosalita's note as she felt sure her mum would try to prevent her from trying to help, would say she'd be worried about her, that it wasn't safe for her to go and see the young woman again. And today was the last college session before the break so it would be her only opportunity to go to the campamento without it being obvious. She'd miss Dr Chavez' final lecture of this trimester which grieved her – it was to be on the great Inca Civilisation, which Santiago had told her was a mine of fascinating information about the genetics of the population and Chavez' call to a return to the past – but she had to act on the note. She wondered yet again what on earth had impelled Rosalita to write. What had gone wrong? Why did she think Allie could help?

Just before leaving she'd finally managed to ask Dr Chavez about the virus. Chavez had frowned.

'Where did you hear about that?'

She explained about the clinic and gave Dr Chavez a slightly edited version of her encounter with the woman on reception. She made a special point of not mentioning Yupanqui since it appeared he knew Dr Chavez and he'd ignored her. She had her pride.

'The Anderlans virus.' Dr Chavez was thoughtful. 'I can't really understand them saying that. It used to exist years ago but, as they said, they vaccinate the girls against it now if they're considered to be at risk.' She sighed ruefully. 'I used to go to the clinic regularly but now –,' she sighed again and spread her hands, 'all the administration…the paperwork. One never escapes paperwork.' She smiled at Allie. 'But enough of my problems. I understand you're off to the mountains, Allie. It will be good for you to get a break.'

The keen dark eyes looked at her and she was aware again of the woman's magnetism, her charm. She wanted to ask what predisposed a woman to the virus but Chavez was asking about her mother and she lost the opportunity. And she didn't know quite why but she felt that to show too great an interest in the clinic and the missing girls might seem in some way accusing.

An hour or so later she was on her way, the bus rocking and swaying as it trundled along the rutted roads. How had they ever managed before hover or eco-drive when all travel was like this, each pothole a jar to the body? Amaru had told her that Rafa would meet her from the bus so at least she didn't need to worry about finding the shack again.

She'd had some qualms about heading back to the campamento, especially in view of her mother's remarks and the shock it had given her when she'd thought they'd spotted her on camera helping Jaime escape. No way did she want to get into trouble with the authorities here and lose her place when it was so very important that she get her degree and then the doctor's job. Given Stick's present lack of success in his search for employment she might be the only wage earner for a bit and if they hoped to set up home together they would need every penny.

But then she'd remembered the way Rosalita had cared so tenderly for Jaime despite the terrible conditions and her concern for Allie when really she should just have been worrying for her own safety. She had to help her.

As she inspected the goodies in her basket she couldn't help wondering if she'd see Yupanqui and, if so, what he'd say to her. The memory of the cold eyes in Chavez's courtyard had left a bitter aftertaste. She'd been kidding herself. That he should have ignored her so completely hurt. She went back to looking out of the window at the now familiar landscape of the shanty town and tried to think in what way she could help Rosalita. At least she could tell her about the vaccine.

The bus suddenly juddered to a halt, throwing everyone forward, those standing in the aisle grabbing at the rails or overbalancing and falling onto those seated next to them. One woman shrieked and a child wailed. Deep in her own thoughts Allie hadn't taken any preventative action and so was thrown forward against one of the stand poles. She rubbed her forehead where it had hit her and wondered what had caused the sudden stop.

The general movement and hubbub on the bus meant that she couldn't see what was happening forward. Then, looking to the side, she saw through the scrum of people outside a woman running past the bus, a small child clasped to her, her face rigid with fear. She stumbled, almost fell, then unfastened the child's hands from round her neck and stood him down. As she did so Allie realised who it was.

Kantuta.! Amaru's twin sister!

Once again the lack of a lab coat had confused her. What on earth had happened?

Kantuta was racing forward again, dragging the child behind her. The driver looked at her out of the window and then back to the door next to him which he opened. A large policeman was climbing the steps, his gun pointing at them ominously.

'Sit.'

They all obediently resumed their seats, those standing crushing themselves towards the back. As they did so Allie could see through the window beyond the policeman's back thick coils of smoke rising from somewhere ahead of them.

Kantuta, visible over the driver's shoulder, was still running for her life, heading in the direction of the fire, the child dragged along in her wake. She'd wrench the poor little thing's shoulder from its socket if she kept that up.

But even as Allie thought it, Kantuta was stopped by another policeman barring her route. Allie could see that one of the newer houses was burning, flames leaping through the roof with smoke writhing above it and dispersing into the upper air. There were no fire engines or firefighters, only a cordon of police officers holding back the crowd from getting to the building.

'What is it? What's happening?'

The old man next to her looked at her with fear in his eyes.

'Punishment,' he said.

'Punishment?'

'Police burn house.'

Allie looked again, seeing past the officer who'd bent down to talk to the driver that Kantuta was screaming and yelling and beating at the chest of the policeman who held her, trying to force her way forward. Next to her was another older woman, also gesticulating and yelling, arms thrown wide, turning and apparently appealing to the crowd standing around the police cordon.

Kantuta was Rosalita's cousin. Was this what the note was about?

Allie put her basket on her seat, wriggled past the old man and headed to the front of the bus. The driver and policeman were still deep in conversation, about what she couldn't tell, hearing only the alarmed murmurs of the other passengers at her action.

They'd alerted the policeman and he turned and grabbed her arm as she went to step down from the bus through the door which still hung open.

'*No comprendido*? Sit.'

'I can't,' she said in English. 'That's our technician, Kantuta, from college.' She saw the confusion in his eyes and thinking perhaps that his English was not so good grabbed her student pass from her bag. 'I must speak to her. We have a very important project.' He still held her arm. 'Dr Chavez will vouch for me.'

He obviously recognised the name. His grip slackened and she pulled away, leaping down the steps of the bus.

'Don't any of you try to follow the foreigner. You will be leaving as soon as it is safe,' she heard him say as she landed in the dust and began running as fast as she could towards Kantuta. He made no effort to pursue her, just following her with his eyes, until he saw her reach Kantuta, then turning back to the other passengers.

Allie, breathless, stumbled up to the college technician. She was still shouting passionately at the man holding her. The older woman next to her turned to Allie, her face transfixed with hatred.

'Now you see the justice in this country.'

She pointed ferociously at the policeman and then threw her arms wide to indicate the ring of policemen preventing people from getting any closer to the fire. 'They're burning my daughter's house because they say her husband is a rebel, a traitor, that he's against the government. Hakan's a teacher, *Madre de Dios*. What danger is he to them? He wouldn't know one end of a gun from another.'

The fire had now taken firm hold and the smoke pall lessened as the flames burned higher, eating everything in their path. Through a crumbling adobe wall you could see furniture, a table and some chairs open to the flames.

The mother's shrieks rose above the crackle of the fire and the shouts of the crowd. Allie could see Gutierrez swaggering towards them, a satisfied smile on his face, while more policemen were going to the aid of the one holding Kantuta back. She writhed and fought like one possessed, trying to get through the cordon to her home.

'It's just lies,' one of the people from the crowd said to Allie. 'Probably one of the officials wants to buy that plot of land. You'll see. No trial. No witnesses.'

He spoke calmly, as one announcing something too well known to be disputed. 'Just lies.'

Allie wondered where she'd heard Hakan's name before. Kantuta had thrust her way forward towards Gutierrez, barring his route, berating him at the top of her voice, her mother beside her. The crowd was grumbling in sympathy.

Where was the child, Allie thought, the toddler dragged along in Kantuta's wake? Intent on her fight with the police, distraught at the burning of her home, she must have forgotten him, let go of his hand. He was not at her side.

Standing at the very end of the cordon and looking round Allie spotted him, right inside the semicircle, hidden from everyone's view by some sort of trellis. He was patting a small dog, a puppy, that unexpectedly bolted away from him towards the house. With unsteady toddler steps the child followed.

The dog had run towards the part of the building, which was only just beginning to catch, passing easily through some slats of wood to the room inside. The tot was going surprisingly quickly. Allie yelled at the policeman at the end of the cordon but realised as he turned that he was too far away, that he couldn't see what was happening. She heard a piercing scream from Kantuta. Most of the policemen, who had their backs to the inner circle and were facing out towards the crowd couldn't see what was happening either and merely grabbed her and restrained her again.

The attention of the policeman in front of Allie was distracted, looking in the direction of the scream, and Allie threw herself under his arm and raced across the semicircle towards the child.

He was on his knees, crawling after the dog. She heard voices yelling '*El bambino*' and '*El perro*!' as she hurled herself towards him, flinging herself to the ground next to him and grabbing one of the little fat legs. He giggled, wriggled and slipped from her grasp, disappearing through the slats.

Had the fire got that far? Allie looked up and saw a flame leap from one side of the roof to their side. It would soon be upon them. She had to tear one of the slats aside to follow the child, thrusting herself through in a panic, scraping the skin from her arms and legs. She could just see him through an open door opposite, standing bewildered in the central courtyard, looking around for the puppy. Heaving herself past the boards, for one agonising moment held back by a large splinter of aged wood, she squeezed herself out and stumbled towards the courtyard.

Clouds of billowing smoke hid him temporarily from view but as she ran forward she spotted him on the far side, heading quite the wrong way – towards the fire rather than away from it. She dashed forward, disentangling herself frantically from a large blanket hanging with some washing on a line stretched across the courtyard, scooping the toddler up in her arms. She turned to head back to their exit hole.

Too late.

The fire had pounced and was ravaging the interior of the room she'd just left. She spun round but on every side there were flames and smoke. Grinding noises of crashing walls and timbers, sparks rising in the air. Only here, in the centre of the courtyard, next to the stone water trough were they safe.

Then one side of the building groaned and sighed and roared as one wall collapsed in towards them. The toddler looked up at her with large, frightened eyes. She stood him down and rushed towards the washing line, wrenching at the blanket. It wouldn't come. It had caught in someone's shirt. The child looked around and began to wail.

The terrified sobbing was lost in a further groan from a second wall and a great timber fell across her path, still burning. She had the blanket in one hand and ran with it, leaping across the burning timber. With the other she grabbed the toddler and raced to the stone trough, clasping the frightened child to her, hurling the blanket into the water. Then she was throwing herself and him forward after it as yet another timber crashed into the courtyard.

Pushing the child down she yelled, *'Bajo el agua.* Under the water. Only your head out.' And then, '*Solo tu cabeza,*' as she heaved the now sodden blanket over them.

The trough was narrow but large enough to hold her and the child, although both could not submerge completely at the same time. The child was gulping in fright ready to scream again. Hearing the shriek of tortured metal, now the only thing holding the building still surrounding them in place, she pushed him down under the water. Landed on top of him. Desperately heaved him up so that his head was free, gasping and spewing water, and then submerged them both again.

She was drowning. They'd have to rise.

'It's a game. It's a game. *Solo un juego.*' She looked into the blinking, terrified eyes and saw the mouth preparing to scream. '*Un juego*, a game. *Bajo el agua.*'

Holding him tightly to her she struggled down into the water again, dragging the blanket back around them.

Another roaring sound echoed above them and a timber must have fallen across the water trough because its flaming weight was heavy on her arm, held to protect the child. She tried to lift it, to push it off, terrified that it would burn through the blanket, but it had already done so and she succeeded only in burning her arm. She tried again to rotate them both into the water but the acrid smoke was seeping in. She couldn't breathe.

The child began to wail and cough as she tried to submerge them one last time, dragging her burning arm down into the water. The smoke was scorching her lungs. She wouldn't be able to hold out much longer. The world was going black. She held the child more tightly.

CHAPTER 8
The Crater

Allie's mother wrenched the cap off her pen and then snapped it back on again, her fingers trembling. Thanking Gutierrez stiffly for his assistance she'd shown him out and then returned to her daughter, striding from one end of the room to the other and back again as she spoke.

'For God's sake, Allie.' Her voice was shaking with the effort to control it. 'What on earth were you doing, getting mixed up in an anti-police riot? I can't believe you'd be so stupid…'

'I wasn't…'

There was no stemming the tide. '…it's incredible. I despair. You'd have lost your place at college. You could have got us thrown out of the country. What were you thinking of?' Her mother's voice rose.

'I wasn't mixed up in any riot. I was stopping a little kid getting burned to death.'

'But you were there.' Her mother's neck had gone red, a sure sign she was under great emotional stress.

'He said you ran past the police cordon. That they were protesting in favour of a known activist.'

'I ran past them to get to the child.' Despite herself Allie's voice rose as well. 'And the people only rioted because they thought we'd been killed. Anyway this 'known activist' is just a schoolteacher, married to one of our technicians at college.'

Her mother grabbed a chair back as if needing support, saying through gritted teeth, 'If you'd stayed on the bus as you'd been told to you wouldn't have got mixed up in it. Somebody else would have rescued the child.'

'But it's wrong, Mum. Can't you see it's wrong? They were burning that poor woman's house. Don't you care at all about the injustice, the way these people are treated. They're sometimes even killed. Rosalita's husband never came back.'

Her mother's face stiffened.

'Don't you dare lecture me, Allie, about social injustice. You've been quite happy to profit from a privileged lifestyle till now. And isn't it possible that Rosalita's husband just took off? You don't have to blame the police for it. There's plenty of deserted wives out there.'

Allie felt a bubble of rage begin to surface and then wondered suddenly if her mother's comment had more to do with her own absent partner, Allie's father, than the present situation. But her mother hadn't finished.

'And just because you've got this boyfriend who lacks the privileges you enjoy you're all at once a bleeding heart for the poor. You didn't *need* to get off that bus in the first place.'

Allie's anger rose again, white hot.

'How can you even drag Stick into this?' She was shouting. 'I never asked for a 'privileged life'. And you can't possibly think it would have been better to let the child burn - because we mustn't *take sides*.' She put as much venom as she could muster into the last two words. How could her mother take that attitude?

Voice still shaking, she said, 'Maybe some other person could have rescued the kiddie, but nobody else had even seen him. Gutierrez is annoyed because it put him in a bad light with the child almost being killed. Anyway, I'd better start my packing.' She didn't want to burst into tears in front of her mother.

Running to her room she flung herself on the bed and buried her head under the pillow. Her eyes burned but she couldn't cry. It was all so unjust. She'd been unable to contact Rosalita afterwards so she was still no wiser as to what the girl had wanted to see her for. Kantuta had apparently been taken to the police station for 'further questioning'. Her basket of goodies for the family had disappeared with the bus and there'd been no sign of Yupanqui either. Where was he when you needed him, she thought sourly.

As they'd been bandaging her arm at the clinic Rafa had appeared, having heard of the fire and Allie and the child's rescue from someone who'd been on the bus. At least Rafa was the same.

'Eh, Allee, you have been hurt bad.'

'No, no Rafa. I'm fine. It's just a little burn, honestly. Are Jaime and Rosalita all right?'

'I not know, Allee.' His brow wrinkled and the glancing smile disappeared. 'They call her back to the clinic the other day and I not see her since – or Jaime.'

Allie's stomach knotted. She'd remembered where she'd heard Hakan's name before. Yupanqui talking to Miramae. Was it true that Hakan was mixed up in this protest group? Had Gutierrez worked out his connection to Jaime and Rosalita?

When they'd first brought her into the clinic she'd tried asking the woman on the desk, different to the one before, about Rosalita's results, hoping to find out something that way. The woman, large and forbidding, with straight black eyebrows and none of the dramatic bone structure of the Indian profile, was unhelpful. Yes, Rosalita was a patient but as far as her notes said all was going well. There was nothing for the Señorita to worry about.

Allie could see Rafa was trying not to panic. 'I hope they not some of the Missing Ones.'

'I'm sure they'll turn up. You'll see.' Her voice, she thought, sounded pale and unconvincing.

Gutierrez had come into the clinic in search of her at that moment so she didn't dare say more, and he'd dragged her away, insisting that she return to her mother. He, of course, wanted to be able to represent himself as Allie's saviour and explain the situation in a way which put him in a good light. She buried her head more deeply under the pillow.

Seated in the back of the large Aggy the following day she had nothing to do but appear to enjoy the trip. Her arm had healed amazingly well – hardly a twinge – and it was true that Alaina was great company. The Aggy ate up the miles in total comfort, especially since, with an embassy allocation of fuel, the expense would be no problem. The ambassador and her husband were following later.

Allie tried to stifle the nagging feeling that she should have turned down the trip and done more to look for Rosalita instead. The girl must have been desperate to send the message. If Allie had backed out of the invitation, however, it would merely have upset her mother and Alaina as well, and probably to no good purpose. Perhaps she could get away somehow later in the break and team up with Rafa to try to find out more from the clinic.

That Rafa loved Rosalita she knew – she'd seen it in his eyes when he'd sat with them in the little shack, although he'd appeared to know nothing about Rosalita's note. And who knew, maybe the girl would have reappeared by the time she got back and could explain what it was she'd wanted. She'd just have to wait.

She wasn't even going to worry that Stick's latest email had been particularly bland with no account of his job search at all. Jake, too, had seemed evasive when he and his mother had come for supper prior to their departure, although it might just have been his excitement at the moon trip diverting his attention.

As she thought of Stick, the long bony body, the flaming red hair, the intelligence in the pale blue eyes, she felt a rush of desire to have him at her side, in her arms. If only he would say something – anything – to let her know he still felt the same way about her she wouldn't feel so…so adrift.

When she was packing for the trip she'd found amongst her jewellery the small SIM he'd given her on that last disastrous day back in Runa Four.

'If it's important, load this,' he'd said, his face even paler than usual. 'It will get to me wherever I am. Don't be misled by the size. It's extremely powerful and fully encrypted.'

She'd loaded the SIM into the little Moby hidden in the belt buckle which she'd bought that day in the Mall and wearing the belt now she felt a little closer to Stick, even if it was only to be used in an emergency. She leaned back into the luxury seat and gazed with pleasure at the view.

Nobody was following them. She'd checked.

'We're gonna go up the Granverde Valley,' said Randy. 'Fabulous scenery all through there. And the river is something else.'

Leaving behind the houses of the rich, built in the old Spanish style and hidden behind high fences, with electrified gates and their own security guards, they headed out of town and began to follow the line of the river. The cliff walls closed in, the canyon narrowing, as they advanced up the valley.

'Well fabulous scenery apart from this bit, that is,' said Randy, pulling a face, as they passed the RUNA barracks – mile upon mile of low concrete bunkers, wire fences and guard towers, hugging the canyon side. 'Apparently half the garrison and the arsenal are hidden in caves in the cliff but you wouldn't have thought they needed to put the rest right on the tourist route, would you?'

But in no time it was behind them and only the towering sides of the Granverde Valley enclosed them, a gorge carved out of the mountain by the green flecked torrent of the Granverde itself. Their route followed the river until they took a turn off in a new direction, heading down towards the Atacama Desert. As the road took them further and further south the air became noticeably drier, the landscape even barer, the hot wind sculpting the soft rock into curves and waves and banking the sand into fantastic snake-like ridges.

They were headed for the small town of San Pedro River, 'Conquered by the Inca in 1450,' lectured Randy in tour guide mode, 'And the Spanish two hundred years later.' Randy could really be a bore, sometimes.

'I've got something to show you at San Pedro.' His eyes gleamed with mischief. 'An ancient Chilean treasure.'

But Allie wasn't interested in treasures or the history of Runa Five. She'd gone back to worrying about Jaime and Rosalita. Stick, she knew, would expect her to do her best to help if she could, as he would have done.

Or would he? Stick might think she was just being a useless do-gooder, as her mother seemed to believe, and have been totally unaffected by the girl's plight. She sometimes wondered if she really knew him at all, although her belief in his essential goodness did not waver. She was so busy fretting that she was quite unprepared for the sight in the museum at San Pedro River of the small, mummified body of a young woman in a glass box. The leathery face stared out at them.

'Kinda gross, isn't it?' said Randy. 'They were famous for mummifying people. It's because the Atacama's so dry, the air preserves them perfectly.'

Allie shivered. She knew that the Inca were renowned for preserving their dead, sometimes keeping them in their houses for years and bringing them out for family celebrations. Archaeologists had often found burial places with hundreds of little bundles of what looked like sacking containing mummified bodies. The girl's skin had a glazed look, the fingers apparently beginning to fray, but the hair still thick and black. Hair was the last thing to rot.

Randy watched her face and smiled.

'Think,' he said. 'She's called the Beauty of Chile. People have been admiring her for hundreds of years.'

'I'm dead sure I wouldn't want to be left on display for hundreds of years or whatever, no matter how well preserved,' said Alaina.

They headed back inland towards the mountains, up towards Lago Noche, the land below them, the salt flats of the Salar de Atacama, shimmering in the heat. The sun's rays shone between the jagged black ridges of the great volcanoes surrounding the flats, turning the salt crystals to brilliant colours. As they climbed higher and further into the uplands the landscape below them changed again, the valley floor becoming a drought-burned golden expanse where even the mustard weed struggled to survive. Looking back at the road behind them, a thin sinuous serpent coiling itself round the side of the mountain, Allie felt like an eagle soaring on the thermals.

On one of the curves was a stone dwelling, sitting on a rocky ledge in a long wall of cliff face.

'A huaca,' Randy told them. 'The Inca used to build them to house their priests. I don't know who the gods were.'

Well, finally something Randy didn't know.

But she had no time to brood on the thought of a week in his company because they were at the crater. As they came round the mountain flank the expanse of the dark lake stretched in front of them, its waters even blacker in the gathering dusk. No wonder it was called Lago Noche, Night Lake. The virgin forest of the Enclave at the far end reached to the very base of the giant crater wall, one of the sides of the extinct volcano into which the lake had settled.

In front of them was a kallanka, a low single-storey stone building with several doorways. The Inca had built them, Randy helpfully informed them, as primitive staging posts for travellers but this one had now been extensively converted into a luxury hideout. More stone cabins stood behind it.

'You two girls can have the kallanka, I'll take one of the little cabins, the other guys can have the third one and Mom and Pop can have the big cabin when they get here. There's piped oxygen in the cabins and so on, so you don't need to worry too much about your oxygen filter levels. Staff quarters are round the corner of that bluff.'

Flinging wide the shutters of the kallanka Allie looked out on a magic landscape. The Enclave was everything Alaina had promised. Even, dipping up and down in the dark water, the black ducks, almost invisible except for their orange feet as they plunged for the scarce weed.

'No air conditioning, ladies, I'm afraid. Up here it's so high it's cool enough, although you'll need to cream up even more.' Randy, who'd come up behind her, making her jump, looked down at the lake. 'They say they're the Devil's ducks. They're found only here.'

'What's the whirring noise?' asked Alaina.

'That's the particle dispersers. They'll stop as soon as it's dark. They're huge things like lighthouses.

They're down at the far end of the forest. You'll be able to see their tops above the trees in the morning. They throw tiny little particles, like pieces of foil, out into the air above the trees all day, and the fragments reflect the sun's rays away from the greenery.' He stopped, seeing that Allie had known this already. 'You can't cover a whole forest of twenty-year-old trees in tinted glass.'

'Well thank you, bro, for that fascinating information,' said Alaina.

Allie also knew that amongst the trees were small autobots and mini drones, perpetually blowing the particles off the leaves if they had settled and hoovering them up so that they could be flung out again into the atmosphere the following day. To think that they were come to this, when even trees had to be protected from the sun.

Looking down into the black water she said, 'Can we swim in it?'

'Sure, as long as you stay fairly close to the edge. Wouldn't want to get cramp further out. The thing goes down a million miles.'

'Quick dip before supper then,' said Alaina, and they changed quickly and tumbled noisily into the water – and then even more noisily out.

'Gosh that's freezing,' said Alaina.

'It'll be warmer tomorrow. Sun gets round the mountain and hits this end of the lake in the morning.'

They picked up the clothes they'd cast off and headed back towards the cabins, Allie studying the rock face immediately to their left and deciding that climbing would be even better than swimming. She wished that she could enter into the occasion with greater enthusiasm, enjoy this very welcome break as much as she wanted. But she couldn't rid herself of the sense of unease that lingered at the back of her mind, born of the events in the campamento, seeing Rosalita's anxious little face, remembering the sensation of being followed and the suddenly shuttered look of the receptionist at the clinic.

As they got close to the kallanka they saw a lad coming out of one of the cabins. One of the staff, Allie presumed.

'Whoops! Didn't tidy up before we went out.'

'Strange,' said Randy. 'I don't recognise him.'

At the sight of them the boy turned quickly away towards the staff quarters, but he'd not been quick enough. As he turned to run Randy rocketed forward, covering the ground more quickly than Allie would have believed possible, grabbing the boy's arm. He twisted and screamed but Randy held on.

'You little devil!' he was wrenching something from his hand, 'You bloody thieving…'

The boy looked imploringly at the girls.

'Look,' said Randy, voice rough with anger, 'he was trying to take my tablet.'

'Señor, I just wanna look,' the boy said. 'I put it back after.'

'Oh, going to put it back, were you? Give me one good reason why I shouldn't get the Guardia out.'

'Oh, for land sakes, Randy.' Alaina was impatient. 'It's only a throwaway tablet and it isn't as if he actually got it, is it?'

Randy's face stiffened. 'It contains my blog. I haven't uploaded it yet'.

Randy rather fancied himself as a literary genius and was no doubt honing his blog for posterity.

'Well take a look and see if anything else is missing and if not you might as well let him go,' said Alaina poking her head into the kallanka. 'We don't want to spoil our break sitting in some crummy police station somewhere.' Allie did a quick check as well but nothing at all was missing, even the money card loaded with cash that her mother, surprisingly, had thrust into her hand prior to departure.

'Take a picture of him and tell Juan, if he's the chap in charge. He'll deal with it'.

Randy made a great show of taking the photo and threatened the lad he'd show it to the police if he ever saw him near the cabins again. They watched as the forlorn little figure trudged away out of sight behind the bluff.

It wasn't until just before bed it struck her and she checked her own blog. At first it refused to open, but on the second attempt, after she'd used the retinal display pass, she found a message from the firewall. It was the one that Stick had set up for her prior to her departure:

Unauthorised entry attempted. Reset Parameters.

Someone had been trying to hack into her files.

Stick ran lightly up the steps to the hospital, stopping one of the white-coated junior doctors as he was leaving.

'Hi Ravi, how's it going? Long time, no see.'

Ravi's thin brown face split into a delighted grin. 'Hi, you old son of a gun. Not my fault you don't see me. You don't come to my parties.' He threw up a hand. 'I know, I know, you're married to your computer, and...' he waggled an eyebrow, '...you've been consorting with one of our surgeons' daughters.'

Stick grinned back. 'She's in Runa Five at the moment and so is her mother, so I thought you might be able to help me instead,' he paused, 'since you're almost a fully-fledged doctor now.'

'No problem, my boy. No problem. On all matters medical I am now the Oracle.' Ravi's smile was infectious.

'Just wanted to know if you'd ever heard of the Anderlans virus and if so what sort of effects it has.'

'Why do you want to know?' Ravi looked puzzled. 'I don't think anybody gets it anymore. There's a vaccine. As far as I can remember you're only ever affected if you're pregnant and that shouldn't be worrying you, should it? Leastways...' the eyebrow waggled some more, '...it shouldn't, should it?'

Stick smiled weakly.

'No, not at all. So what would be the effect on our hypothetical pregnant lady?'

'Miscarriage, as far as I can remember. Not my specialty.'

'Not amnesia?'

'No nothing like that. Mark you, I'd have to look it up.' Ravi's face lightened with an ecstatic smile. 'Don't tell me you've decided to take up medicine?'

'No, no, just tracking something down for a friend. To be honest I've started on the twelfth level of the Feather of Destiny and I wouldn't have time to take up doctoring.'

'Wow!' Ravi laughed. 'Up with the big guys, I see. That's a game that's way beyond me. They say you can make a lot of money at it though.'

He looked at Stick's threadbare coat and Stick grinned. 'I play the League of the Dead.'

'Funny you should say that. I was in an online poker game the other day and one of the other players called himself that.' Ravi affected a falsetto girlie voice. '"I represent the League of the Dead". Wasn't a nitwit when it came to the play, though. He cleaned us all out.'

Stick frowned. 'Odd.'

'Yes. Usually the Gamekeeper weeds out the suspect players before you get to the higher levels so she must have checked his credentials.' Ravi flung a quick look at his wrist. 'Look man, much though I'd love to spend hours with you swapping gaming anecdotes, I must fly. We should really catch up some time. Text me.'

'Will do. And don't forget to let me know about the Anderlans virus.'

'Do my best.' He was already halfway down the steps.

Stick threw a final question. 'What was the name of that game again?'

.

Chapter 9
The Royal Road

When Allie came out onto the veranda the following morning the mighty blur of the distant crater edge had already become sharper, darker, more solid, etched against the blue of the sky. The sun was warm and the lake sparkled.

Alaina was excited. 'Juan's told me there's a market on today down at San Andreas del Punto and he says they've got the most wonderful fabrics from real vicuña wool. They used to run wild but they've managed to semi-domesticate a few. It's only about twenty miles or so down the valley. We could be there in half an hour.'

'Sounds amazing. You almost make it sound more attractive than climbing.'

'It is. You've got to come with me. You have such excellent taste.'

'Flattery will get you everywhere.'

Randy was grabbing a coffee and sitting down with them.

'Allie's booked with me and the boys. We're going to try that northern side since it looks as if it'll be an easy climb.'

Whether it was his assumption that she, as a girl, would need an easy climb or the memory of his ineffectual pass at her the night before after supper, but Allie was decided.

'No, sorry, guys. You know us girls. Must have some clothes to wear. Alaina's promised to take me with her.'

Randy, clearly irritated, looked as though he would have protested but then said, 'Well, watch out for the mine buses, little sis. They're lethal on corners.'

'Not as lethal as me, bro,' said Alaina with a broad grin. 'Come on, Al, drink up. All aboard.'

They'd just pulled away from Lago Noche, on the first of the many snake back bends, when a mine bus roared past from behind them, ignoring the fact that it was impossible to see if anything was coming the other way.

'Those guys really do have a death wish,' said Alaina, wheels spinning on the edge.

Allie, looking down over the vertiginous drop said, 'Why a mine? I thought there weren't any more minerals in the ground worth digging out.'

'They've still got silver up here, would you believe. All government controlled of course. Gold too, so they say. But you'd need to be a Runa Rep to get into a gold mine and what they put those miners through at the end of their shift to make sure they haven't snaffled a nugget or too doesn't bear thinking about.'

Alaina waved a hand, demonstrating some of the undoubtedly attractive metal in the form of several intricate filigree rings. 'All the gold ever mined is still here in the world somewhere, of course. You can melt it, slice it, turn it into jewellery and then drop it back into the ground, and it'll be more or less the same as it came out. It's a very stable element but easy to work with. Softer than silver.' The rings flashed again. 'They say a single gram of it can be drawn into a wire thirty metres long. Quite apart from being beautiful. That's why the Inca worshipped it of course.'

Odd the things Alaina knew, although, perhaps not so odd that as the ambassadors daughter she should be familiar with one of the most coveted elements in the world.

The narrow road wound down the mountain, hugging the rock walls. Allie gazed entranced. The view in front of them was a whole universe of peaks, spurs and ridges, distant crags disappearing and then reappearing through wisps of sheer morning mist. It was almost other-worldly.

Although she'd decided not to worry any more about the hacker and his attempt on her blog, the road itself was giving her plenty of cause for concern – especially when another vehicle came the other way. As lay-bys hadn't always been cut out of the cliff face at the side of the road the two vehicles had to inch perilously past each other, the one on the outside having to run right to the edge, towards the drop of thousands of metres. It was no comfort to know, Allie thought, looking down, that the auto-correct on the steering and the sensors on the wheels along with the automatic grapples which would shoot to the ground and retain them if the wheels lost contact – it was no comfort at all to think that they would save them.

They'd been passed by a large mine wagon in this way a few moments before when coming up the hill towards them was a small bus.

'Gee, our lucky day. At least it's a small one,' said Alaina.

It had something familiar about it. It went past, following the mine wagon, and just as it was almost through Allie realised it was the clinic bus. Spinning round she saw, in the rear window, the pale despairing face of Rosalita.

'Stop! Turn round.'

'What?!'

'Turn round. Turn round.'

Alaina screeched to a halt.

'That was the clinic bus. We've got to follow it. Rosalita's on it.'

'What, your girl from the campamento? What's she doing up here?'

'I don't know. I must find out. She asked me to help her. Turn round quickly or we'll lose them.'

'Gee, you do like to set people interesting little tasks,' said Alaina, slamming the manual button. She began to negotiate a turn on the narrow road, desperately trying to avoid the heart stopping drop on the one side and the giant cliff face on the other. 'Just pray no other mine buses come up right now. This thing doesn't have sensors everywhere, you know.'

She swung the Aggy expertly right up to the cliff wall. 'You sure you saw the girl? All there is in that direction is the silver mine, and that's miles away. They wouldn't take pregnant women to a mine. What would she be doing out there?'

'That's what I'd like to know.' Rosalita had seemed so innocent, Allie thought. 'There's something odd going on at that clinic and I want to find out what it is.'

Alaina had turned the Aggy, gravel spitting from the tyres as they sliced next to the very edge of the ravine.

'Rosalita didn't look happy.'

Alaina turned the throttle to maximum. 'I can't spend too much time on this, you know. I don't want to miss the market.'

'We're in plenty of time.' Allie's voice tailed off. 'Anyway, we've probably lost them.'

They could see no sign of the bus. She slumped in her seat. She'd failed the girl again.

Alaina was just saying, 'We'll give it another mile or two and then we'll have to head back,' when they saw the little bus on a snake back bend in the distance above them. Alaina accelerated and said, 'According to the satnav there's only the mine up there, miles and miles away. They can't be taking them there.'

But the bus, still visible some way ahead, was already turning off, long before the mine. When, some minutes later they arrived at the spot, they found only a broken-down hovel at the side of the road, with a caved-in roof and a peeling *LIBJU* poster hanging down sadly from a cracked adobe wall. It didn't look as if the track beyond it would go anywhere civilised. It disappeared into a small canyon. Alaina, going at close to full speed, swung the Aggy into the opening taken by the bus but soon had to throttle back as the road narrowed. The canyon walls rose steeply on either side of them, the road in shadow, the rock above them glinting in the sun. A condor, visible in the specially tinted glass of the Aggy roof, soared and drifted in the crack of blue sky.

Leading deeper and deeper into the canyon, the road narrowed even more, twisting and turning, finally becoming little more than a dirt track.

Alaina was glancing at her wristcom and muttering to herself. 'Hope this gets somewhere soon.'

But it didn't appear to. Allie's gut churned. The shadows from the canyon walls darkened down. Coming round a corner, past thickets of wizened, scrubby trees, the track opened out into a larger circle of ground, enclosed on all sides by rock walls. It was a dead end. There was nothing there.

Just a circle of rutted gravel, completely empty.

Nothing.

Nowhere where you could hide a whole bus. It was a cul-de-sac. Alaina backed up, preparing to turn the Aggy, saying, 'I never saw another turn off. Did you?'

Allie was jumping out.

'No, I'm pretty sure there wasn't one.'

Alaina had turned their vehicle and was jumping down as well. She wandered some way back along the way they had come, looking for another track leading off the main one. Allie was inspecting the dusty ground of the turning circle and found what she was looking for.

'Look! There go the tyre marks.' She turned round but Alaina had disappeared along the canyon. She ran after her and called. 'Look, I've found the tyre marks.'

Alaina returned and joined Allie in following the tyre tracks, saying, 'It can't have disappeared, can it?'

The tracks led right up to a thicket of interlaced dead branches directly in front of the giant cliff face. Allie scrambled across the sandy ground towards them but they were an impassable barrier.

'It has to be some kind of camouflage. On the other side there must be an entrance into the rock.'

Now that she looked more closely Allie thought she could see fault lines in the rock through the cracked and bleached wood, fault lines which might indicate an opening, a kind of rock door. But of the clinic bus there was no sign. Even if you'd pulled in off the road to picnic you'd never know that there must be a tunnel on the other side of the cliff face.

'We could wait to see if they come back out.'

Alaina's face told her that this was not a good idea.

Looking to her right Allie could see a track leading up across the scree, heading past the canyon wall towards the shoulder of the mountain. 'Look, there's a path. I'll just go up and see if I can get round the hillside that way. See, it leads to the ridge up there. Perhaps I can follow it and find out what's going on around the other side.

'What?' It cracked out. 'You want to go up into the mountain?' Alaina's eyebrows had shot into the stratosphere.

What was the problem? 'No, sis, not up. Round. I should be able to get round that bluff no problem and get in the back way. We can rendezvous on the main road when you've had a look at your market.'

'Are you crazy, girl? Who knows what weirdo's are up there.'

'That was a clinic bus, Alaina, wasn't it? And Rosalita was on it so we know it must be okay. Chavez practically owns the clinics, from what I hear.'

Alaina was tugging at one of her braids, twisting it back and forth. 'You're not listening to me, Allie. It could be real dangerous.'

For Pete's sake! The girl was beginning to sound like her mother.

'And anyway,' Alaina was continuing, 'I need you with me when I'm looking at those ponchos. It won't be much fun on my own.' She would have carried on but then saw the look on Allie's face.

'That girl's really got to you, hasn't she?' She sighed. 'You do just rush in, you know.'

Allie smiled at her friend, willing her to see the problem her way. 'Oh, you know, us Brits trying to be saviours of the world.' She paused. 'And you'll have a whale of a time with all those lovely materials. You don't need me.'

Alaina's brow creased. ' I still think it's too dangerous. Your mom will cut me into tiny pieces and fry me with the eggs and bacon if this gets out. Couldn't I go back and fetch Randy?'

Randy had been entirely too friendly.

'No, you'll miss all the best bargains at the market. If I do it's my own fault but I don't want you to miss out. I'm sorry...'

Allie stopped, seeing that Alaina was seriously concerned as well as annoyed, and then said, 'I really feel I must try to find the girl. She wanted me to help her in some way but then she disappeared and I never found out how. I should have gone to see her sooner.'

Alaina's face was still shadowed.

'I feel guilty about it. This way I might be able to find out what it was she needed me for.' Allie paused again, thinking back to the scruffy piece of paper, clearly written in haste, and its message – the fact that it had been written at all. 'I got the impression it was important.'

Seeing Alaina's frustrated expression she added, 'If I can't get anywhere with this I'll head back out. The enclave buses stop anywhere to pick up passengers, so I'll be able to get one to San Andreas on the main road and find you in the market.' She laughed. 'That won't be problem since you're about two foot taller than everyone else round here.'

Alaina still looked irritated but then she'd never been much interested in Rosalita and her problems anyway, Allie thought.

'If I'm too late to meet up with you I'll catch an enclave bus back to the cabin. I'll give you a buzz on the wristcom or text you. Hang on a moment and I'll look at that path and then you can just go straight on.'

'What do I tell the folks back at camp?' Alaina was seriously grumpy.

'I don't know. Tell them I've decided to commune with nature. Or something like that. Whatever....'

Alaina sighed. 'Here.'

She handed over one of her precious bars of chocolate and fetched a water bottle from the back of the Aggy. 'Provisions for the explorer. I'll tell them you've met a friend.' She was still frowning.

Allie turned to look at the path.

'Just a sec. Take this.' Alaina was removing a thin, delicate strap from her wrist. 'Put this on. It's the embassy rescue button. Fantastically powerful and will contact every satellite known to man on your behalf!'

'What about you?'

'My wristcom's good enough for the short distances and on major roads – which the one to San Andreas is, although you'd never believe it. Just remember you're bringing out half the American army if you press it. You have to hold for four seconds.'

Allie laughed and said, 'Thanks, sister. Although I'm sure I won't need it.' She slung the bottle over her shoulder, tucked the chocolate into her travel pouch and checked that she had enough battery, topping it up with the mini power pack she always carried with her. Fixing the rescue strap to her wrist it occurred to her that she was wearing the belt with the buckle and hidden moby. But of course, she wouldn't need that. And Stick was on another continent anyway.

'It looks as if this path has been used. I'm sure I'll be perfectly safe,' she said, heading up the slope and checking to see if it carried on.

Alaina's grunt behind her indicated lack of belief in this theory.

Turning back Allie said, 'I'll just see if there's anything round the back of this bluff and if not I'll head back. Even if there are weirdos up there, or even worse, government military, I'm sure they wouldn't touch me. After all, Mum's practically part of the embassy staff - diplomatic immunity and all that. You just go on to your market. If I get stuck I'll call you.' Allie paused. 'And thanks a bundle for the provisions.'

'Okay, sis. On your own head be it. I'll be coming back up at four or so this afternoon so meet me on the road here if you need to. I'll be watching out for you. And give me a buzz lunch time to let me know you're alright.'

Allie smiled. 'I'll do that. Just enjoy yourself.' Then she said, laughing, 'Don't buy too many ponchos,' and turning back to the path headed up the slope.

Despite the heat of the sun it felt good to be in the open air, the path in the shade of the mountain's edge above her, sheer against the blue sky. With her oxygen pack clicking companionably on her arm, she concentrated on placing her feet with care as she made her way upwards. She didn't want to have an accident in this remote spot. Apart from having already annoyed Alaina it would be too embarrassing to have to call Randy out to rescue her, given that she'd well and truly snubbed him the night before. His inept pass at her had been all the more irritating as she'd never promised anything more than friendship. And he'd thought she'd just drop into his arms like a ripe plum. Well, sorry, buster. You knew I love Stick. She was struck by the sudden thought that it might be because she could do nothing for Stick that she was so anxious to help Rosalita.

Looking ahead as she came over the hill she saw that it was part of a ridge forming one side of a huge canyon. On the red-brown slope opposite was a maze of criss-crossing paths, making a crazy quilt pattern on the mountainside. And to her amazement, looking down at her feet, a road running away in front of her, a road made of giant stone blocks.

It must be one of the Inca highways. She knew that the whole Incan empire was spanned by such highways running for many thousands of miles, linking all the major centres of the territory.

Maintaining the roads had been a task undertaken by the *ayllus*, roughly the equivalent of local parish councils, family groups who supplied the labour. The huge stone blocks of which the highways were built, were so carefully linked together that they formed a level and completely solid surface. Barring earthquakes most had lasted for thousands of years and some had even survived those. This one, she estimated, was about three metres wide, about the average width for an Incan road in the mountain regions. On its far side the ground fell away into the canyon below.

As she jumped down onto the paving she felt a thrill. She was on a *Camino Incaico*, perhaps even the *Camino Real*, the Royal Road.

It ran close to the mountainside, narrowing as it curved round its flank but providing a comfortable walk none the less. She followed it for nearly an hour, the sun beating down on her now she was no longer shaded by the mountain, glad of the visor and the creams and happy to have chosen the loose-hanging sun jacket. The massive mountain range in the distance was a sheer wall of brown and gold rocks, rearing towards a deep blue sky. Far below was a river, a glinting thread winding through pale, sun-bleached stones.

The road narrowed further and was now edging its way along the cliff face, the sheer rock on its far side falling away below her. The bottom of the canyon seemed so far away that with a total lack of logic she gave up worrying about it.

Her steps kept pace with her thoughts, the strange fact that the clinic bus was up here in the mountains….and had disappeared. Rosalita had looked distressed. She was heavily pregnant, for Pete's sake. And what had happened to Esteban? Was it possible that he'd just gone off with some other woman? Or had he been involved with Hakan and the rebels – whoever they were – and been picked up by the police?

She stopped for a moment and took a swig from her water bottle. As she did so she heard a small sound from above her, something scraping, and a handful of small stones dropped from an overhead ledge above onto the path in front of her.

She froze. Was someone up there? Following her?

She waited, listening for footsteps, but heard nothing. It was probably some small animal, one of the tiny rodents that managed to live in these barren mountains. But she was out here alone. Should she go back, grab a lift, go down to the market and join Alaina?

She listened again, heart beating unevenly. Still nothing… It had been some small animal. It was a long way back. Just press on, girl.

With the thoughts tumbling over and over in her mind she'd scarcely noticed the distance she'd travelled but now began to worry that this route would never lead to the other side of the mountain. Perhaps it didn't curve round to the back and she should have gone over the top. But that would have been impossible without the right equipment. And who knew what or who was up there? Yet this road must once have been used. She would give herself another few minutes.

Her thoughts reverting again to the campamento she asked herself again about Yupanqui and the stolen briefcase. It had apparently come from the Ministry of the Interior, a department renowned for its oppressive tactics. They were probably the ones ultimately responsible for burning down Hakan and Kantuta's house. How could her mother not see the injustice of it all?

As she came to yet another bend the view changed, the needle-sharp distant peaks looking almost like a child's drawing. She took another drink from her water bottle and nibbled a piece of chocolate. Ahead was the corner, curving inwards she noticed gratefully, so that the path would perhaps lead to the rear of the mountain, which was what she'd hoped.

Her attention taken by the view; she hadn't registered a slight unevenness in the paving. As she came smartly round the bend she realised to her horror that the road beyond had abruptly finished. Nothing lay in front of her. She was teetering on the edge of a plummeting drop into the canyon below.

She backed away from the precipice, heart dancing a salsa on its rib cage. The great seismic shift which had sheered Avila in two had also split the mountain she was on and let the great slabs of stone from the *Camino Real* slide into the abyss below. She could see the road on the other side of the fissure, but she wouldn't be able to get to it.

As she shuffled away from the edge small stones and grit trickled from beneath her feet and dropped into the gulf. She grabbed at the cliff wall next to her and as she did so her grip loosened on the water bottle. It tumbled to the road and rolled over the rim. Some of the broken paving where it had fallen loosened and slid down with it towards the depths thousands of metres below. The noise made by the bouncing bottle and the stones it took with it tore at the silence.

For an instant she felt dizzy but once her heart had steadied and she could better take in the scene in front of her she realised that the ravine had once been spanned by a bridge, undoubtedly one of the hanging rope bridges for which the mountain people were famous. They were of such strength that they could easily bear the weight of a man and his mule and were thought to be sacred. The punishment for anyone tampering with one was death. What had happened to this one she couldn't think.

Now that she looked more closely she could see the holding pillars but nothing linked this side of the crevasse to the other. No way forward at all. She wouldn't be able to get to the other side of the mountain. Her knees weakened.

It was a long way back without any water.

Her muscles slow and unwilling she began to turn and as she did so she heard the noise again, a slight scraping, as if someone's shoe had slipped on stone. But it was behind her. Someone was following her.

Her heart jolted manically into activity and she looked desperately back at the plunging ravine. There was no escape. She saw herself being thrown into the depths, tumbling past outcrops and the tiny dead bushes still clinging to the cliff face, smashing into the great boulders and stones in the valley bed, hundreds, perhaps thousands of metres below.

Then she saw it. A narrow path, partially hidden by a large outcrop above it, leading off to the left, back down into the fissure. And it was heading towards the place where she imagined the bus might have come out. It was not the *Camino Real*, more of a widened ledge, but still looked negotiable. She sprinted under the outcrop and forward along the path, hardly worrying about the danger of falling, anxious only to put some distance between herself and the strange noises.

As she shot round a second corner she saw, on the opposite side of the crevasse, a huge stone doorway. A doorway the height of several men, the lintel and side supports intricately carved. As she ran she could see, even at this distance, the animal forms and human figures etched into the monolithic blocks of stone surrounding the black hole.

And lying on the ground a brightly coloured scarf.

So people must use this portal as a back entrance. But it was on the other side of the crevasse.

She didn't dare linger but stumbled onward again only to be brought up short. The track finished. In front of her was a sheer wall of rock blocking her way forward. Behind was only the mystery follower.

But before the track ended she could see a bridge. A bridge to the other side. Just a narrow strip of stone, or rather stones, a corbeled bridge such as the Inca had built hundreds of years ago, where on either side of the span each paving block was partially balanced on the one behind it, jutting forward until the two sides met in the centre. Despite the large slabs of stone it looked fragile, narrowing to less than two metres in width where the central blocks lay.

The bridge had no side walls, no railings, no posts, not even a rope cable. Only the strip of arched stones going across the chasm.

She looked frantically back up towards the *Camino Real*, heart pounding, but saw no one, heard nothing.

To her right was the thin line of stones over the ravine. The path she was on went no further. The bridge was the only way to the other side.

Could she do it?

She put her foot on the first slab.

When you're climbing you just have to ignore the drop, the tumbled rocks hundreds, perhaps thousands, of metres below. Fix on your destination only.

From somewhere there came another faint scraping sound.

She launched herself over the bridge.

Stick had a bad feeling in his bones. He'd been tracking the lab technicians' activities because Velasquez, Kantuta and Amaru seemed to be the only link between Rosalita, Allie and the campamento.

Kantuta meant Flower of the Incas, he'd learned, and her only interests appeared to be old Incan ritual and history. It made her easy to follow on the web. But since Allie's report of the destruction of her house she hadn't visited any of her usual sites and she hadn't got a blog. Perhaps she was in prison. Of the husband, Hakan, he'd found no mention in official listings, other than his job as an English teacher at the one of the local colleges.

In contrast to Kantuta, Amaru her twin had his digital activities extremely well concealed. His avatar was a coiled snake, an ancient Incan icon, which at first had made him seem very easy to follow. After a couple of dead ends, however, Stick realised he would have to work harder and use more of his tools and technique to find out where Amaru was going. He'd spent some time tracking him through the various false trails he'd laid and had begun to wonder why an ordinary lab technician should have his details so well guarded. Unless it was the fact that he appeared to be in contact with someone from *LIBJU*. Was it anything to do with his brother-in-law Hakan, the alleged rebel? Was that what Miramae was talking about when she spoke of an uprising? *LIBJU* stood for *Libertad y Justicia*, Freedom and Justice, so perhaps it was true what the police had said, that Hakan had been inciting rebellion. Perhaps Amaru was too.

But you can wriggle as much as you like there's always someone a few steps behind you, Stick hummed to himself, as he followed the trail. Amaru had also been trying to contact the League of the Dead but had given up.

Or had he? Nothing guaranteed the fact that the man purportedly representing the League of the Dead really was a member of some mythical organisation. Perhaps he was just someone making use of the name, a well-known fairy tale, and Amaru had discovered this. But Amaru had also visited a variety of sites that were causing Stick even greater anxiety. He was investigating anthrax, ricin and novichok and the latest in chemical nerve poisons. Why?

It appeared to have nothing to do with Rosalita or the clinic – and yet…Stick shivered, a cold lump of dread in his stomach, pulled his old coat round him, and returned to his screens.

Chapter 10
The Mine

Allie was almost there, almost at the other side of the chasm, when her foot turned on a small stone and she slipped. Swayed. Struggled to maintain her balance and then threw herself forward, landing with the top half of her body flat on the ground in front of the great stone portal, her lower half dangling over the abyss.

Her lungs seemed to be no longer working. She couldn't breathe.

Clutching at the ground in front of her she found a small tuft of the mustard weed.

Hang on, she thought. Breathe. Lever self slowly forward.

She wedged one knee against the rock below and wriggled forward a few inches, fingernails of the one free hand scraping for purchase in the gravelly surface.

This will ruin my manicure.

Wriggle some more. Grab for the next tuft of weed.

The weed didn't hold, tearing off at the root, and she was obliged to make a grab for another. As she did so her wrist scraped savagely against the edge of the bridge, the sharp stone scraping the skin, tearing loose the rescue strap Alaina had given her. It slid from her wrist and dropped into the canyon below, too light to make a sound as it floated the hundreds of metres to the floor of the crevasse.

For a second she was immobilised, thinking in that moment that she now had no quick means of summoning aid. But she couldn't worry about that now. She had to get onto the ledge.

Breathe again. Get her pelvis over the rim.

She remembered Stick's maxim. 'It's always the best swimmers who drown, the best climbers who fall.' It had something to do with overconfidence.

But I wasn't overconfident, she thought indignantly, as her knee came slowly over the edge. It was just bad luck.

Dragging herself upright and still shaking, she looked back along the crevasse, to where the track curved away in the direction from which she had come. Nothing. No one. To the left of the portal an almost invisible track disappeared up into the mountain. To the right, the path which led to the Royal Road had collapsed into the fissure, leaving only the sheer cliff face. It made re-joining the highway impossible, so the portal was the only way forward. She limped towards the black gateway.

The great stones loomed over her, the carvings sharper and more powerful now she could see them close up, the jaguar and the snake and in the middle of the upper lintel, the condor. On the sides were smaller human figures, accompanied by llamas and other more homely animals. Within the entrance all was darkness.

Using the wristcom's light she peered in. It looked as if people had blocked the entrance off from the inside at some stage, but the great stones had fallen or had, perhaps, been knocked down by others. They lay beneath the entrance on the floor of the cave which was several metres below the level outside. She'd have to climb down over them to get into the passageway disappearing off into the darkness.

She checked the time. It was already past midday. She wouldn't make it back in time to coincide with Alaina's return from the market, even though Alaina could be counted on to be late, picking through the wonderful local materials. And what about the unknown watcher? And that dreadful bridge? The scarf told her that there was someone nearby. She'd just peek in and try find them. If the worst came to the worst she'd just have to head back.

But first she had to let Alaina know what was happening. Standing in the shadow of the great stone doorway, ready to disappear into the cave if anyone should appear on the other side of the fissure and thoughtful of her battery, she sent a text.

"Have found what I think is a back-way in. Here's my latest GPS. Am going to locate one of the locals and find out what's happening and then I'll let you know more. Don't worry, so far I've been perfectly safe (slight untruth there) *and have seen no one, but there's signs of life over here. See you later this evening maybe but will phone later on xx"*

The response pinged straight back.

"Glad you're okay. You're missing a treat here – material fabulous. I've got you a poncho! See you tonight xx"

That was all right then. Alaina was clearly happy enough and she could carry on with a clear conscience. Sending a quick *"Thanks for the poncho. See you later xx"* Allie took a final glance down towards the Royal Road and, seeing no one, headed past the great stone guardians into the cave. The noise had probably just been some small animal looking for her lunch.

As her eyes adjusted to the lack of light she found it easy enough to clamber from one stone slab to the next, heading down to the cave floor. A carpet of small skulls and bones, birds or bats maybe, crunched underfoot as she gingerly explored the cavern. It was icy cold after the ferocious sunshine outside and she shivered.

On the walls more animal figures had been carved, crouching, ready to spring. Although the passageway had clearly been used at some point it had the dusty, cobwebby feel of neglect. Definitely only a back door then.

Another barrier – more stone, cold and damp, the light from her wristcom now her only way of seeing her way forward. But ahead, through a crack, a distant glow.

She froze instinctively. She didn't want to run into someone without having seen who they might be. Peering nervously though the crack she could see only dark shadows but heard a distant rumble, the sound of great machines. People must be here.

She hesitated for a few more minutes but, after telling herself not to be a wuss, she slipped through the crack. She was in a rock corridor. One which was clearly used. Flashing the wristcom light ahead of her she could see large crates and containers stacked along the walls, some draped in tarpaulin. Good. Something to hide behind if someone appeared she didn't like the look of. The noises she'd heard seemed to be getting louder as she inched her way forward.

It seemed an odd place for crates and containers to be found and she wondered if they contained the weapons that Miramae imagined they'd use to overthrow the government. Several had been torn open already and as she flashed her light quickly into one she saw not rifles nor machine guns but brown plastic sacks containing what might be a powder and what she imagined were sticks of dynamite. Or was it gelignite they used nowadays? Were they for sabotage?

Another case held detonators. She knew this because it said so on the box. What had she stumbled into?

Heart catching in her throat, muscles taut, ears strained and listening, hearing only the sound of her own cautious steps and the distant rumble she crept forward, prepared to leap behind one of the crates if anyone should approach.

Lengths of fuse wire.

And then, amazingly, a broken wooden chest with a treasure trove of golden Spanish doubloons. She knew that they'd once found such a chest in Cerro de Pasca in Bolivia, eighty feet below the main street in one of the old mining galleries. It had been a marvel. But this one was left lying around unguarded.

Yet the Indians had worshipped gold. They called it the Tears of the Sun. It was what they were famous for, and what the Spanish invaders had coveted. In Cuzco, the old capital of the Inca world, many of the buildings in the main square, Huaycapata, had been sheathed in the precious metal, including the great Temple which housed a huge, golden image of the sun, the Punchao.

How entranced she'd been, when studying the history of Runa Five, with tales of the Curicancha, The Golden Enclosure next to the Temple. One of its greatest wonders had been a garden containing figures of animals, flowers and plants, llamas and their shepherds, all exquisitely made from gold and silver. None of these miracles of artistry had survived the conquest. The sheets of gold on the temple went to ransom the Inca Atahualpa from Pizarro. The golden animals and shepherds, the flowers and plants were all melted down and sent to Spain and only the enormous golden image of the sun had escaped, so well hidden that it had never been found.

Perhaps these weren't real doubloons and that was why they'd been left lying there.

She carried on down the passageway following the sounds. Lights were on ahead, at the far end of the tunnel. In front of her on the left was an upright box, about the size of a tall man, with a door.

Leaning next to the door a rifle.

A rifle? Her initial euphoria at the thought that she'd found people evaporated. This wasn't good. She certainly didn't want to be on the wrong end of a rifle. Perhaps someone had been guarding the doubloons after all. She should go back.

She had turned when she heard the scraping of a door opening and leapt back behind the nearest stack of cases, crouching down so that she was shielded by the sacking which had been roughly thrown over them. A man came out of the hut, clearly adjusting his clothing, and grabbed hold of the rifle, heading back in her direction. It must be a workers' toilet. The man appeared to be making for the entrance through which she had come, presumably to guard the way into this tunnel.

She bit her lip in frustration and fright. Now she was cut off. He was between her and the way out. As the man headed up the tunnel a woman appeared from a corridor branching off to the side and he turned and grunted a greeting, each going to their separate tasks. Her brain scurried about in panic. Would the man come back? Could she get out while his back was turned. Even the bridge seemed a better option if she could get to it. Or perhaps she could take that little path up into the mountain and, if the worst came to the worst, get Alaina to come and rescue her.

Shrinking back into the darkness of the cave wall, she saw the woman pass. A pale moon face, the roundness accentuated by the anti-dust mask she was wearing, her clothing hard-wearing with big elbow length gloves. Her work must be some form of manual labour. But at least it was a woman and perhaps there were more and she would feel safer.

What were they doing down here?

The woman was letting herself into the toilet and Allie froze. Should she go forward, hoping to find some more women or should she head for the exit and try to avoid the man with the gun? Crouching in her hidey-hole she tried to send a text but got only *No Reception*. Would the rescue strap even have worked underground? She'd have to get out of this one on her own.

She jumped as a louder rumble indicated that the machine she'd heard before had kicked into more violent activity. Peering round the corner of her packing case she could see at the far end, visible in lights strung along the cave walls, a conveyor belt and realised that the sound was that of a mighty crusher, grinding rock and spewing it onto a conveyor belt which rumbled away out of sight.

Amongst the rubble and crushed rock lying on the belt the lights picked out a gleam of yellow.

Was this a gold mine? She knew that anyone who found a seam of gold or indeed of any metal was supposed to declare it to the authorities. A quota system applied to all metals, especially precious metals, in every Runa and all mining had to be government sponsored. What was it Alaina had said? That apart from the workers only Runa Representatives could get into a gold mine, that gold had a value above all else.

So that was what the explosive was for – rock blasting for the mine. But they obviously did a lot of the hacking out the hard way here with picks and shovels as well, if the ancient tools leaning against the tunnel walls were anything to go by. That didn't look like government sponsored mining. So this mine was probably illegal. Hence, perhaps, the lack of interest in the doubloons. Maybe much more gold was still there in the ground.

Alaina's voice echoed in her head. "And what they put those miners through at the end of their shift to make sure they haven't snaffled a nugget or too doesn't bear thinking about."

If this mine was illegal she was in even greater danger. She'd have to give up the notion of finding Rosalita and just get away from here. But it would soon be getting dark outside and she wouldn't be able to follow the path in the dark, let alone go over the bridge. She must leave now.

She'd half stood when she heard the door scrape across the rock floor. The young woman coming out looked up, her face slackening in shock, and then opened her mouth to scream.

'No, please!' Allie stretched out her hand, her heart turning somersaults.

The scream seemed to fill the cave. The crusher feeding the conveyor belt at that moment chose to belch into activity and the scream was almost swallowed up.

Not completely, however.

A man peeled away from the group at the far end.

'Please, please, *por favor*, I don't mean any harm,' Allie gabbled. 'I'll just go away.' She turned to run.

But it was too late.

The man, used to the terrain and the darkness, caught her easily and swung her around. He looked at the girl.

'*Que pasa*?'

The girl, almost it seemed to Allie as frightened as she was, stammered a reply in what she now easily recognised as Quechua. The man holding her arm in a vicious lock was only young, with a round, chubby face that he was evidently trying to make scarier by the cultivation of a fierce moustache.

'*Que pasa*?' He looked at the girl again and Allie caught the word '*Inglesa*' in the reply.

145

More men ran up, one or two grabbing her arms. Older men, more powerful, jostling each other, shouting things she couldn't understand. Her heart began to pound. The guard was running towards them, his rifle in his hand. Someone behind her had got his arm around her neck, crushing her throat so that she could hardly breathe. He smelt rank.

The first man, shaking her roughly while fending off one of the others who was clutching at her elbow, shouted, 'You, English? What...' he sought for the words, 'What you do here?'

The man behind her said, *'Es una espía.'* She's a spy.

She tried to speak but could only croak, her blood thundering in her ears in her panic. The younger man fired off a lot of Quechua and the arm around her neck loosened.

'No, no, I'm a friend,' she said hoarsely. *'Soy amiga.'*

What would happen if they knew nothing about Rosalita, if the clinic bus was nowhere near here? If she'd stumbled into an illegal gold mine where they thought she was a spy? A rivulet of ice ran down her back.

The man behind her said again. *'Es una espía.'*

Her mind spun frantically. They were Indians, the *indigenas*. She thought of the golden half disc in her travel pouch. Could they be Yupanqui's people?

'Soy amiga,' she said, 'Friend, *amiga*,' and then, praying it was the right thing to say, 'Yupanqui.'

At the name several of the men holding her arms loosened their grip and she tore herself partially away. Dragging her travel pouch to her front she took out the small half-disc. The eyes widened.

'Yupanqui,' she said again.

More of the workers had noticed what was happening and had come to see what was going on and soon a crowd was gathered round them, the large, protuberant eyes swivelling in the round pale faces as they followed the to and fro of the argument. Yupanqui's disc was passed from hand to hand and, as the men holding her saw it, they gradually released her.

'English?' Allie said. 'Someone who speaks English.'

But they'd already fetched another older man who was pushing his way through the group. He was clearly some sort of overseer, the others backing off in front of him, and he too grabbed her arm. His own were heavily tattooed, his face covered in rough stubble, and there was a dark stain on his chin where the brown spittle of chewed coca leaves, the local stimulant, had run into his beard. He was looking at her in puzzlement.

'You have Yupanqui's disc. They say you need help? How did you get in here?'

As people backed away she began to feel a little safer, although her heart still pumped unmercifully. No question now, though, that she had to give up on her quest and get back to Lago Noche. What should she say for the best?

'I was looking for a friend. I came on the Inca Road.'

'What! The bridge?'

She felt rather smug, her heart beginning to settle down. '*Si.*'

A murmur rippled behind her as the news was passed back and she heard the tones of disbelief. '*El Camino Real*' and '*El punto*!'.

'But,' the man shook his head, clearly amazed at her taking such a risk, 'Why?'

'*Mi amiga,*' she said, 'my friend, Rosalita, is here.' And then, seeing his frown, 'She came on the clinic bus. *La clinica.*'

'From the clinic.' He turned to murmur a question to the man next to him in Quechua, Allie recognizing the odd word like '*clinica*' and 'Rosalita'. The overseer turned to her and said, 'His girl works in the hospital and he says he thinks a new mother was expected.'

'That would be Rosalita. She came this morning on the clinic bus.'

'You want to see Rosalita?' He was frowning, visibly suspicious. She wasn't in the clear yet. Why, he was obviously thinking, hadn't she come with Rosalita straight to the clinic?

'Yes, I wanted to see Rosalita, but…' what could she say for the best? '… I don't think I'm supposed to know she's here. I don't want to get her into trouble. I just wanted to see her and make sure that she's alright so I came by the roundabout route. But I didn't really know the way.' She took a calculated guess. 'And I didn't know there was a mine and I can see now it wasn't a good idea.' She adopted her most conciliatory tone. 'Your managers probably don't want anyone knowing about the mine – so I'll just go back the way I came in.'

A babble of discussion broke out. Some were clearly telling him he should have nothing to do with her. Or hand her straight over to the supervisors, whoever they might be. Even, perhaps, just dispose of her. How easy, would it be to drop her off that bridge?

Again she felt the shard of ice on her back, the cold lump of dread in her stomach. In the welter of talk she heard Yupanqui's name and that of the clinic and what sounded like the name Atahualpa but understood nothing else. Once more, she thought, she'd underestimated the risk.

The man came back to her.

'We cannot let you go without checking.' He seemed frustrated, irritated. 'The *curacas* will be angry if they know you have seen the work here. We will have to find this Rosalita to see if she knows you. Yupanqui expects us to help and we can get you to the next level but someone else will have to take you to the clinic.' The man who thought she was a spy was protesting violently. The man ignored him. 'It is difficult. There is only one lift and it is guarded top and bottom. It is better if they do not know that you have been here. Only trusted workers are allowed. We will see what can be arranged but once you're at the next level we cannot help you after that.'

'I'm very thankful for any help,' said Allie quickly, thinking that Yupanqui must not be as all powerful in the mine chain of command as he was in the campamento. The servant had called him 'My Lord', but perhaps there were others even more powerful.

'For now we must hide you.'

A flurry of activity took place, the other workers retreating toward the conveyor belt and their work, and she was unceremoniously shoved into the disgusting toilet. She could see through cracks in the wood, the reason for the alarm, a large man, obviously a more senior supervisor, shouting and swearing at the workers.

She waited for what seemed like hours in the foetid-smelling, gaseous hole, until they came to release her.

'We have to wait for the shift change to help you,' said the overseer who spoke English. He was accompanied by another young girl with the same round face and faintly bulging eyes as the other workers. 'Very dangerous. If you are found we'll have to say we know nothing.'

Great, thought Allie. Locked in the can till I expire of methane poisoning and then disowned when anyone finds me. Thank *you*.

The girl looked at Allie with great interest.

'Cusi will look after you. She speak a little English.'

'Come,' said Cusi, smiling shyly, the eyes shining. 'I take you to my room. The end block. No one look for you there.'

'Thank you.' Allie smiled at the girl. She'd been one of the group who'd been so impressed at her coming over the bridge. 'The name's Allie. And your name is Cusi, is that right? Is it a Quechua name?'

The girl smiled. 'Cusi Coyllar, Happy Star. Famous Inca name.'

'Lovely,' said Allie, thinking that Cusi probably never got a chance to see the stars. Poor girl. The whole set-up was more than weird. What was a clinic doing up here? She must find a way to contact Alaina and let her know that she was okay. And she needed above all else Stick's expertise. He'd be able to find out who was masterminding this operation.

'Are there any reception boosters down here?'

Cusi looked at her puzzled and Allie sighed.

'I imagine not.'

She needed the open air. She'd tried several times but could get no signal in the mining gallery. She'd entered a text, '*All okay,*' but she knew it wouldn't go until she was closer to the outside.

This lack of communication, in a world where you were always in contact with others and in so many different ways, was unnerving. She could die down here, and no one would know. She'd become one of the Disappeared, the Missing. She shivered.

'Do you ever go up to the next level?' Surely they didn't stay down here in the dark forever.

'Oh yes, I go up to eating hall and Domingo, Sunday, I go to see Asiri, my cousin. She is clever. She can work on the next level.' Her eyes shone. 'Her room is in the living quarters and I go there. Once I got to walk outside in the valley, but they don't like that. No one must see.'

I bet not, thought Allie. All this illegal mining. "They" must be making a fortune.

Cusi's room turned out to be nothing more than a large niche in the rock wall with a dirty piece of sacking hanging across it, an old mattress on the floor and a rickety card table and chair against one wall. A wooden box sat in one corner and a change of garment hung on a nail banged into the rock.

'So if there's only one lift up to the next level and there's always a guard how will you get me up there?'

'We have a way of sending messages if we not want *curacas* to see. We send it on the rock belt. Sometimes people too, the boys, if they want to escape for a night out.'

'Do you go sometimes?'

Cusi looked puzzled. 'I not need. Asiri invite me on day off. And I go up to the food hall each day for food. Then I can go in lift. I go work now. Break in a little while all men go to room for cards and beer. Then I come back for you, show you.'

She left and Allie looked round at the walls of the cave. They were covered, not with images of pop stars and actors and Hollywood glitz but with pictures of animals and trees, and soft rolling landscapes which

Cusi could never see. No people. No family. Yes one, a young woman, very similar in looks to Cusi, probably Asiri.

It seemed forever but eventually Cusi was back, grabbing her arm and dragging her in the direction of the conveyor belt.

'Quick, quick, before anyone come back. I show you.'

Allie watched as the belt rumbled past them carrying the tons of rock with the gleaming yellow fragments. Cusi was patting the edge with one hand.

'When time to go I slow it down. You get on very quick. You lie on this. Must stay very still and keep below the...' she pointed up and along to where the conveyor belt disappeared through a hole in the rock wall. 'Very small space. Must lie very flat. Understand? The belt will not stop. Very important to get off before the hopper. One boy crushed.'

So – no safety mechanisms, the belt doesn't stop even if something – or someone – is jammed and turning to mush, and you can't tell when you've got to the hopper till you fall into it. Great.

Cusi must have seen her face. 'It all right.' The little voice was anxious. 'Boys often go. I will send message first to Asiri. She will help you get off at right place.'

'How do we know if she's got the message?'

'Don't know. We must trust. I send it now.'

Allie took a deep breath. 'Righto. When do I leave?'

'Two hours.'

'Why then? Why not now?'

'Because Cobo, top *curaca*', Cusi sought for the word, 'boss man...'

'Supervisor?'

'Yes, supervisor. Because Cobo stop working then and another will come. Better.'

'Cobo not so helpful, I gather?'

'They call him Rumiñaui.' She saw Allie's blank look. 'Name of general of Inca Topa. From old days. It mean "Stony Eye."'

'I get the message,' said Allie. 'We wait.'

Cusi scratched a few symbols with a lump of chalk onto a piece of slate, turned it over, drew a line across the back and put it carefully on the belt, close to the edge. The belt rumbled on and disappeared out of sight into the upper level. 'Asiri or Juanita will see it,' she said confidently. 'You will see.'

Wish I could, thought Allie, and settled down to wait.

It all went better than she might have expected, although the conveyor belt had been very, very scary. She hadn't dared raise her head above the level of the rock and so couldn't judge how close they were to the hole in the wall or the hopper. Quite apart from the fact that at one stage they were travelling in mid-air across one of the galleries and she feared she would be tipped from a great height. The belt wasn't stable and the rock walls they passed glinted and seemed to move as they trundled past.

The journey seemed to go on for ever. Just when she was beginning to panic, imagining herself tumbling through the air and being sucked into a crusher, with tons of rock falling on top of her, somebody tugged her shoulder and she dropped to the floor at Asiri's feet, recognising her instantly from the cracked and blurred picture in Cusi's room.

'You okay?'

'Yes, yes, I'm fine.' Staggering up and starting to brush the earth and pieces of rock and gravel from her clothes, she realised that something was wrong.

'It is all right,' Asiri was saying, looking over Allie's shoulder to someone behind her. *'Es una amiga.'*

Allie turned and was looking into the eyes of an older man, sullen and suspicious. She wondered if he was this Cobo – Stony Eye.

'It is okay,' said Asiri to the man. 'She has Yupanqui's disc.'

'Ah.' He exhaled noisily. 'I heard. That of course makes it a different matter.' A flow of Quechua passed between them, but Allie, watching the interchange, was sure the man was saying he wanted nothing to do with it.

'I'll take her to my room and hide her. I'll come back straight away.'

The man nodded, clearly relieved that no more was expected of him.

Asiri fished in a cupboard and brought out a large black rag and thrust it into Allie's hand.

'Take off the cloak. Cover your head and arms. If someone looks at us keep your head down.'

She was clearly a lot older than Cusi and dressed in clean overalls with her hair tied back in a bandana. She had the same eyes, though, and the same smile.

Allie did as she was told and Asiri stuffed the cloak into a bag and led the way into another tunnel. It seemed to go for miles twisting and turning, gradually rising in level, until eventually they came to another portal. It looked as if it had been filled in with stone slabs, but when Asiri held her hand against the side wall a huge rock door slid back, rumbling on steel runners. Asiri stepped through, gestured to Allie to follow her and then moved her hand again against the other side of the portal. The door slammed shut.

Now it was just a stone wall again. As the sound echoed along the corridor Allie felt a hollow in her stomach. Now she was irrevocably cut off from going back the way she'd come. She'd never find the mine again. She could only go on.

As she turned to follow Asiri, passing what looked like a heap of rags piled against the corridor wall, a bony hand shot out and grabbed her arm in a pincer-like grip.

Ravi waved to Stick through the corridor window. Stick returned the hologram's wave as he read the message Ravi had sent.

"Nothing beyond what I thought on the Anderlans virus. There's a vaccine, so it's no longer a problem. Paediatrics and obstetrics tell me that memory loss has never been reported in connection with either the vaccine or the disease itself. I see you found the site. Made a fair bit on it in my own small way. They've got all sorts on there, not just poker. Last time I was on the League of the Dead were a no show."

He smiled and waved again and the hologram faded.

Stick looked at the group around the virtual table. It was clever the way the programmers had it all set up like a real hospital, even to the glass fronted corridor outside, through the windows of which Ravi had waved. Of course, with a game name like *Plague 7* one might expect a hospital. Various medical devices sat on shelves behind them and opposite, phials and test tubes in racks next t0 boxes of medical gloves. In front of each player was a nameplate and space for their avatar. Some had chosen to remain anonymous, their small avatars only displaying animals, vehicles or flowers. There were a couple of men with greatly enhanced pectoral muscles on display and one of the women was impossibly scantily clad. Perhaps she hoped it would divert their attention from the game. If it was a 'she', of course. Several wore surgical masks. Their names were flashed on a circling LED display in front of him. Some he recognised from other games, some not. One of those he'd never come across before was Beautiful Fruit, another Loot.

'We know what *you*'re here for then, Stick thought. And the fact that Aleister, whoever he was, had joined this game as well struck him as curious. Was he following him?

He'd sent out his Hijame worm the minute they were all logged on and hastily reviewed the data it had brought back. Ah, the glorious internet of things, he thought, as he inspected the fridge contents of the wizened old crone opposite him, listed as a Mrs Philips. Nothing in her fridge but four six packs of lager. The vision monitor was even more revealing – wall-to-wall porn movies. Stick congratulated himself on his discernment. Might need to watch this guy.

The gamekeeper laughed and called them to order.

'We welcome two new players to *Plague 7*, Aleister and Mrs Philips, so I will repeat the rules. The world has been swept by an untreatable plague. It has been discovered that one small tribe near Kisangani in Runa 7 is immune. If you are a researcher your job is to find the tribe, sort out the variables that make them immune – DNA, antibodies and so on – so that your company can create a vaccine. The chemists will help you there. Of course, the great pharmaceutical companies will be interested in your results and may try underhand methods to get hold of your findings. Some governments might be interested, for nefarious reasons. The other participants' roles are self-evident. The Shaman may fear the newcomers will undermine his authority in the tribe. Who knows whose side the Chief is on?'

She giggled.

'Please ensure that your sensors are correctly placed. Wrongly placed sensors can be quite dangerous, so this is extremely important. You were issued with a number of chips according to your scores in previous rounds and you can use these to purchase what you feel you might need during the game. And, of course, you can accrue more at each stage.' She giggled again. 'Use them wisely.' She took out a pack of cards. 'Usually you would choose your role but at this level you are what the dice tell us. If you are a researcher and are – um – liquidated before the end of the game, the liquidator takes your role and inherits your chips, if he so chooses.'

Stick watched as she placed a card in front of each of them, saying eventually, 'We now have a chief chemist, and his assistants, five researchers, three pharmaceutical experts, the members of the tribe, the Shaman, the Chief, the porters, a pilot.' She paused. 'There are also several unnamed players who may or may not be helpful to you.'

Stick turned over his card. He was a researcher, which was a lucky break. He read his instructions.

'Here are your assistants and your headquarters.' A small group of white clad workers appeared in his VR screen along with a building saying Research

Department. 'The aim is to find the tribe, take samples, cross-check with the data base, get back to the research station, get the chemists to analyse your data and then register your vaccine. They may not be honest employees. Some will sell it to the highest bidder.

Your tools are your syringes, your first aid pack, your keys, your data set, and your map. You're also allowed a weapon, a ball of string and a torch. If you get to the forest then you're allowed to change any of these items for something more useful. If you accrue enough points you get to choose from the Loot Boxes. Or the Easter Eggs. Or you can, of course, buy more points to spend on medical devices. You might even want to sell your points for cash.'

Stick dwelt on this point with satisfaction. He'd already traded points for cash in previous rounds and had begun to dream that if he got close to winning the game he might get enough to go to Runa Five. It would be worth every penny just to see Allie. He'd even pinned the flight times on the wall above his desk.

'No army,' said Loot, looking at his card. 'What a bore.'

The worm had brought back nothing on Aleister except his surname Crowley and the name of a book, *The Blue Equinox*. Stick had no time to see more as the holograms disappeared and their screens went black.

It was time to begin.

Chapter 11
The Village

The convulsive grip on Allie's arm did not slacken as she looked down into an ancient face, shrivelled and wrinkled, criss-crossed with lines like the maze of paths on the mountainside.

Every nerve shrieked.

The old lady looked up at her with small bright eyes.

'You have seen my son?'

'Leave the lady, Aunty,' said Asiri. 'She will talk to you later.'

Allie dragged her hand away as the old lady released it reluctantly, muttering something in what sounded like Quechua. Following Asiri as fast as she could, her pulse still beating in irregular rhythm, Allie stumbled on.

Asiri was leading her through a warren of stone corridors, heading constantly upwards. 'The old lady's a little bit mad. No need to worry. She doesn't cause trouble.'

'She thinks I've seen her son?' They were passing a set of doors.

'Many years ago the great father had many children. He took them away from their mothers.'

'Grandfather? Her husband?'

'No. Great Father.' You could hear the capital letters. 'He…' Asiri sought for the words, 'he took the babies. They never saw them again. When Maria Rosa heard they were coming to take her son she grabbed him and ran into the mine. They said she found a way out to the other side and came to the little bridge. She dropped her hat and shawl down into the valley.' Asiri's voice indicated approval of the strategy. 'Then she hid in a crack in the rock for a long time. They went past looking for her and then went back over the bridge and saw the hat and the shawl in the valley bottom. They needed many hours to get down there and check and in the end they gave up looking for her.'

'But now she is here?'

'Yes, I don't know what really happened but after six years they found them and brought him back. But he screamed so badly they had to let her come with him and now she stays with him.' Asiri's voice was respectful. 'He is one of the Seven.'

Allie was about to ask who the Seven were and why the old lady thought she'd seen her son when Asiri grabbed her arm and rushed her past a doorway which led to a large communal eating area. She was clearly worried that Allie would be seen. In the seconds it took them to pass Allie saw several people seated at tables, and from what must have been the kitchen came the smell of cooking. This must be the refectory, the food hall that Cusi had talked about.

'No one must see you yet. We'll go to my room.'

In the next corridor there were thin slots for windows on their right, looking out onto the outside world. Allie was trying to see where they were when Asiri dragged her away from the window and into a side passage, back against the wall. A large, thickset man went past in the opposite direction to them. He looked like the overseer she'd seen through the crack in the ancient wood of the mine toilet, shouting and swearing at the workers. The grim expression on his face was probably permanent and he paid them no attention.

'Rumiñaui,' Asiri said, once he was safely past.

'The unhelpful one? Stony Eye?'

'He works for the *Panacas*, for Atahualpa.'

Who on earth were the *Panacas*? Allie had vague memories of having read about them when researching Runa Five prior to leaving England but could no longer quite recall what. And who was Atahualpa? Asiri grimaced and pulled her onwards once more.

She caught a glimpse in the dim distance, through the narrow slots, of a mountainside and, far below, a valley floor.

'Panacas?'

'Big bosses.' Even moving at speed Allie could hear the contempt in Asiri's voice. And she'd remembered who the Panacas were – relatives and advisers to the Lord Inca back before the Spaniards came, who'd represented the inner circle of government. Big bosses indeed. So who was the Lord Inca now? This Atahualpa?

Following Asiri closely Allie continued to speculate as they came to a line of doors, all, as far as she could see from some that were partially open, leading to small rooms. They seemed more like cells in the rock than living quarters but looked comfortably furnished and had views through the slit windows out over a valley. On the opposite side of the corridor more doors. A whole village was hiding here, buried inside the mountain. What were they all doing? And what had happened to the children that the Great Father had stolen? Slave labour for the mine like poor little Cusi?

Asiri interrupted her thoughts by opening a door and saying, 'This is my room. Please, you can stay here for now.' She smiled shyly, pointing at a second bed. 'Cusi only sleeps here at weekends so you can use it if you like. I'll come back soon and take you to Rosalita. She's in the hospital.' Then, clearly concerned, she frowned and said, 'If we are asked I'll say you're my cousin, that you're a bit simple, that you don't speak.'

Allie laughed and said, 'It's very good of you to look after me, Asiri.'

The young woman smiled. 'Yupanqui entrusts you to us and we are happy to do it. But it is more dangerous now with the new *curacas* so we need to be careful. I must go now but I'll be back in an hour or so.'

She didn't wait for Allie's thanks but disappeared at a run and Allie was left alone. At least she wasn't locked in a foul-smelling toilet.

Sitting on the edge of the second bed she reflected on her situation. She'd wanted to find out what was going on and it seemed that she had in indeed found something – although whether this hidden village and the mine had anything to do with the unrest in the campamento or Rosalita's problem with the clinic was not clear.

It appeared that the young woman was here, at any rate, so at least she'd be able to find out what her message meant. Something to do with this place? She hadn't looked happy on the bus. Was the Great Father, presumably the new Lord Inca, still stealing children and, if so, was Rosalita worried that her child would be one of them? It seemed suspicious that she was here, in a secret mountain hideaway, rather than having the baby at the local clinic. And who were the Seven? Did she think they'd take her child?

Allie tried looking through the slit window but could only see the bare valley floor and the jagged surrounding edge of a crater wall. How did Yupanqui fit into all of this? Was he one of these *Panacas*? A leader of some kind, one the people would be happy to follow, who'd be worthy of their trust?

Yeah, right, jeered a voice from within her. Very trustworthy. Keeping in with you till he was sure you wouldn't betray them. Rejecting you once he didn't need you any longer. But surely he wouldn't be as ruthless as the present government, she thought, remembering the gentle way he'd touched Miramae's shoulder, chiding her for believing everything that Hakan had said. And he'd given her the disc – which may well have saved her life, if not worse. She shuddered to think what might have happened had she not had it. Well, now she was here, maybe she'd find out what was going on.

She turned back just as Asiri returned, bringing with her a little box of food which Allie was able to eat while Asiri busied herself. It was amazingly tasty and apparently fresh – a salad of some kind, with various vegetables, tomatoes and peppers, courgettes and even quinoa, the protein rich grain which had been so common in the Andes before the Blind Ages. Allie suffered a momentary qualm, wondering if these things had been grown in contaminated soil, but in the end, seduced by the delicious smell and taste, gave in and wolfed them down. It had been many hours since her breakfast coffee and churro.

Asiri burrowed into the back of a cupboard and found an old cloak which she gave Allie, tucking the elegant sun jacket into the cubbyhole in place of it. She looked anxiously at her visitor and then rummaged in the cupboard some more.

'Nobody here has yellow hair.' She waved a black scarf at Allie and wrapped it round her head bandit style, covering her hair completely. Then, squinting at her disparagingly, 'You're too clean…' she sought for the word, '…too white. We'll use the juice of alo berries. Colour your skin – like in the army.'

After Asiri's ministrations Allie looked at her new, slightly smeared, brown face in the piece of polished metal which did duty for a mirror and sighed. Almost as bad as the aged crone. And since, although she wasn't in Alaina's league, she was undoubtedly too tall as well as too white and too yellow she'd have to stoop. One thing on top of another. She sighed again.

Asiri looked at her and laughed. 'Much better,' she said. 'Now I don't need to worry we'll be caught.'

Taking Allie's hand she led her off through another set of corridors and rock tunnels deep into the mountain until they came to some large double doors. To Allie's amazement they opened out into a big reception area and waiting room. The fact that there was no-one behind the reception desk met with Asiri's approval. 'We can go straight to Rosalita.'

She went ahead and Allie followed, lurking at the back, head down. They passed a room with a row of incubators lined up, and another with MRI on the door. It was, as far as Allie could tell, a fully equipped miniature hospital, only the rock above revealing that they were inside a mountain.

Only one nurse was looking after the six bays which included the one where Rosalita was the single patient and she took Asiri's explanation that Allie was just family visiting her from beyond the village without question, leaving to look after other patients as soon as she had shown them where Rosalita was. Asiri launched into a flow of Quechua until the woman was well out of earshot.

Rosalita's face was transformed, holding her baby in her arms.

'Allie! You come; you make me very happy!' She patted the side of the bed so that Allie and Asiri should sit next to her. 'See my little Esteban. Isn't he beautiful? He have my Esteban's eyebrows.'

Allie had never worked out how people saw family likenesses in babies which were all more or less little pink blobs. Must be love, I guess. She shucked the tiny infant under the chin, seeing the startling blue eyes wandering in her direction in the unfocused way that babies have.

'He's beautiful, isn't he?' Allie tried to sound casual. 'But why are you here, Rosalita? Why didn't you have your baby in Avila, like the other mothers? Was that what you wanted to see me about?'

Rosalita looked a little uneasy. 'They send a message from the clinic, that I must go to see them. They said the baby can have problems. I very worried and not know what questions to ask when I go. Jaime still poorly and cannot help me so I think if you go with me then you can explain to me what is wrong.'

'I don't suppose I'd have been much help. It's my mum who's the doctor, not me!' Allie was trying to sound light-hearted.

'No,' Rosalita's earnest little face shone with admiration. 'You understand much better. So Amaru take note for me. But later they send someone to collect me very quick and I not know how to tell you. Amaru was at police station trying to help Kantuta. I not see Rafa. So sorry.'

She looked anxiously at Allie who said, 'That's all right. No harm done,' while thinking that she sincerely hoped that that would be the case.

'At the clinic they say that I have the virus and the baby will be much better here. They are going to help me. They send message for me to Jaime, tell him not to worry. And they send the bus all the way up here for me.'

Her face brightened. 'Ignacia is here too.'

'You've seen her?'

'Yes, she is here.' Rosalita's beautiful little face clouded with doubt. 'But she did not remember me. She had the virus but,' she brightened again, 'she has a beautiful baby and she has married one of the... the... *metalisteros*.'

'Metalworker?' Allie suggested.

Rosalita shrugged. 'Better. He very clever.' She sought for the word, 'Artist. He make beautiful things. Ignacia is very happy. The baby is fine but Ignacia remembers nothing. She did not remember her man in Avila even. She is happy. The baby is beautiful.'

Allie was wondering if she should mention that nobody seemed to believe in this virus, that Dr Chavez had said that a vaccine existed, when at that moment somebody bobbed his head around the door.

It was Rafa. Allie's heart leapt. A friend in a strange land.

'Rafa, Rafa! Oh it's good to see you. What are you doing here?'

The flashing smile. 'More like, what you doing here, Allee?'

'I came to see Rosalita.'

Rosalita's eyes sparkled. 'They tell me she come on Royal Road, the bridge.'

'I hear.' Rafa's eyes were admiring.

'So how on earth did *you* get in?'

He laughed. 'I come on clinic bus. I looking for Rosalita and see her with nurse from the clinic. I hear that bus has come for her so while they fetching her I hide in back in big box with lots of equipment. Rosalita have baby just as we get here. Everybody so excited and busy no one see me climb out. I lucky. I find cousin here; he help me stay. Say I am a good worker, know how to keep my mouth shut. Knows I will do anything for Rosalita.'

'How is Jaime?'

'Much better. The old ones hid him. Gutierrez come back. Not find him.' His smile faded. 'Raoul still in hospital but...' his natural ebullience returned, 'but he bit better.'

'That's good.'

'We have to get him out of there before they take him to jail.'

Rosalita smiled. 'Jaime and me, we both lucky.'

How beautiful she looked when she was happy, thought Allie. She stroked little Esteban's velvety cheek, admiring the blue eyes.

Back in the room Asiri made a better job of the skin stain and dyed her hair.

She looked at Allie and laughed. 'Don't go out in the rain. It'll all come off and I'll get into trouble. I must go to the mine now, but I'll come back later, one hour maybe, or two.'

With a cheerful smile she was gone and Allie was left alone again. She wondered what she should do.

What was this place? Apart from the conveyor belt, the mine had seemed very antiquated with few modern pieces of machinery. Most of the equipment was old and rusted, the mine workers performing tasks done by robots in modern mines. Nobody used pickaxes and shovels any more. And the mine appeared to be completely cut off from this area which was, in essence, a whole village, a small town even, hidden inside the mountain. She would never find her way out without assistance, and even then, she thought, those in charge, whoever they were, might be reluctant to let her go.

The little hospital seemed to be equipped with all the latest technology. The food Asiri had left her from the refectory was excellent. Better, even, if she was honest, than the food at home. It looked as if her oxygen pack was replenishing as well, so that meant they had piped oxygen. Who was responsible for all of this? Who really were the *Panacas*? The Seven? She still had to ask Asiri about them.

By dint of dangling her arm outside the small slit window in the rock she managed to send a text to Alaina. Should she mention how dangerous it had been? She seemed to be quite safe at the moment. She didn't want Alaina coming in all guns blazing if it would get Asiri and Rosalita into trouble, especially with the baby. Perhaps she should just find out what was going on first, and then they could plan on how she could leave safely.

"Hi! Really sorry about this. I'm okay but I've only just got above ground so I'm staying with a girlfriend overnight."

She'd been about to put *Rosalita* but then thought of the attempt on her blog. She'd better not mention anybody by name but knew that Alaina would guess who it was.

"Give my apologies to your parents if they've got there already. Hope you got some gorgeous material and thanks for my poncho. Am looking forward to seeing it. Say Hi to Randy and the others for me. See you tomorrow! Allie xx."

It seemed very bad-mannered, but it was the best she could do and at least they'd have her GPS if they needed it. She hadn't mentioned that she'd got in but was unsure whether she'd be able to get out.

Just as she finished sending the text a loud banging on the door made her jump.

She stiffened and stayed as still as she could. Had someone seen her arm waving about? The noise would surely disturb everybody. If the person couldn't hear her then perhaps they'd go away.

The banging continued, if anything getting louder. Whoever it was wasn't going to give up.

Allie summoned up her courage and opened the door by a crack, prepared to slam it shut again if need be.

The old face in front of her cracked into a thousand wrinkles as the woman smiled. She was holding the hand of a toddler who wandered beside her, seemingly unworried by the noise. He was attached by a thin leather line to the old lady's hand.

'*Hola!*'

'*Hola.*' Relief washed over her and she smiled. What was the woman's name?

'It's Maria Rosa, isn't it? Is this your son?'

The lined brown face creased into laughter.

'He my little baby. He called Paquito.'

The child looked up at her and her heart lurched. He had the same vivid blue eyes as little Esteban. And Yupanqui.

She looked at the old lady. 'Yupanqui is your son?'

'*Si!*' the old lady smiled in satisfaction. 'We go to fetch Paquito's cousin. You come? You tell me about my big boy.'

She had an hour or so for reconnaissance and thus far nobody had paid her any attention. Accompanied by the old lady she might be even less noticeable. If she wanted to help Rosalita she needed to know what was going on.

'If it's not far. Asiri is coming back later so I must be back.'

'We go to school. Just near, round corner.'

'Right, let's go.'

Nobody gave them a second glance as they wandered along the corridor, Allie making sure that she draped the black shawl in such a way as to almost conceal her face. She told the old lady about her meeting with Yupanqui and of his visit to Rosalita.

'He was very helpful.' It sounded a bit bald but the old lady had obviously heard the story before and, after establishing that Gutierrez had been well and truly put off the scent, lost interest.

'So you visit Rosalita,' she said. 'Very good. She good girl. Now we fetch the cousin.'

'Who's the cousin?'

'Aylen. Son of a *metalistero*. His *cuidadora* works in the food hall. School finish soon so I fetch him, take him home and keep him till she come back. Paquito go in morning only.'

Allie looked down at Paquito and he looked up at her and laughed, the intense blue eyes sparkling. A couple of small children, not much older than Paquito, came out of one of the doors on the corridor and ran past them. The old lady stopped at the door.

'I bit late,' she said. 'Hope he not gone.'

She peered into what was obviously a classroom and said with satisfaction, 'No, he still there. He doing something with Milleray.'

Allie, looking over her shoulder, saw two smallish children sitting together at a desk at the front with small screens in front of them. Playing games? Some sort of kindergarten?

Maria Rosa waved at a young woman standing at the front and she looked up, saw them and waved back, saying something to Maria Rosa.

'She say they almost finished,' the old lady said. 'They just loading their homework.'

The two children turned round to gaze at Maria Rosa, almost twins they looked so alike, their faces somehow unwelcoming. They didn't smile but went back to their homework.

Allie looked at the large white screen with a jolt of surprise. That couldn't be what they were downloading, surely? It was covered in groups of equations, what looked like integral and differential calculus, and symbols which were from quantum physics. Arcane knowledge, far beyond anything she could have managed.

But these were just small children.

Somebody was coming up behind them, a young woman in workers' overalls, opening the door opposite the classroom and coming out with a small autobot, a mini vacuum cleaner.

'*Hola*, Maite.'

'*Hola*, Maria Rosa.' She was obviously in a rush and smiled apologetically. 'I late, must finish.'

She put the bot on the floor and started the motor and then pursued it down the corridor, guiding it with a remote into the areas she felt needed attention, before disappearing round a corner. Allie and Maria Rosa ambled after her. The old lady said, 'They always late in that lesson. We go to the end and then come back.'

Maite appeared from out of one of the rooms. The small bot, now unaccompanied and brushing ahead of her, headed into the next opened classroom door. A few seconds later an angry teenager erupted in front of them from within, hurling what sounded like a load of abuse at Maite.

Maite stopped the bot and stammered what was clearly an apology.

He was incredibly beautiful, with the thatch of blue-black hair above the broad forehead, the sharply delineated cheekbones. Allie had a sudden flash of memory of a face opposite her in the alleyway next to Rosalita's, the profile of the youth who had tripped up the escaping Manco. She was sure it was same person. He had the same brilliant blue eyes as Paquito – but these eyes were like glass. And, the thought came unbidden, they were like Paquito's, like little Esteban's, like Yupanqui's. But without the humanity.

'Brusca,' muttered the old lady. 'He say bot stir up dust, spoil his experiment.'

Maite said something else, probably trying to explain, and Brusca sneered. She scurried off down the corridor and Allie and the old lady followed her, the young man glaring at them as they went past. The force of his arrogance was like a wind behind them.

At least he appeared not to have recognised her from the campamento she thought. Going quickly round the corner away from him they heard giggling coming from one of the rooms ahead and then girlish screams of mirth.

Maria Rosa ambled up to the classroom door and looked in, Allie behind her, preparing to move out of sight if anyone looked in her direction. A small pig squatted on the floor, gazing at the group of girls seated in a ring around him. It had a small box attached to its head.

'Come on,' the girls laughed. 'Again.'

A small tinny voice emanating from the box said:

'La Cucuracha, La Cucuracha

Ya no puede caminar.'

Allie recognised it. *La Cucuracha* – The Cockroach. An old Spanish folk song that she'd learned in junior class when Spanish had been popular. *Why can't the cockroach walk*?

'Next,' the girls chanted.

'Porque no tiene…' the voice stuttered, *'…porque le falta…porque le falta...'* It stopped.

'Limonada que tomar,' the girls shrieked back at the little pig, collapsing with laughter again.

Allie had always wondered how the lack of lemonade made the cockroach unable to walk.

The pig moved its head, looking in her direction and Allie, saw to her horror human comprehension in its eyes and deep sadness.

They had allowed chimera embryos here?

Maria Rosa withdrew, saying matter-of-factly, 'It will finish as *Caldo de Puerco.*'

'What's that?' Allie asked, thinking only of the human anxiety in the little piggy eyes.

'Soup,' the old lady said.

Maite reappeared on her way back, studiously carrying the bot, and Allie was happy to have her thoughts diverted.

'I just go now to water the plants,' Maite said, putting the bot back in its cupboard, 'and I must feed the animals. They have to be fed on time.'

'And I must collect Aylen,' Maria Rosa said and chuckled. 'Feed him on time too.'

Something terribly wrong was going on here. It turned her stomach. If she wanted to find out who was responsible this might be her only opportunity to see more. She came to a swift decision.

'I'll go with Maite to feed the animals if that's all right with you, Maria Rosa. Maite can show me the way back.'

The old lady was unworried and, accompanied by the two children, waved them goodbye cheerfully.

'We water the plants first.'

Maite was leading her through yet another doorway cut through the rock, into what was obviously an enlarged natural fissure. Amazingly it was lit by natural light, although looking straight up only the rock was visible and then, as they went further forward, green tracery on thousands of ledges, ledges so narrow that it seemed impossible that anything could survive on them, plants of every description clinging to the surface. Drops of water splashed on her face from above, cool and refreshing, as Maite opened and closed taps along what seemed like miles of corridor. Small fruit trees stood in corners, fruit bushes tumbled from their ledges, ledges that were so well terraced they could hold all kinds of vegetation. Each ledge was shielded by stained glass above it.

No wonder they had enough food for the village and more beside. The old Inca techniques of terracing, along with the husbanding of water and channelling it to where it was needed, were now used to feed this mighty vertical farm. It was hidden cleverly from above but lit by natural sunlight as rays fell at different angles at different times of day. So this was where the food in the refectory came from. Everything smelt cool and green and pleasant.

Maite sighed with satisfaction, as she closed the last tap. 'Plants have water. Now we feed the animals.'

As they came out into another corridor Allie was surprised to see a life-sized painting set in a specially carved niche in the wall. She looked at it in shock. It was Dr Lieberhart, Chavez's father. Framed in gilt, it had several little bowls of quinoa and fruit and vases of flowers in front of it. Although similar to the photo in Chavez' study, in this image Lieberhart was standing with his hand on the head of a small Indian boy next to him, an expression of pride on his face. The boy had blue eyes.

So this must be where Lieberhart had come. Stick had told her that he'd disappeared years ago. He must have found the Indians and the mine and lived among them. Was that the connection between the clinics, the one in the campamento and the one here where Rosalita had had her baby? Was Lieberhart still here somewhere? Was, she wondered, the child in the picture his?

She couldn't linger or think about it too much as Maite was hurrying her on, anxious no doubt to finish her job. Perhaps Brusca would report the young woman if she took too long. The air had been so fresh and sweet-smelling in the planting area that Allie was completely unprepared for the smell when Maite opened another door, leaned in and pressed a switch on the wall. She was almost overwhelmed by the rank stench issuing from the cage which ran the length of one of the walls inside.

'Ouch, that's awful.'

'He always smell bad.'

A huge grey wolf paced up and down the cage with ill-controlled savagery. The name, Wulfi, was engraved on a copper rectangle screwed above the cage door. Maite opened a fridge and took out a large lump of what looked like replacement meat, in essence just a hunk of protein, and swung it cautiously through the hatch towards the animal, hastily closing the hatch door. Wulfi inspected her with ill-concealed contempt.

'I bit scared of Wulfi. He too clever.'

As Allie approached the cage to look more closely at the animal she saw with horror that it had open suppurating sores on its side, and older scars.

'It must be in pain,' she protested to Maite. 'Look at those wounds.'

Maite still held back. 'Brusca's boss have to punish him sometimes. He wicked.'

Allie was about to say that any animal imprisoned in such a way would be violent when she saw that the yellow eyes looking back at her were human and despairing. In a sudden paroxysm of rage Wulfi hurled himself against the bars, fangs clashing on the metal, missing her pointing, outstretched hand by inches. Maite dragged her back and the human eyes looked at her and the slavering lip curled in what she could swear was a grimaced smile.

'He dangerous. Leave him.'

Maite carried on down the corridor to further cages, throwing in the substitute meat and the vegetables while Allie stood transfixed in the middle of the corridor.

This was not possible. The Eringaard laws permitted no genetic engineering of this kind. And certainly no human/animal chimera embryos were ever allowed. Perhaps that was why the villagers were so scared of being spotted out in the valley. Someone had been practising genetic modification, if not worse.

Her mind sped back to Yupanqui's odd oxygen implant. Perhaps he didn't really need one. She knew that years ago everyone had been working on the ability to breathe in the thin atmosphere or to find some way of protecting human skin from the sun. Especially as these changes might offer some military advantage. Hadn't Lieberhart got his Nobel Prize for his work on the Crispr technology for gene therapies? At one time there'd been government sponsored programs in many of the Runas working on ways around the oxygen deficiency, or some means of mitigating the sun-damage, but they'd only produced grotesques – people with grossly inflated chest sizes, thick elephant hide skin, other atrocities. The Species Protocol had eventually put an end to all such experiments, a Protocol enforced in every Runa. It was why, in Avila, the four-eyed came into town so rarely, scared of the Eugenics Police who implemented a savage sterilisation programme.

She looked back at Wulfi. Even in the Blind Ages they'd known that wolves kept in cages went mad. How much more so if they were, in some way, human. Her mind spiralled back to the poor pig. It was horrible. Stomach churning. Human intelligence imprisoned in an animal body. Were the rebels responsible for what was going on here? And she'd wanted to help them.

'*Que pasa?*'

The voice behind her was loud and angry and as she spun round she saw that it was Brusca, the handsome face contorted by annoyance.

'*Que pasa?*'

Maite ran back saying something and Brusca swung towards her, clearly asking her who this stranger was, what she was doing there. He obviously hadn't recognised her from the alleyway so Asiri's alo berry juice and ancient cloak must have worked. He was pointing at one of the notices on the wall, which probably said *Off Limits*, or words to that effect.

He turned to Allie again and she could see he was asking what she was doing there.

What was 'lost' in Spanish for Pete's sake, let alone in Quechua? She mumbled the Quechua phrase Asiri had taught her for 'I don't know,' and Maite must have been saying that she was just a friend visiting when they were saved by one of the other teenagers leaning out of the doorway, laughing, telling Brusca to come and see something. After looking at her in indecision he pointed towards the exit corridor.

'*Vaya*.' The voice was harsh.

'Come, come,' Maite was dragging at her arm, 'We go back. I finished the jobs.'

Brusca waited to see that they went in the right direction and then ran away from them towards the other teenager.

Who were these children? The feeling of dread in her bones began to worsen. Was little Esteban doomed to end up as one of these freaks like Brusca, supremely intelligent but lacking all normal feeling. What was it that Maria Rosa had said about Aylen? That his *cuidadora* worked in the food hall. Not his mother. *Cuidadora* meant carer. Had his mother been one of the failures. Had she died? Ignacia had kept her baby but only, perhaps, because of the amnesia. How could the children show real feeling when they'd had no normal family life? Yes, they were beautiful but what other genetic material had gone into them? In what other ways were they deviant?

And their mothers hadn't known.

Her mind a rage of anxiety and revulsion she ran back to Asiri's room, aware that she must now be late.

As she burst in the door, heart still beating unevenly, she saw that someone had preceded her – a man, seated at the desk, waiting for her.

Stick found himself standing on a vast plain. In the distance was the forest, the one shown on the map where the tribe was hidden who might or might not have the disease, who might or might not be saved and whose DNA might yield the information to save the world. To his left stood Aleister and behind him Loot and he wondered whose side they were on, and what roles they were playing.

His points score was more than satisfactory and he had his eye on Aleister's more detailed map, wondering whether he should offer to trade, when he heard Loot yell.

''Ware the taser.'

He was struck a tremendous crippling blow on the shoulder from behind and found himself toppling towards a crevasse which had just opened in the ground at his feet.

Ah! he thought, I see we're playing dirty. Retrieving himself at the last moment, he rolled away from the edge of the crack in the ground, ignoring the excruciating pain, and swung the first aid bag at the legs of the man behind him. Aleister Crowley, he'd just remembered was a renowned twentieth century Satanist. Undoubtedly from the League of the Dead.

Chapter 12
The Punchao

The man seated at the desk was Yupanqui. His eyes, the vivid blue eyes of Paquito and Esteban, were angry. Allie paused in the doorway as he spoke.

'What are you doing here?' The voice was harsh.

She hardly knew what she said as she spoke stiffly. 'I came to see Rosalita.' He'd ignored her. He hadn't expected her to use the disc. He wasn't even pretending to wear an oxygen pack today. 'I wanted to know that she is here by choice.'

The voice hardened even more. 'And what did you decide?'

She sighed, feeling that she was in a false position. 'Yes, she's delighted to be here. And her baby is beautiful. But... Yupanqui...,' she looked at him, trying to find again the charming man who'd promised to help her, hoping against hope that somehow he would not have been party to the grotesque experiments taking place in the village. 'Why the secrecy? Why are these mothers buried away? If it's

what I think it is then these women have been used....'
Her voice trailed off '...it's immoral.'

'You think Rosalita is unhappy with her little Esteban? The police have killed her husband. Don't you think she stands a better chance here than in the campamento?'

'Yes,' hotly, 'but she was never given the choice.'

'You think anybody has complete choice in what happens to them? You are naïve, Allee.'

'I might be naïve but at least I never practised genetic experiments on people who didn't know what was happening to them.' Her anger made her voice shake.

He stood abruptly, away from the desk. 'I cannot explain now. You must leave here.'

'Well that would be great if you think your fine friends are just going to let me walk out of here.'

'Ah, Allee...' he sighed and it seemed to her that the trenched lines deepened, leaving a silhouette of steel. 'Nevertheless ....' He looked blankly at the wall behind her, seemingly readjusting his thoughts. 'I will arrange for you to leave, I promise. There's an important meeting of the *Panacas* tomorrow,' – he must have seen her expression and smiled ruefully, '– the great and the good, the leaders of *LIBJU* and my brothers – and I must get organised for that. Then I will get you out of here, truly.'

The blue eyes looked keenly into hers. 'For myself I cannot claim it has made me unhappy not to have to wear an oxygen pack nor to have skin that didn't suffer in the sun. As for Rosalita...' He shrugged. 'She must decide.'

She was once more aware of the charm and the wonderful body, but saw his frown deepen and his voice sharpened again.

'It's not safe for you here, Allee. You have come at a bad time.' Something flashed in his eyes and she wondered if it was concern. 'How does this boyfriend of yours allow you to wander into danger like this? Why is he not here, protecting you? Were you mine...' A shade passed over his face and he moved towards her, towering over her, his voice angry again.

'I will see what can be arranged for you to leave.' The bright blue eyes looked down into hers, the voice rock-hard. 'In the meantime, stay out of sight.'

He left Allie frightened. What had she got herself into? Was there nobody here, apart from Rafa, she could trust? She felt a rush of desire for Stick, for his thin bony body, for his blade sharp intelligence. He would know what she should do. But first she would phone Alaina and talk to her. It would cheer her to hear a friendly voice although it must be said that Alaina's answer to the text she'd sent had been brief to the point of non-existence. *"Okay"* didn't really tell you very much. She was obviously still annoyed.

Practically hanging out of Asiri's window and struggling to get any reception she could see the distant crater edge, a barrier of pinnacles like dinosaur teeth outlined against the gun-metal sky. Below her stretched the barren, empty valley floor but, as she pushed her arm and shoulder further out, she saw a figure on one of the almost invisible paths below. Boulders and intermittent overhangs prevented her confirming what she thought she'd seen but it was a woman, she was sure, almost directly beneath her, some levels below. Foreshortened by the angle of sight she couldn't make out who it was. Nobody she would know, anyway, she thought.

A second figure appeared from some exit leading out from the base of the mountain below her and the woman said sharply, 'Finally!' her head jerking as she spoke.

The man, for it was a man, was mumbling a reply as Allie's heart jolted with surprise. She'd seen that same movement before, the head jerking on the thin neck. But where?

'We have it,' the man was saying. 'Straight from the army's own commissary in fact.' They were speaking Spanish, not Quechua, and it was this which jogged her memory. Was it the Undersecretary at the reception? The elegant woman who'd been in deep conversation with Dr Chavez at the beginning of the evening? She would like to have confirmed it but couldn't lean out further as the window slit was too narrow and she feared she might be seen.

The woman was clearly irritated, dragging the man back under the overhang, the strange movement of the head no longer visible.

Small scraps of conversation floated up to her, the man also becoming angry, clearly rebutting something she'd said, the Spanish so fast she could only partially understand.

'There's no danger...I've used Amaru's account.'

The woman's reply was sharp, and the man's truculent.

'It will be impossible to trace...'

A door banged back and Asiri was in the room, grabbing her arm.

'What is it?'

'They have come! We must go to the Chamber... Quickly!'

She was dragging Allie away from the window and across the room to the little bowl of alo juice, rubbing it with great force into the skin on her face and arms, shoving the shawl into her hand. Her lips curved in a smile. 'Camouflage! We must go.'

Almost running, she pulled Allie out of the room and along the corridor, through a tunnel Allie hadn't previously noticed. Then they were heading down roughly hewn stone steps, winding through tall stone walls, through the heart of the mountain.

To her surprise, they emerged into the open air of the valley bottom, running towards the shelter of an overhang which appeared to have been built into the mountainside. Glancing up as she ran she saw that the mountain face at this end of the crater was an almost perfect ziggurat, a pyramid, like those in Egypt and ancient Babylonia, and common in Runa Five. It was composed of enormous blocks of carved stone of all different sizes, some clearly hundreds of tons in weight, yet fitted together so snugly not even a razor could pass between them, blending seamlessly into the surrounding mountainside.

'Quick,' said Asiri, pulling her forward to below the protection of the overhang. 'We must not be seen. We're going to the Chamber.'

The stonework was incredible. Allie patted one of the immense blocks as they went past.

'It's amazing,' she said. 'They didn't even have the wheel or mortar or anything.'

More people were heading in the same direction as they. Asiri hardly broke step but turned and smiled at Allie. 'The Old Ones say there was a time when the earth was lit only by the moon and there were strange men who could move stones by force of will.'

'Mmm. I heard it was log rolls and pivot stones but it's still difficult to see how they managed it.'

The blocks looked as though they'd grown together over the centuries, becoming immovable, defying storms and sieges and earthquakes. The fact that the ziggurat was man-made had been well concealed. Numerous boulders sat on the ledges creating an uneven contour, some of the giant stones lying apparently where they had just come to rest and merging with the rock of the crater walls, so that the illusion of natural formation was complete.

She could only see part of it since they were hidden by overhanging rocks much of the time, almost like the galleries in cloisters. Whenever she attempted to step outside Asiri dragged her back in under the shadow of the stone.

'We must not be seen.'

It was as if the mighty structure had been built to be invisible from the air, camouflaged by the very mountain itself. But, she thought, it had clearly stood there for hundreds, perhaps thousands of years, when the only things flying overhead were condors. She knew that in the Nazca valleys in Peru a plateau existed that had huge images of animals and birds etched into the sand and gravel of its surface, surreal outsized figures of condors, spiders, and llamas. Geometric patterns as well, some of the lines running for miles. Strangely none of these images was truly visible at ground level but could only be seen from the air.

But this ziggurat had been built not to be seen.

A construction designed thousands of years ago to be hidden from a sky in which flew only birds.

At least, now they were outside the mountain, it felt less confining, no longer so hemmed in by the rock. But the respite was only temporary. The people ahead of them had already disappeared.

It was hardly an entrance, more a split in the rock, a slash so narrow that they could no longer walk side by side, the walls too close to sustain an answering sound.

'Be careful. Keep close to me. We go to the Chamber.' Asiri's face was serious. 'Nobody can find it who doesn't know the way. Many, many tunnels. Some people got lost forever.'

Under the rock, enclosed by stone once more, they were entering a labyrinth-like maze, a natural formation, its passages carved out by ancient underground streams long gone. Tunnels disappeared off to the left and right but they followed what was obviously a chosen path, heading ever downwards, deeper under the ziggurat and the mountain.

The passageway they were on eventually widened out and took on greater height so that they could walk side by side, coming at last to a small chamber. In the centre was a great circular stone table, onto which small pools of light fell, somehow channelled from far above. Intricate carvings were etched into the table's edge and as Allie watched a flash of much brighter light fell onto the table, casting a shadow towards one of the etchings. She realised with surprise that it was a huge sundial and that somehow they had managed to filter the light down into the heart of the mountain. Looking up she could see silver channels disappearing above them. People went past them, all heading in the same direction.

'What is this place?'

Asiri smiled. '*Intihuatana*. The Hitching Post of the Sun.'

'It's wonderful.'

'We are the Sun's Guardians.' Asiri spoke unselfconsciously, repeating what must be for her an evident truth.

Allie looked at the dark walls and the single blade of light. The Sun's Guardians? In this gloomy cavern?

She would like to have asked more but they were hurrying on, deeper and deeper under the ziggurat, trying to keep up with the group. As they rounded a corner they saw a small boy in front of them leading a llama. In the light from the sconces they glowed with colour. And then she saw that they were, in fact, statues, life sized, perfectly formed and gleaming in gold. Surrounding him and down the corridor in front of him the walls were adorned with flowers and plants made from gold and silver. Intricate filigree work, shining in the darkness, lit only by flaming torches, worthy of any of the great palaces of the world.

Allie drew a stunned breath. Just like Curicancha she thought in amazement.

Around every corner they came upon a new wonder. A long, lithe, golden puma with silver whiskers and a silver tuft to the tail, three small silver mice in a nest of filigree gold, a vase of flowers in a niche, golden petals and leaves beautifully veined, all in gold, with silver stamens waving delicately in the moving air.

From ahead of them they could hear a hubbub of voices and above it a continuous roaring and rushing sound. The flaming sconces smelled of tar. Following the noise they came out through two great doors into a huge, vaulted chamber already filled with throngs of people. Her senses were assaulted by the babble of voices, the incense-like smell and the roaring of water,

water which she could see gushing from channels fissured into the rock high above them and plunging into a great pool on the far side of the cavern. To the right and left of the entrance, in wall niches, shone ritual figures sheathed in silver and gold.

Something else glowed at the end of the chamber but she was unable to see what it was, only a spiked crescent of gold on the far wall, the rest hidden by the mass of people in front of her.

'Go closer to the water. You'll see better.'

Indeed there was the water, battering the brain with noise, the Granverde itself, the vertical walls of the gorge through which it ran echoing its roar. Here must be the river's source, gouging its way through the mountain, carving out runnels and basins as it twisted through the mountain's heart, its mighty descent accompanied by a continuous thunder as it plunged into the great pool. She could just see through the moving and jostling bodies the foam flecked surface into which the liquid green sheets fell, bubbling under the force of the tons of water falling into it, the foam swirling in the rocky basins worn into the stone at the pool's edges, the river plunging again, deep out of sight, at the far end of the cavern.

And reflected in the water was a huge, glowing, golden sun. It filled almost the entire end wall of the chamber. The Punchao, she thought, amazed – the Punchao from the Temple of the Sun. So this was where it had come. And the Indians had come with it to guard it.

'We are the Guardians,' Asiri had said. No wonder this was all hidden from the world, such tremendous amounts of gold, such incredible artistry, worth a king's ransom. What was it that Rosalita had called Ignacia's new husband? *Metalistero*, metal worker, artist. And given the way the original Temple of the Sun and Curicancha had been pillaged would they want another government to do the same? No wonder they hid. Somehow they'd managed to conceal this marvel from the Spanish and hide it away in the mountains for hundreds of years, even from the present spy society. And they'd found the mine and used the gold and recreated Curicancha underground.

She tore her eyes away from the great golden sun and looked around the chamber. In front of the burning image was a raised section, a dais, with a stone table upon it. And upon the table a huge slab of rock with zigzag channels carved into the side.

Was this another Chamber of Sacrifice with the same channels as the huaca at Quengo? Were they to take away the blood of the sacrificed llamas or other animals? Or even humans? She shivered.

Now everybody was looking towards the dais above them. She felt the tense expectancy as silence gradually fell on the crowd. Despite its great size the chamber was now almost full of mineworkers and their overseers, people from the village, some of the older children, crammed right to the edge of the great pool and held only by a flimsy railing. They were all looking towards the dais with the stone table. On it was a large box, half a man's height, covered with a black cloth.

A small figure in ornate black robes, his face hidden by a golden mask, stepped forward to stand beside the box. Perhaps some kind of priest? The Indians began to chant, very quietly at first but gradually increasing in volume. Their faces were flushed, flames flared in the wall sconces, and the smell of burning pitch permeated the air.

They were stamping in rhythm.

'Hermanos, solo un momento,' said the Priest.

A murmur rose as the great doors swung back and a magnificently garbed procession marched to the dais and mounted the platform, the individuals standing in line and looking down at the people.

It was Yupanqui, but not just Yupanqui. Six others, all clothed in golden tunics and gold-threaded cloaks, all with the ceremonial daggers at their waists, all wearing the golden and feathered headdress of the Royal Inca. He must have changed before joining them. The six more, all exactly the same.

'Hermanos, vosotros dios!' said the Priest.

At first Allie thought that she was dreaming or that they must have introduced some hallucinogenic substance into the air. Seven magnificently sculpted bodies, seven patrician features, all identical. The water roared, the people swayed and moaned and the great, golden Punchao flickered in the light of the torches. The Priest gave a command and a thin piping rose on the air. She recognised the sound as that of single reed flutes, the *qenas*, and several of the other instruments that gradually joined in.

As the Seven stepped forward one by one the crowd called their names and stamped. 'Roca,' they chanted, 'Viracocha, Pachacuti, Huascar,' the stamping was louder, 'Topa, Yupanqui,' and finally, louder still, 'Atahualpa!'

Did they recognise them? Could they tell which one was which? Or were they merely saying the names? Wasn't Atahualpa the one Asiri had mentioned, the one Rumiñaui worked for? She remembered Asiri's grimace at the name. 'An angry man, Atahualpa,' she'd said. But surely Yupanqui wasn't like that.

The people rocked and moaned, the panpipes and *qenas* wailed and the floors and walls vibrated to the sound of the drums and the great pipes, the *zamponas*. Common sense told her that the Punchao cave was a natural formation of solid rock, the ground beneath her feet granite, and that it was not possible for it to vibrate. Perhaps it was the strange, incensed smell, the heavy scent of gardenias and orchids, or the hypnotic chanting and rhythmic movement of the crowd which were affecting her senses so that her surroundings seemed to move.

Perhaps it was the movement of the water in the great pool, the white flecked surface, the mighty boiling under the force of the tons of water falling into it. The walls of the cave on the far side were black and shiny like mirrors, diamond drops of water glinting, magnified in the light of the flickering sconces, the walls beyond sheets of darkness.

Two black clad servants came forward at the Priest's command and took hold of the cloth and began to remove it. The chanting stopped. There was a hush. As the cloth slithered to the ground Allie's breath caught in her throat. On the table stood a large glass case in which sat hunched the body of a man.

He was dressed in modern clothing, a suit jacket of the old style, matching trousers, a collared shirt and he appeared to be looking at them naturally, the lips apparently moving under the handlebar moustache. Despite the sunken cheeks and the same glazed skin as that of the young woman at San Pedro River, she recognised Lieberhart.

A deep voice echoed round the chamber. 'My people, my children, you have come.'

One of the arms jerked and the jacket sleeve slipped back to reveal horrible, raised tendons under the stretched skin at the wrist. They must have the mummy wired in some way so that it appeared to move.

The stamping and chanting started again; the responses shouted back.

'We have come.'

'You have come to serve.'

'We have come to serve.'

'I, Dr Lieberhart, will guide you.'

The voices were rising in ecstasy.

'You will guide us.'

'Listen to the Guardians.'

'We listen.'

The voice died away and the stamping began again.

Some sort of recording? His own voice? Somebody else's?

So it was true. Lieberhart had found the village and its hidden treasures and had taken it over to become their god. The Lord Inca.

Then, having found a perfect source for his experiments, hidden away from government reprisals, he'd tried to create Superman and having perfected one had cloned him so that there were seven. The Great Father who stole the children. Allie looked again at the beautifully sculpted bodies, the easy breath, the intelligence in the eyes and, at the same time, the ghastly, replicated state.

The voice echoed around the chamber again, booming in the high vault. 'My children, our hour is nigh. Follow your gods.'

'We follow,' they chorused. 'Our time is coming.' The stamping and movement resumed, louder and more forceful. 'Our time is coming. Victory is ours.'

So on Lieberhart's death the Seven had taken on the role he held and become gods in his place.

What had it taken to produce these creatures? How many of the children had been 'unsuccessful', how many destroyed, aborted before ever having seen the light of day? And their mothers hadn't even known they'd been used.

Was Yupanqui any different from the others or, like a cloned animal, only able to think as the others thought. The thought was distressing and her brain whirled with wild speculation.

Had Martin Carvajal, Lieberhart's right hand man, worked at the village with him and followed in his footsteps? By their ages the Seven must be the work of Lieberhart, the village children like Brusca and Aylen the work of Martin perhaps? Or, given the ages of the younger children, those who'd followed him.

Had Dr Chavez known what was going on? Had she played any part in these experiments? Lieberhart was her father even though she'd been working abroad when he disappeared. Rosalita had said she hardly went to the clinic anymore. And yet the genetic engineering must owe something to her expertise after Carvajal had died. Allie suddenly remembered what Rafa had said when Rosalita had been singing Dr Chavez' praises. 'She so good. The clinic cost lot of money. She fighting for the poor.'

'Chavez,' he spat. 'She not fighting for the poor. She just want *cobayos* – how you say – guinea pigs.' At the time she'd thought his judgement harsh.

And Chavez had greeted Yupanqui in the courtyard at the reception like a relative.

Allie felt ill. She'd worshipped the woman. She'd almost betrayed Stick to study under her. If she'd helped with this 'Program' could she not see the blighted lives? Ignacia with no memory of her previous husband, Carla's baby miscarried, Rosalita not realising the significance of the blue eyes. Did Chavez know? Did she care? She would not, surely, have sanctioned this grotesque use of her mummified father?

Allie remembered her comment on Martin, in the hallway. 'Talented but too much into politics, my father said.' Lieberhart must have stumbled on the miners and their families and taken over the village somehow. Martin had wanted to take over the whole country. For that he would have needed more than the miners, and at some stage after Lieberhart's death had co-opted the leaders of *LIBJU*, some of whom must be powerful in their own right, into his plan. Although the mine was clearly ancient the hospital was new and expensive so the rebels must have considerable resources.

And they had gone along with him, seeing the huge advantage of Lieberhart's research, the headquarters buried in the mountain, the gold, the fact that most of the Indian tribes, not just the miners, would follow the Seven. And on Martin's death the rebels had simply taken over and, along with the warrior gods, had become the *Panacas*, the Lord Inca's privy council. After all, they still had Lieberhart.

So this was where the great Nobel prize winner, had finished up. Mummified in a glass box. She felt sick. At least the ceremony seemed to have ended as some were moving towards the great doors so she'd be able to get back out into the open air. She'd be glad of the coolness of the tunnels again and to escape what had become a troubling environment.

But the mummy jerked and the voice echoed round the chamber again, this time speaking in Quechua, not in Spanish. Asiri translated in a whisper.

'Guardians! Guardians from the mine. Wait for judgement.'

A hush fell and then there was movement. At first one or two waited and looked around but then most headed for the exit, leaving, Allie thought, in almost obscene haste.

What was happening?

An uneasy silence fell and Asiri whispered again, 'Only mine workers must stay.

Something must be wrong.' She looked around alarmed and then back at Allie. 'You won't find your way out on your own. You'll have to stay with me. They won't notice you.' Her voice had an uncertain note.

Allie dragged the shawl closer round her head, her heart racing, thankful for the alo berry juice which changed her appearance so much.

The chamber was emptying rapidly, only the Incan mineworkers with Rumiñaui and the Seven on the dais left behind. A young worker, clearly only a teenager, was being marched by two black clad servants towards the platform. He stumbled and was dragged upright and thrust forward One of the Seven stepped to the front of the dais, waiting implacably for the youngster to be brought before him.

'Atahualpa,' Asiri whispered. 'You can tell by the armband.'

The mummy's voice rang out again, echoing in the vaulted roof.

'A traitor,' the voice said, the mouth moving in a horrible simulacrum of speech. 'A traitor in our midst.'

The servants yanked the boy up onto the dais in front of the warrior and threw him to his knees in front of the magnificent gold-clad figure. The boy, lifting his head, just looked shocked, breaking into panic-stricken speech.

'No, no, my Lord,' he is saying, Asiri translated. 'I just took a little bit of gold. Just a little bit. For my girlfriend. The young man's voice rose in his terror. 'I would never betray us.'

The warrior grabbed his hair and bent his head back, looking deep into the eyes of the youth cowering before him.

'If for your girlfriend why try to sell it in the market?' The boy began to babble but Atahualpa cut him short. 'You knew that no-one, no-one must speak of the gold outside.' The voice became harsher. 'And you tried to sell it in the open market. Luckily for us the man was one of ours but had he not been our plans might have been revealed – our people exposed, our home raided, the sacred Punchao taken. It was theft and treachery.'

'No!' the boy shrieked. 'No. Just for my girlfriend.'

Atahualpa flung the boy contemptuously back into the arms of the servants and another dark-clad figure stepped up behind the lad.

It happened so suddenly that Allie had scarcely time to register what was happening, the swift movement of the executioner, the thin garotte around the boy's throat, the frantic struggles and guttural sounds, gradually subsiding until the lifeless body, still twitching, dropped to the floor.

None of the others on the platform moved. Total silence fell, broken finally by the harsh voice of Atahualpa.

'Treachery will be rewarded,' he said and turning his back, his features carved in stone, stepped past the mummy's box, down the steps and away, followed by his brothers.

Allie was in shock. What had she just witnessed?

As one of the servants flung a cloth over the body a wave of nausea swept over her and she felt the bile rise in her throat. It was murder and Yupanqui had done nothing. He had not intervened, he had not tried to save the young man, he had just stood there and watched with the others. She was shaking and her blood had turned to liquid lead in her veins, dragging her to the floor. She mustn't faint here, she thought, sweating and panicked. It would betray her absolutely. If Yupanqui hadn't prevented the attack on the boy he certainly wouldn't protect her.

She could feel unbelievable terror rising and shut her eyes, not looking at the forlorn little heap on the dais, trying to blot out the sickness and the horror. She was dimly aware that Asiri had grabbed her arm, the fingers digging spitefully into her flesh, and was dragging her fiercely into the centre of the throng heading for the great doors. Safety in numbers, she thought. Some were muttering to each other in low tones, some sounded almost jubilant, as if something great had been achieved. She was thankful for the coolness of the tunnels.

Her queasiness was only just ebbing when they stumbled back out into the open air, her brain churning with the nightmare she had seen. She had to get out of here. She couldn't stay, having witnessed murder. But it was getting dark so she wouldn't be able to get over the bridge, even if Asiri could get her into the mine. She must contact Alaina, although how much could she safely say? Despite what had happened she didn't want to bring the army in, wreaking havoc. Most of the people here seemed quite innocent, Cusi, Maite, Maria Rosa. And given the way the village was hidden would any rescuers even know how to find her?

She'd got herself into this situation so it seemed unjust that a whole community should suffer because of it. Once she'd got out she could let the right people know what was going on.

Again it was impossible to get any kind of reception under the rock but by hanging back and letting the others go ahead she finally managed to contact Alaina.

'Gee, kiddo, you do like to keep a girl hanging on. So give with the explanation.'

How much could she safely say?

'Well, I've been underground in a whole load of rock tunnels for a lot of the time, and there wasn't any reception, but I did eventually find my friend. She's living in a sort of commune. There's a clinic here as well. She's had her baby and they're both doing fine. The baby's cute.' Was the mystery hacker listening in – her wristcom was reasonably encrypted. She risked, 'I've been quite safe so far and a friend is going to help me get back to you. If he can't, I'll ask you to come and collect me if that's alright. But it's kind of difficult – it's getting too dark to leave now and I'm not sure I can find the way out on my own, to be honest. I'll have to let you know tomorrow.'

'Jeez.' She could hear the frustration in Alaina's voice. 'Well just get back here as soon as possible. Quite apart from the fact that Randy's friends are all dead bores I can't convince Mom much longer. She doesn't know who this friend of yours is and she doesn't see you communing with nature. She feels responsible and I'm running out of excuses.'

Even Allie thought that her response, 'I'm doing my best,' sounded weak. But she had to wait for Yupanqui, and despite the events in the Chamber she felt that if he was on her side she was safe enough.

'Make my apologies to your mum and dad,' she said. The reception was breaking up. 'Just one more day,' she yelled and then Alaina was gone.

Asiri was waiting for her at the stair entrance, looking troubled.

As they made their way up to her room she said little but once there she looked sadly at Allie and said, 'It was not nice that you saw that, Allie. I'm sorry.'

'He was just a boy. How could they?'

Asiri looked at her.

'He deserved it you know. He knows how much danger he brings on us all, showing the gold outside.' She thought how best to explain. 'We have hidden all these years, we have looked after the Punchao, since – oh, early times – and because of that we cannot live like other people do, we must stay inside the mountain like... like in prison. And we all know we must never, never tell of the gold. Perhaps when *LIBJU* are in government we won't have to hide any more, we can go out like all the other people but for now it's not safe.

She seemed to realise the enormity of what had happened for Allie and her brow creased. 'The police killed Atahualpa's older boy when he was just tiny, you know.' She looked sad again. 'He has been angry ever since . I'm sorry you had to see it though.'

'I'm sorry too, Asiri. I suppose I shouldn't judge but surely they could have found a better way?'

Though it was true what Asiri had said, she thought. How else had they been able to keep this whole community hidden for hundreds of years. And what was that about *LIBJU* taking over the government? Some sort of uprising as she'd thought, as Miramae had seemed to imply? Anyway she certainly couldn't stay here and she no longer wanted to wait for Yupanqui. For a second she thought of his touch, light on her arm as they'd left Rosalita's, his mention, yet again of her boyfriend, his final words on leaving. 'Were you mine…' he'd said. He thought she was beautiful. Did that mean he'd cover for her?

'Have some sense, sister,' her mind jeered. 'He might have offered to get you out but he just let them kill that kid and he's on their side. You can't trust him.'

'I really need to leave, Asiri. You must see that. I've seen more than I should, but I promise not to involve any of you.' She thought hastily. 'I'll try Rafa but if he can't help me can you get me to the mine somehow? I could maybe go back the way I came in.'

Asiri frowned and shook her head thoughtfully. 'It's not possible to get you into the mine now because of the guards on the lift. They are not ours; they are from *LIBJU*. And, anyway, by the time you get to the bridge it will be too dark.'

Anxiety gnawed away at her and, with flashes of the garrotted teenager before her mind's eye, she said, 'Please, Asiri, I cannot stay here. Is there any other way out?'

Asiri brow creased and eventually she said, 'There's an old shaft at the back of the kitchen area. It's not used anymore and it's very dangerous but it comes out on the track on the mountain. The one that leads down to the bridge. I know some of the boys go out that way.'

Allie remembered seeing the little path disappearing off into the mountain not far from the great portal.

'Could you or Rafa take me?'

Asiri sighed. 'It would be much too dangerous at night and tomorrow I cannot. I start very early in the mine and they'll come and fetch me if I'm not on time. Then they'd see you. Rafa is working as well and I doubt if he knows anything about that shaft. He's only just got here.' Her brow wrinkled. 'Maria Theresa could take you. She's a good friend of mine and she's used that shaft before. She works in the kitchens. Usually she serves coffee, drinks and so on at their meetings along with girls to help. But tomorrow she has time off – someone else has been assigned to serve at the meeting – so she could take you.'

Allie remember that Yupanqui had spoken of a special meeting and began to feel more hopeful. 'So people would think I was one of her girls if they saw me near the kitchen area?'

Asiri looked dubious. 'They're all very small.' She reflected and then her face lightened. 'Paola helps sometimes. She's tall.'

'Do I look like her?'

Asiri's voice took on a cynical tone. 'We're just servants. All *indigenas* look the same to the *Panacas*.'

Allie had an alarming thought. 'What if someone talks to me?'

The alo berry stain and the black hair covering wouldn't protect her for long if that happened.

'Paola only speak Quechua and a little Spanish.'

'My Spanish is okay. And you can teach me one or two words of Quechua. I'll have to pretend I've got a sore throat.'

Asiri nodded. 'If Maria Theresa agrees.'

While Asiri went in search of Maria Theresa Allie returned to the small bed and tried to sleep for the few remaining hours of the night but found it impossible. As the thoughts churned round and round in her head, the ceremony in the cave, the identical warrior Gods, and then the hideous garrotting of the child, it was becoming clear where the real power lay. Not with Yupanqui and the mine Indians but with Atahualpa and the rebel leaders.

Now she knew what had happened when Rosalita and Miramae believed Yupanqui had been, miraculously, in two places at once. There'd been two of them. Or possibly even more than two, Topa, Atahualpa, Viracocha or whatever they were called. It was the same at the reception. The figure she'd seen in Chavez's courtyard had been not Yupanqui but one of the others. Yupanqui, raised by his mother in his early years, exposed to real human emotion, was different. If only she could count on that. Her safety in this place rested with him.

Such was her anxiety that she would have liked to leave then and there and could hardly contain her impatience until Asiri returned, looking at her eagerly as she came into the room.

'It's okay, Allie. Maria Theresa agrees. She can take you. I'll get you to Rosalita's first thing. She has her own room now so it will be safer for you there. Maria Theresa will collect you from Rosalita's. Before we go I'll work on the camouflage and teach you some words.' She looked at Allie with concern. 'But for now you must get a little sleep. Try not to worry. It will look better tomorrow.'

But, as Allie followed Asiri to Rosalita's room on the following morning, she found her sense of danger heightened. She'd become even more acutely aware of the people who might be watching her, wondering who she was, what a stranger was doing in the village, whether she might be a spy. Maybe this Maria Theresa wouldn't come at all, she thought fearfully. Yupanqui couldn't be trusted. Perhaps Rosalita would know where Rafa was and he might have some idea of how she could get away from this place.

In Rosalita's room Asiri gave her a quick hug, saying, 'I hope all goes well for you, Allie. Maria Theresa will come soon,' and with a final smile and, 'Stay safe,' she'd left, heading back to the mine. Looking sadly after her Allie turned to see Rosalita laying out a series of tiny garments on the bed cover.

'Look, Allee, they have given me these beautiful clothes for little Esteban.'

'Yes.' said Allie, 'they're very cute but, Rosalita, I'm very sorry, I'm going to have to leave you. Does the clinic bus go regularly? If Maria Theresa doesn't come could I get a lift in that?'

Rosalita looked troubled. 'I not know, Allee. I wanted to go myself because I worried about Jaime but they told me they want to keep me just for observation. They said they still worried about the virus.'

Or, more likely, since they knew the virus to be no longer a true concern, Allie's instinct told her they just wanted more time to administer whatever it was that caused the amnesia. The whole thing was evil. Should she tell Rosalita that nobody seemed to believe in the virus? That even Dr Chavez had said that nobody got it anymore? That Ignacia's memory loss was just part of a plan to keep the mothers from realising what had been done to them?

Rosalita was bent lovingly over her baby. Perhaps it was best not to worry the girl, especially when she was so thrilled with her little boy. Later, when she'd got her away. Because she'd have to get her away as well, though how she couldn't tell.

'That's a shame,' she said instead. 'We could have gone together. When is the clinic bus coming next?'

'I not know, Allee. It may not come at all. And Esteban have a little cough. They say he might have to go to special room, so they can keep an eye on him.'

Allie's heart tightened. She couldn't contact Alaina until she knew something definite. Her options were reducing all the time.

'Rafa, he working now, so perhaps he can tell us when he finish.' Rosalita was calm, unworried. 'It is so good, isn't it, that they look after all of us from the campamento. It would cost much money to stay in a private clinic.'

Allie thought again of Rafa's guinea pigs and bit her tongue. It looked as if she'd miss Rafa. Anxiety cramped her gut. Surely Maria Theresa would be able to get her to the old shaft.

And then they had no further time for talk as someone had come into the room – a tall thin woman, older, but with the same aquiline profile, the same almost haughty expression. She looked at Rosalita and asked a few sharp questions in Quechua. Allie could see she didn't really approve of the situation. Rosalita eyes flashed and she launched into what was clearly fervent justification and Allie recognised Jaime and Rafa's names in amongst the flood of Quechua as well as that of Gutierrez. The woman turned to Allie, her face softening.

'Come,' she said, 'we must go.'

Chapter 13
The Meeting

Allie followed Maria Theresa down the corridor, keeping her head down and the shawl as far as possible over her face without it looking odd. Asiri's efforts with her camouflage and make-up seemed to be paying dividends as nobody appeared to notice them. Maria Theresa strode confidently forward, following what Allie imagined to be a very circuitous route, mingling for most of the way with a large group of miners and other workers returning from the food hall to their duties.

'We'll stay with the crowd,' said Maria Theresa, 'since we need to stay on this level until we're past the kitchens and the office.' She nodded a greeting to somebody in the group alongside them. 'We break away for the shaft just after that.'

The people, mostly women, were all chatting happily amongst themselves, occasionally throwing a remark to Maria Theresa, having a laugh. They didn't seem to be interested in her at all.

The smell of cooking told her they were passing the kitchens and she knew that the office area was further down. As they came to the junction Maria Theresa surreptitiously tapped her arm and slowed to a halt. When someone looked round she bent down and pretended to fiddle with her boot, allowing the group to carry on. She had stopped next to what looked like an unused tunnel, unlit and gloomy, with a broken timber half-blocking the entrance way. It had a large *No Entry* sign nailed to the wood.

Maria Theresa looked at Allie with concern. 'It's very dangerous, Allie,' she said. 'I cannot go all the way with you but I'll get you past the worst bits and then you should be able to find the way to the path yourself.' She still looked worried. 'Yupanqui will want me to make sure you get out alright.'

Allie smiled at Maria Theresa. 'That's fine. I'm very grateful for any assistance. I don't want to get you into trouble because of me.' Yupanqui's word must be law for at least some of the villagers, she thought.

Placing a hand on the broken timber she was just preparing to make her way into the shaft, when a voice called them from back in the corridor, the sound of footsteps hurrying towards them echoing in the tunnel.

'Maria Theresa, Maria Theresa!'

Allie's heart lurched.

'Wait. Wait!'

Maria Theresa turned, her hand on Allie's arm, watching the man coming up the corridor. She sighed. 'It's Pepito,' she said. 'One of the kitchen supervisors.'

He was a little man, flustered, untidy, balding, with the air of a frightened rabbit. He scuttled up to them, out of breath from his sprint down the corridor, breaking immediately into speech as soon as he was able. He must be asking Maria Theresa to do something and it was clear she was protesting. The man cast a glance at Allie. He said something to her and she looked at Maria Theresa in anguish, her blood thundering in her ears. What had he said?

Falling back on one of the painstakingly learned phrases Asiri had taught her she mumbled, 'I don't know. I'm sorry,' but the man had turned aside instantly, was not even listening to her, all his attention centred on Maria Theresa. He appeared to be telling her something important, his voice insistent and eventually she reluctantly said something in reply. The man, looking relieved and mopping his brow, said, 'Thank you,' and turned and fled back up the tunnel.

Maria Theresa looked at Allie and frowned. 'This is difficult. I was supposed to have this time off, but Pepito says I must look after the meeting after all. The other worker has not turned up. Apparently she's ill and I haven't got my usual team.' She looked anxious. 'He's rounding them up but perhaps you can help with the serving, at least until Isabella comes. That's what he was asking you – if you'd be prepared to help. He obviously has no idea who you are. Once Isabella gets there you can leave. You can wait for me at Rosalita's or Asiri's afterwards.'

No, no, not yet more delay.

'Couldn't you just leave me here and I'll make my own way out?'

Maria Theresa thought for a second and then said, 'No, Allie, it's much too dangerous. There are many tunnels, you'd never find the right one and we've mined deep here for years and years. 'There are a thousand places, hidden shafts, sink holes, things like that, where you could fall and never be found. And it's dark in there. You'll never be able to do it on your own. And anyway…' her face relaxed into a smile as she said cheerfully, '…I need you as a server.'

'What? Go into a meeting with all the *Panacas*?' Allie didn't think this was a good idea at all and it must have shown on her face.

'Don't worry. They're not at all interested in us. These *LIBJU* people don't come very often so they don't know who we are. Rumiñaui will be there and Atahualpa but even they hardly know who I am although I give them their food every day.'

Allie remembered the cynicism in Asiri's voice. 'We're just servants. All *indigenas* look the same to the *Panacas*.' This place definitely had some serious divisions in the community, she thought. Perhaps that was why the miners had been so worried at the supervisors finding out about her presence.

'If anybody asks Asiri says I'm to say you're Paola's sister. She's a tall girl.' Maria Theresa laughed. 'I'm going to say you're simple so it means you won't have to talk. And you can have the cold.' She laughed again.

Her brain shooting off all kinds of warning signals Allie's couldn't think of any more excuses but actually putting her head into the lion's den didn't seem like a savvy move at all. Maria Theresa had set off purposefully down the corridor and Allie reluctantly followed. What else could she do? She really had no idea where all these tunnels went.

While they retraced their steps Maria Theresa explained the set-up in the office and in what seemed no time at all Allie was swathed in a maid's overall and heading into the meeting room, eyes cast down, slightly stooped, coughing pathetically.

She hoped the cough was convincing as she balanced the whisky, pisco and glasses carefully on the tray she'd been given. They chinked as she made her way into the room, cautiously raising her eyes as she prepared to place the tray on a side table next to the door, seeing for the first time the group around the table.

For one paralysing moment she couldn't move, almost dropping the tray, transfixed by the sight in front of her. At first she thought that the group members must be the result of some horrendous genetic experiment, like the poor pig imprisoned in the animal body. She heard the rustle of feathers, saw the fur covering the eyes and blending eerily with the pale flesh beneath. Or that they were some hideous mutation, the condor's head and shoulders on the human trunk, the wings arcing back, the tips of the feathers sweeping the floor. She saw a jaguar, a puma and a jackal. A dog and a maned wolf. More animals of different kinds. A raven.

Then, as her heart slammed back into action, she realised that they were merely elaborate masks, fancy dress, animal heads over ordinary clothes. She couldn't tell who the people were although Rumiñaui, with a simple Zorro-like face-covering and the large, thickset body, was easily recognisable. Seated at the head of the table, clearly the leader, the Condor was waving a thin hand for silence. A woman's hand, a bracelet gleaming on the wrist. On her right, also at the head, was another Indian but much taller than Rumiñaui and, indeed, most of the others there, with powerful shoulders beneath the warrior's tunic, his face hidden only by a simple mask like Rumiñaui's.

Atahualpa, Maria Theresa had said. He was not looking at her but was deep in conversation with the Condor for which Allie was grateful. He might have been the one in Chavez's courtyard.

The other members were all looking expectantly at the woman as the great feathered head curved towards them. Allie dropped her eyes hastily to the floor and concentrated on balancing her tray correctly. Now was not the time to draw attention to herself.

Maria Theresa took her tray to the top end of the table, gesturing to Allie to serve the bottom end and she was busy offering the Puma a whisky when she realised that the conversation had ceased. The voice welcoming them, to Allie's surprise, spoke in English, but also clearly not in the person's own voice, but from what looked like a small loudspeaker in the centre of the table.

As the Condor spoke a red light came on above the narrow ring of consoles surrounding the table. They must have microphones and earpieces so that when they spoke the sound was translated into cultivated English. So despite their disdain for the workers they didn't want them to overhear what was said. Or perhaps the voice and the costumes were just to impress the simple mineworkers with an added air of mystery. Maybe there'd been a time when they didn't particularly want to be recognised by the others in the group either, only the red light indicating who was speaking.

The slender, elegant hand waved again, Allie saw the great ruby ring flash and was now sure who the Condor was. The woman below Asiri's window. The Undersecretary at the Ministry of Business and Agriculture who had been talking to Dr Chavez at the reception, her head jerking on her thin neck, furious at being passed over. Perhaps it wasn't surprising she was one of the rebels. Here she had power.

Allie offered the one with the dog's head a drink and a large brown hand grabbed the pisco bottle, pouring a generous slug into one of the glasses. She looked up into the eyes of the great bird glittering at her through the slits in the mask and she had the frightening feeling that the woman knew her, could

221

remember her talking to Velasquez. As those around the table settled down with their drinks and tapas the woman spoke privately to Maria Theresa, both looking her way. Allie, heart thumping, caught the word 'Paola'.

'Why is Paola not here?' she was sure. She hoped Maria Theresa was saying that she was Paola's sister, that Paola was poorly, as they'd agreed.

Allie coughed again and in a hoarse voice said, 'Sorry,' in Quechua, lowering her head. Nobody paid her any attention and when she looked next the Condor was talking urgently to Atahualpa.

She presented the drinks tray to the Maned Wolf and then to the Jackal, along with the selection of savouries and the mechanical voice said, 'Just one,' as its owner reached for the tapas on the tray. He'd been speaking to the man next to him and as he took one he laughed at something the man had said.

It was an odd laugh. She recognised it. She must have heard it before.

She carried on round her side of the table, presenting the drinks to the Raven and the Jaguar, waiting patiently while they chose their tapas. The Jackal laughed again and she knew where she'd heard the sound before.

In the lab! Velasquez! The Jackal was Velasquez.

Her heart leapt at the thought. Velasquez would help her if need be. She remembered how helpful he'd been to Isidora and how he'd been going to try and find Rosalita's results for her. But what was he doing here?

Was he also a rebel?. She remembered his comment at the reception about the little care the government had for the lives of ordinary people, the implication that he was opposed to the present regime. And these people were the leaders of the rebel group, *LIBJU*, for whom Yupanqui and Jaime, she now suspected, had stolen the briefcase. She thought of Miramae and her comments about crushing the oppressors, living in the houses of the rich.

She offered the Puma another whisky and, as her mind whirled, her thoughts in turmoil, her initial sense of relief gradually began to fade. She'd thought Velasquez had been trying to be helpful but perhaps he'd just wanted to find out for the rebels what she knew. And the rebels clearly sanctioned what was going on here, even the murder. Allie shivered.

And Velasquez, she thought, her brain working overtime, was one of the few people who might have had access to her log-in details at the college. She remembered what the person speaking to the Condor beneath the window had said, that he'd been using Amaru's account. As senior lab technician Velasquez would easily have been able to do that. Her relief turned to dread and she was more than ever thankful for Stick's careful building of her blog, making it impregnable to cyber-attack, ensuring that nobody else could read what she'd written.

But – her stomach constricted – Velasquez would certainly be able to recognise her if he paid her any attention, despite the camouflage. As would

Atahualpa perhaps, if he was the one who'd seen her in the courtyard. She really didn't want to be found out by *him*. She stayed as far behind them both as was possible.

The Condor tapped on the table.

'Comrades, sisters and brothers, we have called a special meeting today because of some new information we have received. I told you the last time we met that Yupanqui had obtained documents from the Ministry of the Interior with the help of two boys from the campamento. These documents made plain that the Ministry had some suspicion of our activities but one was encrypted under a system different to the one they usually use. I have just received the decrypted version.' It was odd to hear the digitally produced English coming from the centre of the table.

'In essence I can tell you that the document contained a list of names which will be of interest to us all. Most of us here in fact.'

There was a shocked silence. Hands holding glasses froze.

The voice continued.

'That appears to be all they have. A list of names. I am sure that if they knew everything they would have taken action. Perhaps not public, not overt. Some of us would have gone missing. For the most part believable accidents, illnesses – suicides maybe – that sort of thing.

But thanks to these children we now know how much our colleagues know. Or, perhaps, how much they don't know – yet. But since they have the names…' She shrugged and the voice took on a harder edge, '…it is up to us to strike first. We have in previous meetings decided something must be done. We all have a great deal invested in this venture and we don't want to lose our advantage now. It is plain we must act at once.'

The Puma's red light had come on. 'I know most of the ordinary people are favourable towards us but they will be useless in the face of the military.'

'That is true but our people are strategically placed, our followers are ready and we can call upon a certain section of the military, although not all by any means, to fight on our behalf. In view of what you say, however, I have already asked one of our members to investigate other options. He has something to show us.'

The Jackal stood and looked around the table. Allie shrank back even further into the shadows. Slowly and deliberately Velasquez donned a pair of heavy-duty, elbow-length laboratory gloves, such as those worn by researchers into radiation or bio-chemical warfare. Allie noticed that the jackal mask was a little askew so he must be wearing more protective gear beneath that. He bent down and picked up a small box from the floor, where it had been sitting beside him unnoticed, and placed it on the table with a faint flourish.

The box was mostly of glass and divided into two compartments, one above the other, with fine tubes connecting the two. In the lower compartment sat a small mouse, cleaning its whiskers and looking out through the glass with curiosity shining in its small boot-button eyes.

Some of those round the table laughed as it fluffed its fur and looked around. In the centre of the compartment with the mouse was a very small heap of powder which the mouse sniffed gingerly before carrying on with its grooming. Some moved uneasily at the mouse's activities.

'Don't be alarmed. The chambers are hermetically sealed.'

The mouse sniffed again at the powder, whiskers twitching and then ran around inspecting the corners of the glass cage.

The Jackal picked up a bottle of water sitting next to the box and carefully opening a small flap poured in an egg cup full of water into a tube in the upper compartment. He shut the aperture hastily and then remotely opened a secondary valve allowing the water to flow along the tube into the mouse's compartment, and drip onto the powder.

'We must now wait for twenty minutes.'

The Dog asked, 'Where did you get this?'

'I contacted the League of the Dead and they were prepared to help us.'

'I thought they were just a rumour.'

'Clearly not. They suggested this.'

She could imagine Velasquez's lop-sided smile, which previously she'd thought quite attractive but now found sinister.

'Do we know who they are?'

'They're a very secretive, private organisation, prepared, as I understand it, to help anyone who can pay, or if it suits them to. *We* were able to pay and I think it suited *them* to help us.'

The Dog turned to the Raven next to him, clearly alarmed at the entry of an unknown quantity into their plans, but the Raven ignored him.

Velasquez smiled again. 'Their motto is *Providing Assistance from Beyond*.'

The conversations around the table became animated and it was only when a sudden sound came from the direction of the box that their attention returned to it.

The mouse was hurling itself against the side of the glass, scampering about frantically, its little paws scraping the floor of the box. Blood appeared on its muzzle, the small body going into terrible contortions. The skin around the mouth curled back in a rictus of pain, the tiny limbs in spasm. It took a long, long time to die.

A shocked silence fell.

'You will have observed that it is only when the substance is mixed with water that it becomes active and it takes twenty minutes for the gas to be released. I have timed the action. The Granverde is presently in spate – as you know it can rise by as much as ten metres at this time of year – and if the substance is released into it from the Punchao chamber it will take exactly twenty minutes to reach the Barracks. Because of the narrow walls of the canyon the gas which is eventually given off will be contained within it. The effects last for approximately twenty-four hours – although gradually reducing over that period – and are usually fatal, or at the very least disabling. In one go we eliminate the UN contingent and by far the larger majority of the military.'

They sat stunned. Even the Condor had been shocked, Allie thought, at the way the small animal had died.

Velasquez said, 'I will remove this. We don't want any accidents, do we?'

The synthesized voice made it sound all the more menacing. As he left the room a babble of conversation broke out, the Condor talking rapidly to Atahualpa and then calling the others to order. She gestured to the Raven.

'Our quartermaster assures me that we have a reliable source of supply.' One could imagine the grim smile beneath the feathered head. 'The military themselves as it happens. Their commissary is as leaky as a sieve.'

The one with the dog head who had been fidgeting during the previous exchange said, 'But there is a campamento on the river estuary. If the poison is carried by the river it will still be a little active, as I understand it, when it reaches the end of the Valley, the campamento…' His voice trailed off.

The Condor was impatient. 'You can't make an omelette without breaking eggs.'

The Dog looked as if he might continue to argue but was clearly intimidated by the Condor's sharp tone.

'As you know, when Martin died so tragically Chavez helped us continue his work, albeit at arms' length, and now we have many young people who will soon be old enough to take up the reins. They've been educated here in the Valley and then, as some of you know, integrated into local communities. To allay suspicion they wear fake oxygen packs and always dress appropriately', she paused, '– sun cloaks and so on. One or two of you have been able to use them in your departments.' There were one or two surprised murmurs. 'We've called them back here prior to any military action as we don't want to risk their lives before we're able to take control.'

'Do you think the UN will let you get away with it?' The Jaguar's voice was deep and guttural, the sound carrying above the machine translation.

'Were there a threat to all of Runa Five they'd probably intervene. But for just one sector I don't think so. It'll be looked upon as an internal matter, although they'll certainly protest. But if this works they'll be too late to respond anyway and will just have to accept a fait accompli.' The Condor's voice hardened. 'Brothers, this is the only recourse left to us. The authorities know too much about us already. Those who haven't the stomach for the fight can leave now.'

A silence fell but nobody moved.

Allie was stunned. These people were happy to kill hundreds, perhaps thousands of soldiers in Avila and who knows how many innocents in the campamento.

The Puma smiled, showing bad teeth, throwing in, 'There's almost always some form of minor corruption in Runa Five anyway. Bribery is usually the best weapon so in many cases we won't need to fight. And we have living proof of our capabilities in the Seven.'

He gestured towards the Indian seated at the table. 'We have *Panaca* Atahualpa with us and he says he and his brothers are prepared.'

The red light came on in front of Atahualpa and the voice from the centre said. 'We are ready...' he paused as if choosing his words carefully. 'We are ready and the people of the campamentos and the mountains will follow us come what may. Our quartermaster,' a nod to the Raven, 'has supplied us with weapons which we have safely stored and are now ready to use. The fighting units are strategically placed.' The voice hardened. 'My heart does not bleed for the Valley. These people have ignored and belittled us enough.'

'There are quite a few of your people who are well-placed in government and industry,' the Dog said defiantly. 'Chavez, for example. You can't blame the whole valley for your community's woes.'

So they weren't all from the same breakout room, Allie thought. Singing from the same hymn sheet.

Placed as she was she couldn't see Atahualpa's face but she could hear his anger. 'Our people are keen to avenge years of injustice. We have been demeaned and belittled for centuries, robbed and murdered. Our hearts burn with the need to right the wrongs we have suffered. It is not enough that a few token members of our people hold positions of responsibility. Now our time has come we are united. We *will* take the positions we are due.'

Allie remembered the teenager he'd had garrotted. No, he'd have no compunction at the slaughter.

Atahualpa threw his holocom on the table and added, 'It must be said that my brother Yupanqui is…' he paused, '… squeamish. He's worried that innocents will suffer. But he'll accept it in the end. It's the communal will that triumphs. He and my brothers are due any minute and they can report on their various responsibilities.'

It was a kick to the gut. Yupanqui was coming. She needed to get out of there.

She coughed again, pathetically, and Maria Theresa frowned at her and gestured to her to take away the tray. They were all talking amongst themselves and she was able to slide from the room without anyone noticing her.

Maria Theresa followed her out.

'I'm sorry, Allie. This has not worked out well.' A girl rushed past them, ignoring Allie, apologising or asking something as she ran. Maria Theresa cast her a relieved glance. 'I must stay,' she said, 'but now Isabella has come she can take your place. It's not safe in there and although Yupanqui gave you the disc, I think the situation has now changed. So go back to Asiri's room and wait. She can take you to the shaft perhaps if she is back, or I can join you later when this is all finished.'

Once again Allie felt despair. More delay. But there was nothing she could do about it.

Maria Theresa disappeared back towards the meeting room and Allie headed for the outer doors leading to the corridor which would take her to Asiri's room. As she passed the office area her heart continued to beat in triple time as the thoughts tumbled over and over in her brain.

How could she possibly have thought she'd get away with it? If the rebels were prepared to massacre half the people in the Valley what would they do to someone who'd been in their headquarters and had heard their plans? Would Yupanqui still be prepared to let her go with *LIBJU*'s preparations so advanced? He knew she'd seen the village, the hospital, the children, even if he knew nothing of her attendance at the meeting. Maybe he even knew that she'd seen the garrotting of the youngster. He'd want to keep her close until they'd done what they intended to do.

Somehow she had to get out. And she had to get out now.

Anxious only to regain Asiri's room and walking as briskly as possible she turned into the exit corridor. She kept her head down and tried to look as inconspicuous as possible as she passed several offices in the outer area, heart fluttering at every imagined movement. It was difficult to walk calmly when she was seething with anxiety inside. Everyone in the Avila Valley was in danger. She had to warn people. It was all she could do not to run.

She'd come to the end of the corridor and had met no-one, turning half-unconsciously at the junction to her left. This would lead her, she was sure, to the tunnel near the food hall and from there it was just a short distance to Asiri's room and the hospital and Rosalita.

The horrific information was only just beginning to sink in. The whole Valley would be slaughtered. And they would die in a hideous manner. And the rebels, the people she had hoped to help, would be responsible. She felt as if her insides had been hollowed out.

A plan. She needed a plan.

First contact Alaina and get her to warn people. That her mother was the Ambassador would help. But to phone she needed the open air or at least Asiri's window. Down here in the tunnels all communication was impossible.

Stay out of sight as much as possible.

She must somehow get out of the village without detection herself and get back to Lago Noche. The clinic bus was definitely out. If Asiri couldn't help her, perhaps she'd be able to find that disused shaft Maria Theresa had showed her and just try to get through it on her own She'd just have to be ultra careful but she had the light on the wristcom and it would surely be plain which way to go.

Or perhaps Rafa would know what she could do. He would probably be with Rosalita once he'd finished work. Would he have been told what was planned? Surely not of the murderous gas.

She'd already told Rosalita she was leaving.

Text Alaina where to meet her once she'd got out. There'd been nowhere to charge her wristcom but it had just enough battery to contact Alaina. First, though, she had to get her to warn the authorities about the planned massacre.

So absorbed was she in her thoughts that she'd reached the end of the second corridor before she realised that something was wrong. She couldn't think, as she turned a corner, what it was that seemed different. There seemed to be fewer doors in this passageway than she remembered and those rows of pipes running along the ceiling – she hadn't seen them before.

Two young Indians in military fatigues clattered towards her from the corner ahead. One of them was hauling a large trunk-like box on wheels behind him, talking excitedly to his companion as he did so. It looked like a container for military ordinance.

She must be in quite the wrong area. Heart jumping she tried to walk past the two soldiers purposefully but without haste. They paid her no attention but as she came to yet another corner she saw two more members of the military coming towards her.

These had smarter uniforms. Were they higher up the chain of command? One cast her a curious glance as they passed and then looked back at her in surprise, turning hurriedly to his companion.

In panic she veered into the next tunnel which branched off and then another. She could hear the two men talking behind her. Speeding up her pace she took the left fork of the next corridor, into a smaller tunnel. After she'd scurried along it for some distance the sound of voices died away. They must have given up.

But now all the tunnels looked the same. She ventured into several which turned out to be only dead ends. Her chest felt tight and she was having trouble breathing. The passageway she was on sloped downwards, like those close to the mine area. It was much colder down here as well and looked unlike any tunnel she'd seen on the way to the meeting room. Her shunt was chattering loudly on her arm so this must be an area which had no piped oxygen. The stone walls hemmed her in. She was completely lost.

The next tunnel would take her down again. It was no good. The living quarters were on the upper levels and no indication showed that this one would come out at the bottom of the ziggurat. Even if it did, once she was outside in the valley, although she'd be able to phone, she'd be trapped. She needed to be on the other side of the mountain.

Now her anxiety turned to panic, her breathing rapid, her pulse racing. Which way should she go?

Stop. Work it out.

Seeing a tunnel to her right which headed upwards she turned into it. It forked again, and then again, but at least the people coming towards her were not members of the military. They looked like miners heading back to work. With a flip to the heart she recognised one of them, one of the bulbous eyed girls who'd been so impressed with her coming over the bridge. She lowered her head and pulled the shawl closer, desperately trying to remain calm, to walk unhurriedly.

The girl paid her no attention, but her senses tingled with danger. The fact she'd already been seen in the mine made it much more likely she'd be spotted. And the rebels were about to start the uprising and would be more on the alert.

She'd come to yet another junction, her heart beating a frantic tattoo against her rib cage. Leaning against the tunnel wall and waiting for her heart to settle she tried to orient herself. She had to get out. Warn people.

Which way? Which way? None of the tunnels she'd looked down had seemed familiar and every passing second increased the danger.

Two people were crossing the junction in front of her and as she flinched back her heart jitterbugged.

One of them was Velasquez.

Chapter 14
Brusca

She couldn't believe it. Velasquez!

He'd taken off the protective clothing and the mask but had on his lab coat. There was no sign of the box with the dead mouse. His companion was Brusca, also wearing his white coat. They were deep in conversation and paid no attention to those passing. If they were going to the labs and if she followed them she wouldn't be far from Asiri's room.

She slipped after them, watching at a safe distance as Velasquez talked earnestly to Brusca. People passing were also talking excitedly amongst themselves. They knew something was in the wind.

Velasquez and Brusca turned left from the corridor they were in and, as she followed them, she was surprised to find that she knew where she was, although entering the area from a different angle. They were passing the animal enclosures, the pig with its nose resting on its trotters, the little box moving to its snores, the smaller animals, and finally Wulfi, pacing in scarcely contained agitation. As the two went by

Wulfi hurled himself against the bars of the cage towards Velasquez, just catching the edge of his sleeve.

Velasquez swore violently and grabbed a kind of tube from the side of the corridor, pushing it through the bars. She saw a flash and smelled burning fur and Wulfi lay twitching on the floor of his cage. Velasquez and Brusca continued unconcerned.

Now she knew where Wulfi's wounds came from.

The lab area was indeed their destination and as they entered the last corridor Allie slid into a side door pulling it to behind her, leaving just a crack. Once they'd gone she could get to Asiri's room. Velasquez had collected the file he must have wanted and had turned to leave, clearly asking Brusca if he was coming. Brusca mumbled something in reply and waited, motionless, until Velasquez had left.

She'd let Velasquez get out of sight. He knew her from college and might even make the connection with the false serving girl at the meeting. She now knew where she was, but Brusca was between her and Asiri's room. And Brusca wasn't leaving. It was strange. He had a furtive air, looking round and checking as if he didn't want to be seen. She shrank back behind the door.

Having peered about cautiously one last time Brusca stretched on tiptoe to a top shelf and took something from its hiding place behind some pipettes. A set of keys jingled. Carrying a bottle he'd taken from the same shelf Brusca used one of the keys to open a cupboard door and slipped inside. The keys rattled again and he disappeared into a space beyond. Allie couldn't quite see from where she was but it looked as if another room lay behind the cupboard. She waited in her hiding place, wondering how long he was he going to be in there.

Time passed agonisingly slowly. One minute. Five minutes.

She didn't want to make the same mistake she'd made in the mine, walking straight into someone.

Another five minutes.

He wasn't coming out. Perhaps the hidden room led somewhere else. And nobody had passed while she'd been waiting.

Pushing herself cautiously away from the tunnel wall she walked quickly past the door through which Brusca had disappeared. There didn't seem to be anybody else around. Perhaps the labs were only used at certain times. Or perhaps the preparations for the uprising had put ordinary lab work on hold. Getting to the end of the corridor she recognised the little sign saying *Off Limits*, saw the passageway that led past the school rooms and, relief loosening her muscles, knew she was not far from Asiri's room.

She didn't hear him coming. She was just peering round the corner into the school room corridor when an arm fastened around her neck from behind, tightening savagely as she tried to struggle. Her protest emerged only as a gasp. The person behind her increased the pressure on her throat and her sight dimmed. A roaring echoed in her ears. She could feel herself going and kicked back as hard as she could, twisting violently as she did so, contacting a leg and hearing a grunt of pain from behind. Something slammed against the side of her head and all went black.

She came to, feeling sick and faint. She was sitting on the floor, propped against a cupboard door, an agonising pain in her head. Her wrists were fastened in front of her and Brusca was ferociously knotting a rope around her feet.

Head swimming, and through a haze of pain, she looked down at the blue-black thatch of his hair as he bent over her ankles and then across his shoulder to the room beyond.

Surely she was imagining things? She hardly noticed the roughness of Brusca's actions in her confusion. Behind Brusca and sitting on top of a cage was a small rat. It had no front legs or forepaws but was holding its lump of coagulate rice with one rear foot. Tiny green-leaved twigs appeared to be growing from one shoulder. It nibbled the rice, the little beady eyes watching her.

Lifting her head with difficulty she could see glass vials on the shelves on the far side of the room behind Brusca, containing what, to her horrified gaze, looked like foetuses of a variety of animals, most quite unrecognisable. As he wrenched at the rope around her feet she toppled sideways, seeing for the first time at the far end of the room the huge microscope, the fridges, and on a large table more equipment. It was a fully functional lab.

Dragged back into an upright position she could see in a glass case on the floor next to the rat's cage a snake raising its face to hers – not human but neither that of a snake – with fearsome intelligence in the eyes.

Woozily she thought that this must be some secret area that Yupanqui or the others didn't know about. She looked a little more closely at the snake.

'I wouldn't get too close to him if I were you.'

The forked tongue wavered in the air then, in a flash of movement, spat directly into her eyes. She recoiled in horror and the gargoyle leered, as the patch of venom trickled down the glass inside the case.

Having finished knotting the rope Brusca studied her, the blue eyes glittering under the black brows.

'So what are you doing here?'

The voice penetrated the pain in her head and she tried to say something, but with her throat still semi-crushed she could manage no more than a croak.

'I know who you are. You don't fool me. You're this English girl they're talking about, the one who came on the *Camino Real*. You're a spy.'

His English was perfect.

'Don't be ridiculous.' Her voice was little more than a squeak. 'I just came to see Rosalita.' It was too high, clearly panic-stricken.

He sneered. 'So that is why you steal into the labs, even into my private area. We will see what Security has to say.'

She took a bet on her hunch.

'You won't dare fetch Security. I'll wager nobody except Velasquez knows about this little cache of monsters in here. You'll lose your playthings.'

Brusca laughed. 'It's true. It's great fun. Look…' He was showing her a box full of baby mice on a bed of straw and picked one of them up, cradling it gently in the palm of his hand. On the other side to that of the rat was a raised box containing a small tree, larger than a bonsai but no bigger than a garden shrub. It was surrounded by a patch of green grass. The branches were odd, stubby, bare and gnarled, only one or two twigs with leaves.

Brusca threw the mouse onto the grass next to the tree and the few leaves trembled. The mouse was scurrying through the grass, quite unconcerned, when one of the gnarls suddenly unfurled at speed and shot out, tendril-like, wrapping itself around the mouse. It tightened its grip. The mouse squirmed and jerked and gave a pathetic squeak. The boot-button eyes bulged and the little body convulsed violently for a few seconds before going limp. The tendril dropped it to the ground.

Allie stared horrified. Nothing happened for several seconds and then what looked like a root crept from the grass and curled around the tail of the mouse, dragging it slowly towards the trunk and under the ground.

Brusca laughed again. 'Venus fly trap genes,' he said. 'With some jellyfish venom. Not at all sentient except in so far as it can detect living prey in its environs. And I haven't worked out yet how to give it a stomach.'

The blue eyes flickered. 'Shame it's a bit too small for you. You can try it though.' He grabbed her by the tied arms and dragged her over towards the box. She fell onto her side but he continued to heave her towards the tree. As she struggled to right herself he hauled her into a position where he could put her hands on the grass.

A second's pause only and then the tendril lashed out. The pain was excruciating. She looked down at the fearsome weal on the back of her hand and flinched back out of range of the lashing branch. More finger-like tendrils pursued her. Shaking in panic, she wriggled out of reach. The back of her hand was blistering and the pain was unlike anything she'd ever experienced.

Brusca laughed. 'When *LIBJU* is in power I can work on a bigger model. They let me do whatever I like.'

It was clearly something he was looking forward to. He emptied the contents of one of the vials into a small dish, and then fetched a container from the fridge and from it measured another liquid into the bowl.

He turned towards her, a syringe in his hand.

'How do you fancy being a jellyfish?' He laughed and waved the syringe in the direction of a large aquarium tank. She saw, horrified, the trailing stingers of a cloud of jellyfish, floating dreamily in the water.

'You know some of them help you to glow in the dark. Shall we try injecting you with some – perhaps a little cocktail.' He'd turned back to his dish. He wasn't even mad, she thought. Was it genetic modification or just the way he'd been raised?

'Would you like to be able to glow in the dark?'

Taking the dish with him he went to the far end and the microscope, carefully studying a tiny spatula of something from the dish he had put onto a glass slide. He looked across to her.

'I didn't think *LIBJU* would be able to get me the microscope but look! They did. It makes all my work so much easier.'

He was doing something with the glass slide and the dish.

'*LIBJU* are fools. They think they are going to use us, me and the others, to help them run the country.' He looked up at her again and snickered. 'They think we'll let them take over once they've used those poor idiots who believe in them to deal with the army. Do they not notice that we are much cleverer than they are?' He'd gone back to stirring the solution in the dish. 'Atahualpa and I have plans.'

Allie looked around in desperation. Her hands felt numb and useless. She brought her knees up close to her chin.

'He's my father, you know, Atahualpa. He'll be the Great Inca. We won't need that rotting mummy any longer.'

He'd returned to the worktable near her as he spoke, still stirring the contents of the dish, adding something from another pipette. His back was to her. One of the obligatory bottles of oxygen sat in its clamp on the table and a rack of knives lay on the bench. Much too far away.

'You have to get the holding solution right,' he was saying, 'or you kill the active ingredients. And we wouldn't want that, would we?'

He was syphoning the solution up into the syringe.

Although her feet were tied together she was able to place them flat on the floor, as tight into her body as she could. She had her back against the cupboard. She'd have only one move.

He was beginning to turn, the syringe in his hand, when she took off. Using the cupboard door as a lever point, thrusting her back against it as she slid up, and then pushing away. Driving with every last ounce of strength in her knees and her back, up and forward. Head down, careering into his side.

Brusca grunted. Staggered.

Taken completely off balance in mid-turn he cannoned back against the box containing the tree, dropping the syringe. The tendril whipped out, lashing the air between them for a second. Allie on the floor rolled frantically out of reach but Brusca, still totally unbalanced but trying also to move out of range, caught his leg on the side of the rat's cage and toppled backwards towards the tree, landing with his head on the grass. The tendril whipped down, found him and fastened round his neck. He screamed and thrashed out with his legs, trying to roll away as Allie had done. The tendril was remarkably strong and a second one unfurled. Brusca tried to wrench the first from his neck and squealed again as the second one attacked his hands.

Allie rolled again to the bench, hauling herself up on one of its legs, grabbing one of the knives with fingers she could barely move. Reversing it and holding it with its back against the table edge, she began to rub the rope back and forth over the blade.

Brusca's body was bucking and jumping, his legs flailing, as he tried to stand and pull away from the tree. He'd uproot it.

But no, the whole box had toppled over, the tree with it. He tried to rise to his knees, his face, hands and arms covered in the blisters of the venom, but his neck was still held in the tendril's stranglehold and he collapsed forward again.

Blood was trickling along her hand where she'd misjudged the angle needed to cut the rope. Major arteries in the wrists, she thought. Keep the knife steady. Fingers still numb, she wrested the gradually parting strands of hemp back and forth over the sharpened edge.

Adjust the angle. Wedge the arm more securely against the table. She continued her furious attack on the rope. Almost through.

A horrid gurgling sound came from Brusca. He was going purple, his eyes bulging. An obscene squeaking and whistling forced their way through his lips.

With a final downward pressure of her wrists against the knife she had done it. The rope parted. Flexing her fingers and reversing the knife again so that she was holding it normally, she hopped forward and slashed at the tendril holding Brusca. As she did so several more of the frond like branches flickered and uncurled towards her. Another slash and she'd severed the main tendril. For a second it tightened even further around his throat and then uncurled, falling to the floor still twisting and turning, writhing in its death throes like an amputated gecko's tail.

A second tendril lashed out towards her face and, as she hopped backwards, putting up her arms to shield her eyes, the whip-like branch flicked her fingers. Again it felt as if someone had gripped her with red hot pincers. Another weal. And another tendril was snaking out. Fear tearing at her chest, she hopped further back, almost overbalancing.

Brusca lay on the floor, gasping and wheezing, his eyes revulsing, holding his throat. She could see the red welts and the blisters.

She slashed frenziedly at the rope at her feet, now down to a few strands. It took only a couple more cuts and they parted.

Brusca had rolled over and away from the tree and began to haul himself onto hands and knees, ghastly wheezing and moaning noises still coming from his throat. He patted the floor around about him, grabbing the syringe.

The oxygen bottle sat in its slot next to the table. She grabbed it and slammed it as hard as she could against the side of his head, hearing the spongy crack. Brusca toppled onto his side, the syringe falling from his nerveless fingers. Allie rammed the oxygen bottle down on top of the tiny cylinder, seeing the glass splinter and the lethal solution soak away into the floor. She would have liked to hit him again as he lay unmoving, but she could see the keys, still in the lock where he'd left them, and leapt for the door. She was through, taking the keys with her and locking it behind her. Then the outer door. Locking that too for good measure. He must still be stunned. But it wouldn't do to count on it.

Sprinting as fast as she could away from the labs, she knew she wouldn't be able to escape. There was no clinic bus. It was too late to find Rafa. But that didn't matter so long as she could warn people, get Alaina to pass on the message. She needed the open air for reception. Later, perhaps, if she were still free, she could get Asiri to take her to the mine shaft. Anything was possible.

But it was just a question of time before Brusca was found and told Velasquez what had happened.

She was almost at Asiri's room when the siren began to sound.

Chapter 15
Capture

'All please stay in your places. Do not move. This is an emergency lockdown.' The voice echoed in the corridor.

Brusca must have recovered enough to contact someone. The stairs down to the valley floor were not far from Asiri's room and she headed that way, seeing through the windows of the double doors leading to the refectory Velasquez talking rapidly into his wristcom. Then he was running through the food hall, coming in her direction.

She didn't think he'd seen her, but she'd have to cross in front of him to get to the stairs to the outside world. She should head the other way, to the far side. If she went high enough she'd get to the upper level of the ziggurat, closer to the outside world. Back-tracking at speed, she raced through a new corridor going in the opposite direction, climbing some service stairs, leaping up two steps at a time, heart pounding, breath coming in gasps, spotting through a slit in the stone above a glimpse of rock and open mountain side.

A tiny back entrance. The door locked.

No, no. She hauled on the lever frantically. With a clunk it responded and she hurtled out into the open air, fumbling with her wristcom as she ran, pressing the button for Alaina.

It rang but nobody came.

Oh come on, come on, Alaina. Where are you?

Looking back to where she'd come from she could see Velasquez and what looked like Rumiñaui on the stairs she'd taken.

Her wristcom had just enough battery to upload and, her thumb twitching crazily, she started to text. But as she raised her eyes from the screen she saw a dark shadow float across the ground in front of her and was suddenly cold. Spinning round she saw who stood between her and the sun and for a second her heart leapt.

Yupanqui! She was saved.

And then the intense cold of the blue eyes registered. Her heart kicked in with a peal which nearly deafened her. Had she actually said the name? The same lineaments, the same blue-black hair, the same eyes, but these quite without pity.

'No,' he said. 'Atahualpa.' The pupils were dark in the irises, the features engraved in metal. 'We met once before, I think,' she heard the savage bitterness in the voice, '– in Avila.'

Oh Jeez. Brusca was his son. She thought of the garrotted mine boy and the merciless manner of his execution. What would Atahualpa do if he found out what she'd done to his son?

She leapt away, back up into the mountain, desperately trying to send the message as she ran. But he was quicker than she and as her hand pressed the button, he'd come up behind her and was dragging her back towards him, his hand clamped over her arm. She twisted in his clasp, released the catch on the wristcom and dropped it to the ground, stamping on it with all her force. But her balance was lost and his grip tightened. She broke free again but as she did so she saw the others spread out in a line below them, the row of implacable faces all turned towards her. She feinted to her left and kicked the remnants of the wristcom into a deep crevice out of sight. Now she would never know if the message had gone or not.

As she zigzagged across the uneven ground she looked back at the pursuit, seeing the pitiless gaze in the eyes studying her. They all moved as one. It must be some form of telepathy, perhaps made possible by the similarity of the brain waves, as cloned cows standing at the fence all turn together as someone goes by.

She couldn't fight them, nor outrun them, and they caught her easily.

In the office the eyes of the woman behind the desk studied her. The Condor, she was sure, although she was no longer wearing her mask. The blood-red ruby gleamed balefully as she carefully rearranged some writing implements on her desk.

'You seem to have taken an uncommon interest in our activities.' The voice, no longer replaced by the harsh synthetic reproduction, was light and pleasant.

'I just came to see Rosalita. We're friends.' Could she risk it? 'Her brother Jaime helps your people.'

'Quite possibly. Although why you think that justifies your wandering about the labs and interrogating the staff and children I wouldn't know. I'd have thought that someone with your intelligence would realise that every area of this establishment is monitored.'

Her heart twisted. She'd never even thought of cameras. They must have been cleverly hidden. Perhaps they even knew she'd been at the meeting, in which case her life was worth nothing, although Atahualpa had shown no sign that he knew she'd been there, nor indeed that he'd known what she'd done to Brusca. Velasquez and the others had surrounded them in seconds and in a gesture of disgust he'd consigned her to Huascar to bring to the office. He'd know by now, though, she thought.

The Condor was looking at her contemptuously and she wondered how she was going to get out of this one. As a last throw of the dice, she'd try flattery.

'I must say I never gave the cameras a thought.' Was that just the right degree of carelessness? 'It just seems amazing to me what you've accomplished here, so I don't see why you should try to hide it. I'd have thought you'd want everyone to know that you've cracked the problems of oxygen deficiency *and* sun intolerance.'

'Mmm. Which is why you found it necessary to have a good look at the labs yourself and gate-crash important religious ceremonies.'

So much for flattery.

'Even trying to get into the military area, I was informed.' The voice was hard as rock.

The casual approach was no longer going to serve.

'I was lost. I'm sorry but I was just trying to find the hospital again to see Rosalita's baby.' She heard herself babbling. 'All those tunnels look the same. I was just lost.'

'Mmm.' Such a small syllable to reflect so much disbelief. The woman pressed a button on the desk and said, 'I'm afraid you've – er – wandered into our headquarters at just the wrong moment. I'm going to have to keep you with us for a day or two until such a time as we make an announcement ourselves. Take her to room 18, Huascar. And make sure it's secure.' The tone was sardonic. 'We wouldn't want our hospitality rejected too soon.'

Was it possible they didn't know she'd been at the meeting? She'd been just one in a crowd on the way there and the woman had hardly looked at her after that first question to Maria Theresa.

'My friends know I'm here, and I expect they're beginning to worry about me. I probably don't need to remind you that I am staying with the Ambassador for Runa Two and her husband.'

The voice was silky. 'And I probably don't need to remind *you* that you told them that you were staying here to visit your friend. You came in on the Royal Road so it will certainly be no surprise if you were found to have fallen from the bridge on the way back. Young people are always so – er – careless, so sure of their immortality…' She paused and then straightened up.

'No, please be assured that nothing will happen to you if you respect our privacy and follow local rules.'

Since the woman was prepared to slaughter horribly half the people in the Valley, Allie took this statement with a pinch of salt.

'They will find you out,' she said but she was talking to the wall, the woman's head was down and she was consulting her desk screen.

Looking up, she nodded abstractedly and said, 'Take her to her room, Huascar.'

The man's fingers dug painfully into her upper arm and there was not the remotest possibility that she would get away. She was being half dragged, half marched along one of the stone corridors leading out of the office area when she saw an open door. And through it Dr Chavez seated at a desk. She looked up and Allie saw the shock of surprise flash across the woman's face as she realised who she was seeing. Chavez signalled to Huascar to stop and said something rapidly in Quechua, hardly registering his reply.

'Allie! For pity's sake! What are you doing here?'

I could almost say the same thing, Allie thought, but contented herself with, 'I came to see Rosalita.' She paused. 'Her baby is very – how shall I put it – interesting.'

'Ah, I see.' Chavez paused, and then looked up and smiled. 'You have met several of my brothers as well so you will have some idea of the wonders we are about to reveal.'

The dark Indian eyes looked at her over the half-moon spectacles. Strange that she'd never had the eye correction operation. She was only too happy to play with creation on other people's behalf but not prepared to do it to herself. Allie thought of the children in the schoolrooms, and those in the labs. The Guardians in the great hall worshipping the golden Punchao. Cusi in the mine. The poor pig. It hardened her resolve.

'Wonders certainly, but at what cost?'

Chavez humoured her. 'Ah Allie, you know that all research has its difficulties, but sometimes the rewards are so great that it justifies the means. Think! The miracle of people able to breathe without oxygen packs, whose skin has natural protection from the sun's rays, whose intelligence is sharper, keener than that of others. Is that not worth fighting for?'

'Their mothers were never given the choice. And the government will just use those children for their own ends.'

'Which is why we have determined to institute a new system. No, not a new system. An old system.' The eyes shone with the fervour of the zealot.

'Think of the mighty Inca Empire, Allie! *Tawantinsuyo* they called it. The Land of the Four Directions. You've seen the map in my office. Did you know that when Inca Huayna Capac died he was mourned by tens of millions of subjects?' The hands waved in wild enthusiasm as she described the colossal power of the man. 'The Lord Inca, representative of Inti, the Sun God, the supreme ruler of an empire stretching three thousand miles. From the top of the western coast of Runa Five, right across the mountains and down to the southernmost tip of the continent. When he died it was the death of a god!'

Her voice rose with excitement and she looked a little mad. 'Think, Allie. Under the Inca no slavery, no capitalism, no money even, no private property beyond a few personal possessions, no taxation other than a form of labour for the state, plenty of food, clothing, housing, a domain of almost perfect happiness.' Her ecstatic smile showed her delight.

'And who's going to do all the work?'

'It was the responsibility of the local chief to see that the family communities, or *ayllus*, were allotted whatever the people needed and that they provided the right amount of labour for working on government land and government projects. It was designed to benefit the simplest peasant.'

Her eyes shone.

'And think what they achieved. They built the mighty stone conduits for water, not just in Cuzco but all over the western part of Runa Five, great aqueducts, mighty irrigation channels, meaning that there was ample food for all the population. Roads too. Roads and aqueducts we still use today. They had their own means of communication as well, the *quipus*, a subtle and complex system. They could send messages, do complicated accounts, calculate and detail tax, record their history, draw up inventories – all by means of simple knotted lines of coloured string, the mysteries of which we are only just now beginning to unravel.'

Allie felt the bile rise in her throat. This was not the brilliant scientist that she had venerated, had left Stick to study under, but a madwoman, a zealot for an impossible-to-replicate past, one so blinded that she could no longer see the harm she was doing.

'And I suppose under your wonderful communal arrangement people will be happy to be slaves, like those poor girls in the mine who never see the light of day.'

'Don't be ridiculous, Allie. The Inca had very precise laws for mining and miners. It will be nothing like it is now. Those Indians never listened to my father. He told them that the mine conditions were dreadful but they weren't prepared to change.' She looked at her desk a second, deciding how to explain.

'In the times of the Great Incas the mines in the Andes were only allowed to be worked during the four warmest months of the year and miners were rotated to different areas and for different jobs if they were particularly arduous. No miner could be made to serve in the mining districts without being able to take his woman with him. They were not slaves. And now, of course, we have modern technology which will free people even more.' She raised her head proudly. 'My brothers and I will ensure that all is fair.'

'And under this perfect system you're still going to be using the women as brood cows for your experiments?'

Chavez flinched.

Good one, thought Allie, but she could see that she was making no inroads into the woman's fanaticism.

'You've met my brothers. My father succeeded in adding the vital genetic material which enables them to breathe without extra oxygen and their skin to support the sun's rays without harm. He made them beautiful, powerful and intelligent. Clearly there were mistakes but my father triumphed in the end. And now my brothers are much revered in the valleys. The *campesinos* and the *indigenas*, the real descendants of the Inca, Indians like my mother, will help us overthrow this vicious government.'

'So you're prepared to slaughter half the people in the Valley for this wonderful new world?'

'What do you mean?' Chavez was clearly amazed. 'It will scarcely be necessary to fight. The results speak for themselves. My brothers are already well-known in the campamentos and the people will support them.'

'If that's the case then why do they need to poison the Avila Valley?'

'Don't be ridiculous. Who speaks of poisoning the Valley? Who would do such a thing?'

She didn't know. She had no idea what the others were planning.

'Your little pals in the fancy dress costumes, that's who. You weren't at the meeting, were you? So perhaps you weren't told what they're intending to do?'

Chavez still looked puzzled.

'They're going to release a chemical or nerve agent of some kind into the Granverde from the Great Chamber. It spreads on the wind but only after suspension in water for twenty minutes, long enough to take it away from the cavern. But it will be active in the air by the time it arrives in the Valley. The effects look to me like those of mustard gas or sarin. People will die horribly.'

'No, no.' Chavez half rose in her chair and then sat again. 'You are mistaken. Perhaps they've used this as a threat but they wouldn't dream of poisoning the Valley.'

'I was there.' Flatly. 'At the meeting. They want to remove the UN contingent and most of the military. I saw the mouse they used as an example of how it worked. Velasquez was the mastermind of that one, as it happens – not a nice death.'

At the mention of Velasquez Chavez stood again, transfixed for a few moments, her eyes casting round the room as her brain sought some means of rejecting the accusation. She suddenly looked much older than Allie would have estimated before.

'No, they certainly will do no such thing. I will speak to them…' She stopped. 'My father would never have allowed it… I will forbid it.'

She pushed the chair back in quick decision.

'I'm sorry. I can't chat with you any more now. Just go with Huascar, will you. He'll look after you.'

She was at the door, had almost left, when she turned back, clearly troubled.

'Be very careful, won't you Allie. Huascar will look after you.'

Alaina looked down at her wristcom. Not even a phone call, she thought in disgust. Just a text. And a video attachment.

'Well I sure want to look at pictures of you on holiday with your new buddy, thank you very much. I'll look at it later.'

And then the two words of the text slammed into her consciousness.

"Warn Them!"

She opened the attachment.

Chapter 16
Alaina and Stick

Stick returned from making his fake-cheese sandwich and tried to work out how he could make his cash stretch to food for the rest of the week. The heating money he'd already devoted to keeping his machines going and to add to his gaming fund.

He was working on the problem of who had attempted to access Allie's private blog and who, at her college, had been trying to contact the League of the Dead. It was odd. The League seemed to keep turning up wherever he went on the web these days. At first, he'd believed it to be Amaru who was the hacker and had been following the coiled snake symbol, until he noticed that the wrong password had been entered on several occasions, triggering reset requests. Could it be that the person trying to contact the League had been somebody else using Amaru's details as a cover. The digital trace certainly came from the college labs. Whoever it was he seemed to have lost interest in the poisonous substances he'd been investigating before.

Velasquez, on the other hand, was ordering what appeared to be heavy duty work wear, suitable for nuclear or chemical experiments. And the commissary of the western part of Runa Five military was stocking up with a variety of chemical and nerve agents. Perhaps cold and hunger were getting to him but he was having difficulty remembering all he had learned about the various poisons, and how they interacted with the environment. Only that they were lethal. And what possible connection could they have, he wondered, with the college or the women at the clinic? The rebels? *LIBJU*?

Were Amaru and Velazquez working with the military or against them or was the League of the Dead leading them all astray? It all added to his nervous apprehension, heightened by the fact that Allie had ceased to post anything to her blog. He ran through his last few screens again. So absorbed was he in what he was doing that he almost didn't notice the small red image on the monitor, telling him that Allie was trying to contact him.

In the milliseconds it took him to recognise what it was his heart slammed against his ribcage. It was Allie. It was the emergency code. Perhaps she was coming home.

'Open it!' he yelled at the machine.

But as he swivelled towards the hologram next to his desk his heart shrank. It wasn't Allie. A tall, statuesque young woman stood before him, the hologram highlighting the sheen of the ebony skin, the vivid red of the ribbon in the braids.

'Hi pal,' said an American voice. 'Are you Stick? You gotta be.'

'Yes,' he said, almost unable to say the word as his anger erupted in his chest. How dare this person casually use his precious contact. He looked again at the hologram, rage tearing at him, tempted to explode the image and send the digital fragments flying out into the dark. But something about the young woman's demeanour, the fact that she was so obviously worried, made him hesitate to throw the command.

She smiled at him, seeing his anger.

'Allie seems to value you a lot so I'm afraid I tinkered with her machine...' she smiled again, 'or to be precise I got one of our tekkies to do it since I needed the contact to be secure. He said he could have got to Mars on the computing power he had to use.'

Despite his anger one half of his mind admired the way they'd overcome the false trails he'd laid. It was a miracle she'd managed to get to him.

'You're Alaina,' he said. 'I've seen you on Allie's videos.'

'That's right, bro.' Her smile had faded. 'And you've every right to look really hacked off that I've broken into Allie's account. Be assured I wouldn't have done it if I didn't think something was wrong and that Allie needed you. I guess you know her pretty well and I know she'd have tried to contact you if she could – so I'd hoped you know more than I do.'

She paused and one eyebrow lifted. 'I'm assuming she hasn't.'

'No, she hasn't.'

Alaina's eyes were sombre. 'The only reason I'm here is because I think she's in danger.'

'I've been following her blog', he said. 'It stopped a couple of days ago.'

'Right. She was with us in the mountains, at Lago Noche, but she went looking for her friend Rosalita, the girl from the campamento. You know about her?'

'Yes, yes.' Allie had seemed almost obsessed with her.

'Well, she found her in this crater, an old volcano just a few miles down from Lago Noche, as far as I can estimate from the last GPS, but Allie played her cards pretty close to her chest when she was talking to me and I wasn't much the wiser. Pretty cheesed off to be honest. Then she sent this message.'

She flicked her wrist and the message flashed up on the wall opposite.

"Warn them"

'It came with this tiny bit of video.' She flicked her wrist again. 'Of course, it's not very good – wristcom video never is – half of it's at the wrong angle and the sound disappears a lot of the time. But you'll certainly get the gist.'

Stick wasn't listening to her. He was watching, transfixed, the images on the wall, the glittering eyes of the condor, Velasquez in his gloves, the terrible, frightful contortions of the mouse. From far away a voice said, 'You can't make an omelette without breaking eggs.'

He thought his heart might freeze over. 'You think she's still in this crater?'

'Yeah. Well, as far as we know. I haven't heard anything from her for a day or so but that's where she was last. I got Randy to send a couple of his best drones along the valley but there's nothing you can see. No sign of life. To all intents and purposes there's nothing in that valley except, perhaps, a tumbled-down ziggurat. But either she's had an accident or someone must be hiding her somewhere near there. It's close to where I dropped her off. I was hoping she'd contacted you.'

Stick's chest tightened. He knew. He'd known all along.

'She mentioned once she'd met one of our technicians from the college labs in the campamento. Guy called Velasquez. He's always seemed to me a nice enough type. Used to help Isidora a lot. I don't know if he's one of those on the video – all that silly dressing up – but maybe he could help. It might do more harm than good just to go in if we don't know exactly where she is.'

Her voice trailed away as she realised that Stick was no longer listening to her.

He was tearing off the greatcoat, thinking feverishly.

Did they have enough proof? Could he entrust any of what he knew to the web without endangering Allie? Would Alaina be able to help?

He turned to her. 'You're the daughter of the ambassador, right? Do you think you could set up a meeting for me with the Minister of the Interior over there, someone with the necessary clout?'

Alaina thought about it. 'Guevara? He's second in command.'

'Guevara, right. I don't know who's in on what's going on over there but I'll start with him. Make sure nobody knows – not Velasquez, not Chavez, nobody. We can't tell whose side anyone is on. If anything leaks and that bunch on the video find out that Allie has seen this they'll kill her out of hand. Can you do that?'

'Can but try. You intend coming to Avila?'

He looked at the list of flights on his wall.

'Tomorrow evening,' he said. 'That's the soonest I can manage, and it's the first direct flight anyway.'

'I'll meet you,' she said.

He hardly heard.

Allie needed him now. Due to his own stupidity and pride he hadn't contacted her sooner. He'd been right for suspecting the League of the Dead of following him. It looked from that bit of video as if they'd supplied poison gas to the rebels and knowing that Allie was in *LIBJU*'s stronghold they hadn't wanted him to look for her there. It would interrupt their strategy, whatever it was.

He would take a bet on the Jackal being Velasquez despite Alaina's apparent approval. He was head of the labs, familiar with chemicals and poisonous substances, easily able to use Amaru's log-in details to hide his activities. Having gone to all the trouble of concealment it was clear that he and his friends wouldn't permit any stranger to know about their plans. And that meant that Allie was in great danger. He needed to be in Avila.

But where to get the enormous amount of cash for the flight. He didn't want to steal it. Even though Allie would realise the necessity she'd be appalled. She'd think he'd gone back to his old ways. He knew as well that since the affair with the auditor the authorities would be keeping some kind of track on him and if he was caught the prison term would mean he'd never see Allie ever again. Jake's mother would have willingly loaned him the money but she and Jake were no longer on earth. In fact, they were not even on the moon but heading for Runa Ten, the Red Planet, where there was an experimental enclave, an extension of the biodome. Even in these days of accelerated travel, trips to Mars and back still took ages. He would need another way to get the money.

And he would need documents, visas, who knew what else for international travel these days? A government computer would probably yield what he needed. But the money for the ticket?

He had one last throw of the dice. He'd reached the last round of the Game and it was possible to gamble all on a successful outcome. He booked his place.

Looking round the table later that evening and studying the other players assembled he felt his hopes begin to rise. They were the usual bunch but perhaps those who played for high stakes always were. And since so few reached this level the numbers were drastically reduced. Directly opposite him was the ancient crone, theoretically a Mrs Phillips, and next to her the black American, Loot, his real name, somewhat to Stick's surprise, Lutyens. In the far corner was Aleister Crowley, the man he was convinced was from the League of the Dead. Was it possible that Aleister was following his digital traces to find out what he knew about Runa Five? It appeared they knew that he was linked to Allie although the link seemed fairly fragile. Certainly Aleister was one of those he had to beat.

The gamekeeper looked round at them, laughing.

'You all know the rules. Points ultimately equal cash so you can cash in your points at this stage or try for the jackpot.

Stick thought of the huge scores he'd amassed in the previous rounds. Cashed in they'd keep him in food, heating and computing for months. But it still wasn't enough for a ticket.

'No? You all want to try for the big one? Then let us begin.'

The screens went black.

Room 18 was, to all intents and purposes, a cell despite its décor in pastel shades and pictures on the wall. Although it lacked iron bars the door was of very solid wood and was locked. There was no window so Allie couldn't really judge which part of the compound she was in. The room did, however, have a comfortable chair and an en-suite bathroom as well as the pallet bed and a shelf of several good modern novels in both English and Spanish. It seemed very civilised and Allie began to hope that things weren't quite as bad as they looked.

Perhaps she could bribe one of the guards. Or perhaps Dr Chavez had more leverage with these people than she'd thought and could stop the slaughter. Or, at the very least, she might be prepared to help her escape.

Her mind went back to the conversation in the outer office. Did the woman really believe they could return to the old ways? The old Inca Empire had been built by conquest – the subjugation of hundreds of smaller tribes and nations, the Chancas, the Soras, the Collao and more, sometimes with treaties but more often by force, creating an empire that stretched from Ecuador to Argentina, and beyond, an empire founded on cruelty. When Inca Pachacuti had the great Temple of the Sun rebuilt not only had he embellished it with gold and silver and devised special sacrificial rituals but also had numerous children, both boys and girls, buried alive in front of the Punchao as an offering to his god. When in need the then Inca Atahualpa had sent an emissary to his half-brother Huascar asking for help, and Huascar had had the man flayed and his skin used for a drum. Was this the world Chavez wanted?

Allie lay down on the pallet bed and tried not to think about the mouse.

Chapter 17
The Ticket

Afterwards Stick was never quite sure how it had happened or even what had happened. He knew that at some stage he'd had the right amount of points to provide him with the cash for a ticket. As a researcher he'd found the tribe, obtained the samples, got his material to the chemists, and had gone to the Patent Office to register his vaccine. This despite continual attacks by two of the pharmaceutical companies and huge offers of cash from the third. Not counting the regular assaults by the Unknowns, whose instruments of torture were exactly that. They were able to inflict tremendous pain. Even correctly placed sensors did untold damage.

Outside the Patent Office, just as he'd been about to go in the door, he'd spotted Loot, also arriving with his vaccine and behind him one of the Unknowns. Loot appeared unaware of the danger, stepping quickly off the pavement, trying to cross before a bus arrived. The Unknown had come right up behind him and was going to push him under.

''Ware the Unknown!'

Stick threw himself forward to grab Loot's shirt front and drag him out of the way and turning back saw Aleister going up the steps of the Patent Office. Going in.

The Gamekeeper explained it to him carefully afterwards, drawing his attention to the small print in the Terms of the Game. 'I'm afraid you lost even though you had the most points at one stage. Only someone with the most points *and* who registered their vaccine could win.'

'But I was entitled to those points. And I registered my vaccine.'

'That is true, but Mr Crowley patented his vaccine before you and therefore accrued extra points, taking him up to your total. So the first one registered wins.'

He looked at the tabletop. She was raking in his chips, his ticket to Avila.

On the other side of the table Aleister Crowley smiled.

Back in the real world, in his untidy, messy bedroom, he felt as if his insides were disintegrating. He was drained, exhausted. All gone. He still didn't have the money for the trip. He felt nauseous. In his misery he hardly heard the banging at the door and his sister letting Ravi in. He didn't bother to look up. He would just have to steal the money.

'My, you look depressed, man! Anything I can do to help?'

Stick sighed heavily. 'I doubt it. Not unless you've just come into a fortune.'

'You've always done without money before.'

Ravi was trying to be encouraging.

'I need to get to Avila. Allie's in trouble.'

Ravi's face lengthened. 'Oh man, international flights cost an arm and a leg these days.'

'True.' Stick's voice was dull. 'So it looks as if I'm stymied.' What he didn't say was that now he would have to break his promise to Allie and steal the money.

Ravi looked at him in concern.

'Don't you have any rich relatives?'

Stick laughed.

Ravi's eyes narrowed.

'I do,' he said.

Stick looked up.

'Ashrafi. My uncle. I'm a favourite nephew of his or I think I am. He's a nice old boy and he's helped one or two of my friends at med school buy what they needed for their research projects. If you were to mention my name...' Ravi pulled a comical face.

Ashrafi was well known as a do-gooder, Stick knew. It was why he'd had so little compunction in the past about hacking into his account and ordering himself a variety of items. Quite apart from the fact that he despised the rich. However, no matter how philanthropic a person was, being asked to help someone with their research was quite different to helping someone who turned up out of the blue requesting huge sums for an untold purpose. He tried to organise his thoughts.

'Can you get me an interview for tomorrow morning?'

'No problem. If he's there, of course. He travels a lot.'

'That would help me, Ravi. I'll try and return the favour someday.'

Ravi chuckled. 'Oh I'll hold you to that.'

He phoned later in the evening to tell Stick that he was good to go but Stick was already hunched over his machines. He would need, he'd decided, a sprat to catch a mackerel, something which would earn Ashrafi's good will, a small fish to catch a big one. If he could find something which would be helpful to the man in one of his business enterprises it might make him look more favourably on his request.

The computers hummed, the printers spooled, Stick's voice became hoarse as he issued command after command, his fingers floating over the screens, the hours went by, but nothing appeared. Spreadsheet after spreadsheet, drilling reports, employee details, profit and loss schedules, but nothing where it shouldn't be. He hadn't found anything of sufficient weight to help Ashrafi in any way. Ashrafi ran a very tight ship, Stick decided. And then, just before dawn, as the morning sun leaked through the shutters, red-eyed and exhausted, he had it.

This was his sprat.

Early for his appointment he presented himself at Ashrafi's business premises and waited in the outer office, just off the huge central atrium, as the secretary reported his arrival. He was a small man, with hamster pouch cheeks trenched by lines from nose to a cupid's bow mouth, with a shorter lower lip so that when he talked into the officecom his whole face moved.

Stick looked round the reception area. The ornamental plants cascading from every niche, the chandeliers dangling semi-precious stones, the polished real-wood tables, the gothic stained-glass windows almost disappearing out of sight into the vaulted ceiling. He decided that Ashrafi could certainly afford the ticket.

After what seemed an age the secretary looked up from the officecom and said, 'You can go in now.'

The room seemed enormous but the man seated at the desk was small and the round face under the bald head with a curly grey fringe looked genial. Stubby fingers ending in beautifully manicured fingernails held a memory stick, which the man, smiling, laid on the desk as Stick came forward. He put out his hand and Stick, rather uncomfortably, shook it.

'Hello Mr Michaelis. My nephew Ravi has asked me to see you. What can I do for you?'

Stick looked into eyes as sharp as a ferret's. He tried to sound bored.

'The fact of the matter is, Mr Ashrafi, that I need your assistance.' He paused. 'Money, to put it bluntly.'

The ferret eyes sharpened even more. 'And why should I offer this – ah – assistance?'

'A friend of mine has discovered something about one of your companies. There is a threat. I need money. You, I think, will be glad of the information. We can make an exchange.'

Ashrafi steepled the little sausage fingers together and smiled. 'Only after I've seen the information.'

Stick chose his words carefully. 'It concerns your Canadian venture. I believe there is an element of fraud on the resource side. One of your suppliers appears to have, how can I put it, diverted your goods and replaced them with inferior materials.'

Ashrafi looked thoughtful. 'The Canadian venture, you say?'

'Yes.'

The man didn't ask which part of the venture but said, instead, 'How did you come by this information?'

'Unfortunately I'm unable to say but as a token of my good faith I brought you this.' Stick laid the memory stick containing one of the all-revealing documents on the table.

Ashrafi looked at it, raised an eyebrow and pressed a button on the desk console. They both waited in silence while it acquired the document and accompanying statistics and then brought them up on the screen. A further silence fell while he read the contents.

Looking down at the screen Ashrafi smiled. 'Ah, I did wonder about that'. He paused. 'And what did you say you wanted in return?'

'I would like sufficient cash for a plane ticket to Runa Five. I can then let you have all the details of this scam.'

The old face became immobile and then Ashrafi said, 'Why Runa Five?'

How much should he say? How much should he give away?

'I have a friend there. I believe she's in danger. I must go.' He couldn't keep the desperation out of his voice.

'Where in Runa Five?'

You'd have thought his precious information was worthless but he could see no other way. 'She's in Avila.'

The pudgy little hand waved.

'I am puzzled Mr...er...Michaelis, is it not? Despite your very kind offer of information – which indeed I will find useful – I am puzzled as to why you are calling on my assistance now. Since...,' the voice was suddenly whetted steel, '...since, according to my calculations, you have already drawn on my generosity to the tune of...' – he pressed another button and looked again at the organiser screen set into the desk – 'certainly the price of a long-haul ticket. All those items on my account.' Ashrafi's voice thinned.

Stick felt the kick to his stomach as the words sank in. Ashrafi knew – probably had known about his activities all along. Before he'd met Allie, he'd been in the habit of hacking into the accounts of the wealthy held with the great warehouses, and ordering items he needed at their expense. He was a past master at covering his tracks, leaving no sign of his entry and exit. And for these people the amounts had seemed so trivial that most of the time they'd never even noticed what they'd paid for. He'd hacked Ashrafi's accounts with a variety of stores and purchased, over time, a great number of items.

His mind still in shock he scarcely heard the pale voice continuing.

'Oh I didn't mind a bit of private enterprise – though I was about to invoke the law when you decided to leave off your – er – predations. I must say the scarf for old Bill did rather mellow me.'

He'd ordered a scarf for Bill at the bottom of the stairwell in his block on Ashrafi's account, Stick remembered. The man had terrible breathing troubles and had been grateful for the scarf. But how had Ashrafi known? He'd been so careful.

Ashrafi smiled. 'Oh I know nothing about the way you people manage to get into our systems, believe me, but the virtue of wealth is that you can always buy in the expertise you do not, yourself, possess.'

Stick felt even more humiliated. Not only had he been caught but he hadn't even known. And clearly this employee was even better at it than he was.

The thin smile appeared on Ashrafi's lips once more as he enjoyed his revenge.

'Of course I doubt if my aide is as clever as you. He just has more resources.' He paused and looked down at his screen again. 'And you were responsible for the destruction of part of our Enclave, I understand.'

The words burned on Stick's lips but he couldn't say them. Why should this old man believe him? They'd been prisoners. The Enclave had been poisoned by the people who were supposed to be guarding it. The fire he'd set had enabled Jake and Allie and himself to escape.

He stiffened his back. 'So I gather you won't help me then?'

The little eyes looked at him shrewdly. 'I didn't say that. I'm just wondering why, when you had so little compunction about acquiring my – er – unwitting assistance before, you didn't just do that this time.'

Stick stood up. 'I didn't, did I?' He was short. Rude. 'So what's it to be?'

Ashrafi had been his last chance he thought. He felt a scream of despair rising in him. He wouldn't be able to help Allie and she would be killed. His mind swooped and soared amongst the myriad possibilities he'd gone through the night before and had rejected.

He'd lost. He'd have to steal the money.

The old man was ignoring him, frowning, scrabbling about in a drawer.

Sounding an alarm? Contacting the police somehow?

Stick couldn't move, couldn't breathe, his muscles paralysed.

Ashrafi was bringing out yet another organiser, a smaller, old fashioned one with a keyboard to type in the instructions instead of the voice command system.

He tapped in a few commands and then studied the display carefully.

'Where is this place?'

'Avila.' He appeared to have lost control of his voice. 'Avila,' he said again more loudly. He couldn't believe it.

The old man typed carefully. 'Avila.'

'You can collect the ticket from the airport.' He smiled. 'Don't mention my name.'

'Thank you.' Stick's legs were trembling and he was stammering. He tried to lay the second memory stick with the remaining scam details on the desk but it dropped from his nerveless fingers and he had to retrieve it from the floor. 'Thank you.'

Ashrafi smiled again. 'What did you say your young friend's name was? Allie? Daughter of one the surgeons there, I believe.'

How had he known that? Stick was filled with internal rage. He ought to have realised that a businessman of Ashrafi's calibre would have had him checked out before giving him an interview. Now he was completely in the old man's hands.'

'No, her name's Cally,' he said. 'I expect you misheard.'

Ashrafi was smiling again. 'Well, give her my regards, won't you?' The old eyes were piercing. 'Come and see me when you get back. I may have a job for you. Miriam, my PA, will tell you what documents you need for the flight.'

Miriam was quite beautiful with flawless skin, large brown eyes and a mane of silken black hair, burnished to a magnificent sheen. She downloaded to a stick all the various documents which she said he needed, filling in a variety of forms rapidly, checking his details along with his ID card, and putting everything into an envelope along with the memory stick.

As she handed them over she said, 'The visa will come to the airport.'

He took the envelope and thanked her awkwardly. 'You like working for the old boy, then?' he said.

Her look was cool. 'He's my father.'

Checking the wristcom outside he realised he would just have time to get to the airport for his flight, leaving no time for lunch. In great haste he bought a sandwich with the last money on his card and then phoned his sister to collect the devices he might need once in Avila. It was always better to be prepared.

At the airport he grabbed the rucksack she was holding out for him, having arrived a few seconds before, and he gave her a quick hug before running to the ticket booth. He was just feeding in the number which would print his Boarding Pass number on his palm when a young man came alongside the counter.

'Mr Michaelis?'

His stomach dropped. Ashrafi wouldn't have cancelled it? Would he?

'Yes.'

'You need this as well,' the young man said.

It was a *To Whom It May Concern* document. The elegant curlicued script on parchment-like paper looked very official, if more suited to a museum.

> *From His Excellency, Count Alredor de Lamanjaras, Foreign Office, Avila, Runa Five.*

> *Please expedite this visa for Mr F C Michaelis, resident of Kington, Runa 4 and send an authenticated copy to our Embassy in London.*

There followed all the details from Stick's ID card and **Reason for Visit:** *Tourism.* It had the most amazing wax seal.

The official he submitted it to, along with all the other documents which Miriam had supplied, was surprised but since it was listed on the official encryption service he dealt with it promptly.

Making his way to the boarding gate Stick wondered about Ashrafi. Was he anything more than a simple businessman? At first he'd been delighted at the thought he might be offered a job. He knew that Allie would be thrilled since she always asked about his employment prospects in her mails – in fact, they'd both been hopeful of the job in the Statistics Office until it had all fallen through – but as he waited in the boarding queue it occurred to him that it probably wasn't a good idea to work for someone who knew you'd engaged in criminal activity. Wouldn't that give Ashrafi a hold over him?

An even nastier thought occurred. Since the old man knew so much about him was it possible that he was somehow connected to The League of the Dead? In which case he'd put Allie in even greater danger. He could feel his muscles cramping up and terror rising in his throat.

Common sense came to his rescue. Ashrafi had bought the ticket which was good money lost if he'd intended to sell Stick and Allie down the river. Plus Ashrafi was Ravi's relative and Ravi was solid gold. He'd never have recommended the man if he'd had reason to doubt him, to be suspicious of him. However, at the very least, Stick thought, Ashrafi might try to pressure him into more illegal activities. He didn't need his job, he decided.

And a job was the least of his worries, consumed as he was by his fear for Allie. The terrible contortions of the mouse kept coming back to him. The constant nagging feeling gripping his gut even overcame his excitement at his very first flight and to try and beat it in some way, as the queue moved forward, he began to plan his interview with Guevara.

Just before going through the security sc⸻
wristcom vibrated and he checked to make sure ⸻
wasn't a message from Alaina at the last minute.

There was just one line. Not from Alaina, nor from Ashrafi but from the League of the Dead.

"Don't interfere".

Allie had tried every possible way to get out of the room but the door was solid and, anyway, a guard stood outside. And unless you have a hundred years and more than a bent teaspoon there is no way you can discreetly tunnel through miles of rock. She was reproaching herself for not having tried to get to the open air the minute she'd found out what the rebels were planning. It wouldn't have mattered if she'd been caught after that. She didn't even know if the message had gone, or if Alaina would be able to do anything about it if it had. The terror lurked continually at the back of her mind that if the conspirators succeeded, then hundreds, perhaps thousands would die, and die in agony. And it would be her fault.

She'd asked one of the guards who'd brought her some food if she could see Dr Chavez again but the man had merely looked at her and shaken his head. Worry chewed away at her insides and made it impossible for her to concentrate on the book she'd chosen at random, desperate to take her mind off what was going to happen. How could she escape? Get away? Warn people? Eventually, with the thoughts tumbling over and over in her brain, she reverted to her original idea of bribery. Nobody had thought to relieve her of her ring which, while not nearly so valuable as Alaina's, might tempt someone. She thought the man who'd brought her food had looked at it covetously. Ramon his name was. He'd more or less said he'd see her in the morning with her breakfast. She'd just have to wait till dawn to see who came.

The bed was much more comfortable than the one in Asiri's room but she gave up trying to sleep. All she could see in her mind's eye were the horrifying, unspeakable torments of the mouse. When, long after midnight, the small square of paper was pushed under the door she heard the little scratching noise immediately and rushed to pick it up.

With shaking fingers she opened it out and read the message.

"This afternoon. 3 o'clock. Be ready. Y"

Chapter 18
The Ministry

As Stick clambered off the plane it wasn't difficult to spot Alaina, half a head taller than nearly everybody else, her chic sun cloak gleaming in the sunlight. She knew who he was immediately.

'Stick. Good to see you.' Her grasp was firm. 'Any luggage?'

He shook his head, holding up his in-cabin rucksack.

'Good.' Her welcoming smile faded. 'No luggage, less checks. In fact, the less time we're out and about the better since the Guardia seem to be on extra alert.'

They slipped through the crowds, Alaina flashing the diplomatic card where necessary.

'I got my mother to submit the request for our interview, and I guess they couldn't turn her down, but she's gone to what's left of Santiago this afternoon.'

'She isn't coming?' Despite his long legs he was practically having to run to keep up with her.

'She said the less she knew about it the better. Apparently there are some odd rumours swirling around our intelligence department and she can't be seen to be interfering in local politics in any way, especially as corruption is such a problem here. As Ambassador she has to be above all that. So it's just up to us.'

Alaina nodded to the shuttle which had been brought to the VIP exit door, dismissing the driver quietly.

'We'll be quicker if we put the diplomatic flag up.' She pressed a few buttons on the remote and the flag rose above the chassis. She grinned at Stick. 'Might as well be hung for a sheep as a lamb. The mother will kill me.'

The shuttle found its way to the Ministry doors in record time and so they were early for the appointment. The secretary seemed to take it as a personal affront and told them to wait in the foyer.

'I will check if His Excellency is ready for you.'

After what seemed to Stick an interminable delay they were finally admitted to a light airy room, with high windows and ceilings. Ornate curtains were held back by silken swags, the light falling on plush carpets and small marquetry tables. Large oil paintings on the walls reflected the eighteenth-century French style, the room dominated by the immense desk behind which His Excellency sat.

The man rose as they entered, extending a hand to Alaina and ignoring Stick. Alaina was tall enough to be able to grasp his hand firmly across the desk. Stick had done his homework and recognised him as Guevara, second in line at the Ministry of the Interior, a man with a slim face, a thin nose and an insincere smile.

'Ms Hamilton. Delightful to see you. We got your mother's note but I'm afraid it didn't explain very clearly what it was you wanted. Something to do with a missing friend, I believe, in a valley near Lago Noche. How can we help?'

Alaina and Stick had carefully prepared what they wanted to say. Stick hadn't wanted to use Allie's name at all, until he was sure who they were dealing with or that they would be on their side.

Alaina's voice was calm. 'Thank you, Señor Guevara. In fact it turns out that we're here for something even more worrying. It appears there's a plan to poison the UN contingent along with the local garrison and by extension the Granverde Valley here in Avila. Since the Ministry of the Interior is perhaps the only department with the power to stop this happening we've come to you.'

'Poison the Valley?' Guevara's voice was incredulous. 'How is that possible? I'm sorry, Ms Hamilton, there are many wild rumours going round at the moment but…'

'A nerve agent, possibly related to ricin or novichok, is to be released upstream into the Granverde. It remains inert for twenty minutes or so and so will have reached the UN barracks and your own garrison by the time it becomes active. Because of the high walls of the Granverde canyon the gas will be contained and take effect.' Alaina paused. 'It is almost always fatal. It represents a danger to everyone in the Avila Valley and beyond that the campamento and even the town.'

'Ms Hamilton, I'm sorry you have been misled...'

She cut him off, her voice unyielding. 'I have proof.'

For the first time he looked worried.

'How did you come by this information?'

'The friend I mentioned, who I believe is being held against her will in a valley not far from Lago Noche.'

'There is nothing in that valley.'

'So you know about the valley, then,' said Stick. '...and undoubtedly what is happening there as well. So why aren't you warning everyone, for heaven's sake?' He glared at the man. 'We will if you do not.'

'We wouldn't want to cause a panic,' said Alaina, 'but I think you'll find the information on this video convincing.' She held up a memory stick.

Guevara's eyes widened and for the first time he looked unsure of himself. Without speaking he plugged the stick into the console and they waited for the security app to confirm that it contained no malware of any kind before the tiny bit of video loaded. After it had finished Guevara gazed desperately at the screen in front of him, as if hoping it would show him the path he should take, but then said, 'I think perhaps you should see the Minister herself. Just wait in the foyer, will you?'

The woman behind the desk, when they were eventually admitted, looked up at them as they came into the room. It was an even larger salon than Guevara's and you knew that here was where the real power lay. She held a small holocom in her left hand as she too shook hands with Alaina and ignored Stick.

'Ms Hamilton. How nice to see you. I received your mother's note and am glad that Señor Guevara has had the opportunity of talking to you. Thank you for bringing this matter to our attention, although I must tell you that we have been aware for some time of what was going on in the illegal settlement near Lago Noche.'

Stick said. 'But it has become urgent now. They're going to poison everyone in the Granverde Valley. We told Señor Guevara. They have some sort of nerve agent that they're going to release into the water – into the river – while it's in spate. It will poison everyone in the Valley.'

The Minister held up her hand but Stick ploughed on.

'Do you know how long it will take to get to the town? The river's in full flow. And what about the British national they're holding?'

The Minister was suave. 'I don't know how you know this, young man, but all is in hand.'

'But Avila…the people at the estuary.'

'I appreciate your concern but the matter is already resolved. Rest assured nothing will happen to the Valley.'

Stick's voice rose. 'I will warn them if you will not.'

Guevara, who had come in behind them and was standing next to her, leaned forward and flicked the desk monitor switch. 'You'd better see this Minister. They brought it with them.' The images flickered on the screen without sound. 'Since they've seen this you'd better tell them. We don't want them to cause a panic.'

The Minister's looked up from the screen, her eyes like glass. She fiddled with her necklace, choosing her words carefully.

'Please do not concern yourself, Miss Hamilton, despite this – er – evidence. As I said, we've been aware of the settlement in that valley for some time and the situation has been neutralised. If your friend is still there she's in no danger. Someone has been assigned to escort her from the area. Don't attempt to go there yourself. Strangers are being shot on sight and I cannot be responsible for er...' – she hesitated – 'tourists in the wrong place. Even...' she nodded in Alaina's direction, 'the daughter of an ambassador. We will arrange for your friend to be brought to the Embassy.'

Stick bent over the desk, leaning right forward into the woman's face. 'I hope you realise the implications of this.'

The woman's eyes blazed with anger.

'Rest assured that everything will be done that needs to be done. And now, I'm afraid, I'm going to have to ask you to leave.' She dragged a sheet of paper towards her across the desk in a final gesture. 'Please convey my regards to your mother, Ms Hamilton. I am somewhat at a loss to know why she didn't contact me by the usual channels.'

They were ushered from the room.

In the outer vestibule, past Security, Alaina let out a deep sigh.

'Jeez, am I going to be in deep doodoo when this gets back.' She looked, for the first time since Stick had met her, less than supremely confident. 'What on earth were you thinking of back there, getting up her nose like that?' Her voice rose. 'Consider the implications! For Pete's sake, that was the Minister of the Interior you were talking to, not some minor official. And when I think of all the trouble I went to, to get....'

She realised that Stick wasn't listening to her, that he was playing with a small device at his belt, putting in an earpiece....and then hastily grabbing her arm and hauling her outside into the street and round the corner of the building.

He thrust a second earpiece into her hand and as she uncomprehendingly slipped it into her ear she heard the Minister's voice.

'Are they all there?'

She saw Stick gesturing and heard him say, 'It was the only way I could get close enough to place the bug.'

Guevara's voice in the earpiece.

'All is going well. They're all there. The priest, that Lamar fellow, held out for a long time but, as you know, our security services have very – er – persuasive, not to say painful, methods of interrogation.' He didn't sound at all concerned. 'The names he gave us cross matched with those on the list. None of the named is at home so we can assume that they are either in that Chamber or can be dealt with by the military later.' His voice became less certain. 'Of course, these are well known and popular people. Some will perhaps rise in their defence…'

The answering voice was suave. 'If they are alive.'

Allie knew that the ceremony was to take place that afternoon and that they would never allow her to be present. She couldn't believe that Yupanqui would come for her himself, even if he'd wanted to, and the obvious time for whoever had been assigned to fetch her was when everyone else had left for the Chamber.

She was pleased that she wouldn't be there when they released the poison, that she wouldn't somehow be party to the slaughter. Perhaps they'd settled matters with the guard in advance, or perhaps Yupanqui's instructions would be sufficient. She was pretty sure the guard would be Ramon. He was a small man, with a thin ferrety face and a tiny moustache. He was probably one of the *campesinos* who had been brought into the settlement, rather than one of the mine Indians. In consequence, therefore, his loyalty to the cause might not be as strong. He looked untrustworthy.

She'd flashed the ring at him very ostentatiously when he'd brought her some breakfast and knew he was hooked. He'd only have to let her slip away and once outside the ziggurat she'd be able to disappear into the crowds of people heading for the Chamber. She thought again of the solemn procession onto the dais, the phalanx of warrior gods clad in gold.

If she could somehow get to a holocom – or even someone's moby once she'd got away from her companion– she could contact the authorities and warn them. For the short time she'd been in the outside world she'd tried the hidden moby but it was no good. It appeared to be completely dead, the battery long gone. And even powerful as it was it couldn't function under the rock. The power pack had been taken along with her travel pouch and the room didn't have a charging point.

She'd have to try and escape by the back route through the mine or hide somewhere. Unless Yupanqui was providing a way out of the settlement completely. It was maddening not knowing exactly what was going to happen.

Since breakfast she'd waited in a ferment of anxiety, terrified all morning that they would somehow move her from the room, that whoever was sent for her wouldn't be able to find her. At midday a small Indian boy brought her some food but she was too strung up to eat it, pushing it around the plate and finally leaving it entirely. More time went by. She slid the ring up and down on her finger. Footsteps went past but never halted, although once someone stopped and talked to her guard but then continued.

Three o'clock had come and gone. Still nothing from Yupanqui. Just as she was beginning to believe that nothing would happen she heard from outside her room the sound of heavy boots approaching and then the guard at her door talking to someone standing at the entrance. Her heart beat faster.

'Who are you? Why are you here? Where is Ramon?' Her guard was pulling back the door as he spoke.

Allie's heart sank. The man who'd come was not Ramon.

'He has the fever.' The new man had a surly look. 'I'm to accompany the Señorita to the Chamber.'

Her guard tried a feeble stalling action. 'I thought the Señorita was not supposed to go to the Chamber.'

Oh no, no. They couldn't take her away. The person coming for her would miss her. Unless this was the person that Yupanqui had sent.

Her guard was still temporising. 'What's your name?'

'Carlo Ruiz. It is not important. Ask Huascar if you think something is wrong.'

At the mention of Huascar her guard shrugged and stood aside so that Allie could pass him.

'Come,' said the new guard, 'We must go to the Chamber.'

Allie regretted now that she'd put on her trainers and made ready to leave.

'One moment.' She thought feverishly. 'I must go to the bathroom.'

She turned quickly away from him and rushed into the tiny en-suite, bolting the door. On a bloc of soap she scratched 'Taken to Chamber', placing it as prominently as she could on the basin edge. She ran the water loudly and flushed the toilet. The guard was banging on the door.

As she let herself out of the room he grabbed her arm and hauled her painfully along after him, out into the corridor. She tried to drag her feet but it was useless and she soon realised he would have no compunction about dislocating her arm completely if she didn't follow quickly enough. Eventually they left the passageway and Allie knew that the person sent for her would no longer be able to find her. Whatever arrangement had been made it had somehow been overridden by whoever had sent this guard to fetch her. Nobody would be able to find her in amongst all those people in the chamber. Her hopes of escape, of getting to a phone to warn people, were once more crushed.

What could she do? What action could she take?

If she was unable to warn the people in Avila could she somehow, some way, stop the leaders from acting.

She was taken with a sudden thought. If she could appeal to Yupanqui, convince him that their plans were known, that she had actually managed to warn the army in Avila and that therefore those threatened would have been able to escape, then their releasing the poison would be of no use. With the thoughts tumbling over and over in her brain she scarcely noticed the guard dragging her down the steps and pushing her roughly in front of him as they came out at the base of the ziggurat.

Yes, that was one last throw of the dice she could try. It might sow a bit of confusion, if she was convincing enough, if she could prove to him, them, that their actions had been recorded and passed on.

It was cooler now with thunder roaring around the dragon's teeth of the crater rim. She stumbled forward as they walked in single file through the narrow entrance to the rock channels. Passing the Great Sundial, *Intihuatana*, the golden llama and his boy companion, the puma, the mice and the flowers, they came, finally, to the great doors of the Punchao Chamber.

A guard stopped them.

'Where are the others, the children?' he said.

'They are following with Ramon.' The man was brusque.

Surely he'd said that Ramon had the fever? There was no point in wondering about it as the cave was already full, an excited crowd pushing and shoving for the best place to see what was going on.

The man on the doors said, 'Well, we've no time for them now. The ceremony is about to start.'

Allie could feel the level of anticipation rising.

Somebody in the crowd must have heard the interchange because he said, 'The Priest will be unhappy if the children and their mothers do not come. They want everyone to see.'

'We cannot wait.'

Someone else at the front said, 'Our people in the town are ready. We must act now.' She recognised that figure. Rumiñaui.

It was final.

The great doors were pulled to. The music started, the thin wail of the reed flutes, the booming sound of the *zamponas*, and above the music the thunderous roar of the Granverde as it burst its way through the narrow walls.

Standing on a corner of the Ministry building, watching Alaina's face as she listened uncomprehendingly, Stick struggled to work out what they'd done.

'I hadn't heard the missing person was British. How do we know she's there?' It was Guevara's voice. He sounded put out, as if he'd been kept out of the loop.

The minister was bored. 'Oh, Gutierrez reported her when he was chasing the children who stole the documents. He knew they came from the campamento. He had no real grounds to suspect the British national but we had her followed for a day or two to make sure she wasn't in contact with the rebels. She seemed to be just a naïve foreigner,' – Stick could almost see the sneer – 'one of these everlasting do-gooders – so we didn't bother with her anymore.'

Guevara was clearly still a bit irked. 'But do we know she's definitely in the settlement?'

'Oh yes. Our watcher on the mountain spotted her on the *Camino Real*. Since nobody uses that road anymore, not even people from the mine, he checked facial recognition and it brought up her picture and Gutierrez's report. So we alerted our informer in their headquarters. The same one who opened the gates for us this morning, in fact. He reported that the English national seemed to be really only interested in this girl, Rosalita, and was not a particular threat to our manoeuvre.' The woman sighed. 'But then these rebels decided to act so we've had to bring our own operation forward.'

'I know the military are in the Valley but, as I said, these people are popular. Can the military be counted on...?' Guevara's voice tailed off.

'Fortunately we don't need to rely on the military.' The Minister's voice conveyed vast disdain for the military. 'We've changed the product.'

'The nerve agent? But, but...I heard...'

The Minister's voice hardened. 'You know what they've been trying to do. That clinic is just a cover for genetic modification. It's plain we couldn't allow such things to continue.'

'But...'

'It's absolutely their own fault. They were prepared to poison the whole Valley. Luckily, some minor lab technician was able to help us substitute the agent they intended to use for one more suited to our purpose. Called Velasquez, I think.' The voice was complacent again. 'And the League of the Dead were very helpful.'

Stick looked at Alaina in horror as he heard Guevara say, 'But they seem to have got so far. I realise it needs to be under government control...'

A sound clattered in the earpiece as somebody burst into the room.

Someone said breathlessly, 'They've taken the girl to the ceremony.'

'What!' The Minister's voice lashed out. 'Do you know what's going to happen in that chamber?'

The noise of the traffic around Stick faded, his oxygen shunt seemed to have stopped working, as he heard far away the frightened voice of the secretary, the hamster squeak of alarm.

And he knew what they'd done. The League of the Dead. The products Velasquez had been investigating. He saw again the sheets of chemical analyses, the ways in which the various gases interacted with the environment, their effects on the human body.

He could see on Alaina's face the mind-numbing fear echoing his own.

'What have they done?'

He was stammering. 'They've s-swapped the gas. I think it will have a similar effect to the one the rebels intended to use, but it's been designed to react with oxygen and not with water. So it will poison everyone in the Chamber.'

He saw his terror reflected in her eyes as they both remembered the death of the mouse.

Even if they'd sent someone to save her, these government officials thought that Allie would be only too happy to escape. They didn't know her. She would try to save her friends. A pain jabbed his heart. She would try to get Rosalita out and this Yupanqui. He thought that dying would be better than the thought of Allie suffering in agonies.

Turning to Alaina, his face ashen, he said, 'Can you get me up there? Up to the crater?'

Now he knew why the League of the Dead had been following him. They'd been keeping an eye on him, scared that somehow Allie would warn him of what was going on, that their plot with the government against the rebels would unravel. They must have been playing both sides off against each other.

Through a fog of apprehension he heard Alaina's voice. She was already talking into the wristcom, asking to speak to a Sergeant Willis. His heart shrank with fear as the multiple transfers went through and it looked as if it was a dead end.

But then a broad American accent. 'Now Miss Hamilton, have you been getting into scrapes again?'

'Worse than that, Sammy. I need you to get me to the far side of the Lago Noche crater. Do you have a whirly bird?'

Chapter 19
The Chamber

In the Chamber excitement was rising. The doors opened again and the animal headed members of the ruling elite entered in single file and took their places on the podium, the Condor's turning her head to look at the massed throng beneath her, swaying and sighing ecstatically. Most of those who had been at the meeting were there, the Puma, the Snake, the Jaguar, the other animals perhaps. Rumiñaui had joined them. Allie looked for but couldn't see Velasquez, the Jackal.

They were followed by the Seven, the warrior gods, who took their places behind them, splendid in gold. Although, in the excitement and with the smoke of the torches swirling and the movement of the heads in front of her, Allie couldn't tell if there were seven.

Now was the time when she should do something. If she could get Yupanqui to listen to her, convince him that she had betrayed them, he would be able to stop them. It was to him she must appeal. She looked at the line of the Seven, hoping against hope that she would be able to see which one was Yupanqui. She couldn't tell.

Surely there were only six? The waving head of the Condor was blocking her view. The crowd shouted their names, names of the Royal Inca. 'Roca,' they chanted, 'Viracocha, Pachacuti, Huascar,' the stamping was louder, 'Topa, Atahualpa...' Amongst them she thought she heard Yupanqui. She would have known if one of them was Yupanqui, she thought, and then, despairingly, that she'd been wrong about him all along and so was probably wrong now. She'd lost the advantage.

The voice from the mummified Lieberhart rose on the air, a voice magnified by the wonderful acoustics of the cave.

'Guardians! Our time has come!'

The Indians shivered and trembled as the sound echoed in the vault.

'We are the Guardians!' they chanted.

'We have been oppressed for too long, robbed of our birthright. It is time to retake the power of our forefathers and the Great Inca himself.'

'We are the Guardians! We will destroy the oppressors.'

'We will lead you!' Lieberhart's voice.

'We will follow!

'We may die but the oppressors will die also. We will lead you.'

'We will follow,' they screamed.

The noise was deafening, the faces flushed, even the pale moon faces of the deepest mineworkers transformed.

'To the Death!'

'To the Death,' they moaned, 'To the Death!'

The voice of Lieberhart slowly died away and the chanting began again and grew louder as, judging by the names she could occasionally pick out, they sang ancient tales of Inca conquest. As the jubilant voices echoed around the Chamber two black-liveried servants brought onto the dais an ornate black box, suspended between them on two ringed poles. The Priest raised his hands over his head and looked down at them, ready to pray.

Now, In the silence which fell, was the time to speak, to shout out Yupanqui's name, to tell them that she'd reported them already. Allie had opened her mouth to shout when the terrible realisation hit her. She would be signing her own death warrant. She'd be garrotted like the boy and nobody would know what had happened to her. She halted, paralysed, and the guard who must have felt her movement grabbed her.

Feeling a shiver of cold air at her back and trying to regain her impetus she thrust herself forward again, yelling Yupanqui's name above the priest's chant. The guard wrenched at her arm with such force, dragging her back, that she almost lost her balance and the shout was lost, a young man beside her looking at her curiously and then turning his gaze back to the dais.

She tried to free herself but the guard's grip was a vice, pulling her to one side as the cold air became colder.

Apart from the young man the others next to her were unconscious of her struggle, absorbed in the moment, watching the black-clothed servants place the box on the table. The Priest began to chant again and the bearers took up their positions. In heart-sinking despair Allie knew that soon they would lift the box, carry it down the stairs, through the throngs of watchers and head for the river.

In her frantic struggle she hardly registered that the wall was no longer at her back, that the guard had pushed at some kind of door and then, glancing over her shoulder, saw the dark crack through which the cold air came.

He pulled her again and she thought of resisting and then realised that it would be useless. She was dragged roughly through the narrow opening and the door began to swing closed, just as the muffled sound of chanting began once more.

She tried to yank herself away but he was extremely strong and as she struggled he turned on her ferociously.

'Come, you stupid little fool,' he hissed. 'Do you wish us to die with the others?'

She couldn't understand him. Perhaps he thought he would be in danger himself for helping her escape. But it was not they who were at risk. It was the people in the Valley. She wanted to tell him this but he was off, pulling her roughly down a stone corridor, ducking and weaving past uneven outcrops of rock, their path lit by his torch and the light from the sconces, set high in the rock wall, flickering unevenly, casting shadows beneath their feet.

She stumbled after him, half dragged, half running, wondering if it would be possible to break away. Not in the tunnels though, she thought, remembering Asiri's little voice, 'Some people lost forever.' It would be madness to try and escape down here. She wouldn't be able to find her way out alone. Only once they came outside could she try.

At least she wouldn't be party to the murder planned in the cave.

Dust swirled up from under their feet as they emerged coughing into the central square in front of the pyramid. The guard stopped for a moment, heaving great gasps of breath, and Allie wrenched at the arm holding her.

'Follow me,' he said, 'we must get to the village mine shaft.'

'No. First you must warn Avila. It's some kind of gas. It's going to be dissolved in the water and sent down the Granverde.' She couldn't begin to describe how horribly people would die when the vapours crept up from the waters and were carried on the wind.

'Come on, you stupid *Inglesa*.' He was dragging at her arm again. 'There will be no poison in Avila.'

'How do you know? You must get them out. You must warn them. Yupanqui sent you. He will tell you what I say is true.' She was wild with anxiety.

For a second he looked puzzled at the mention of the name.

'No need for warnings. We have been sent to rescue you and the children. Some of the mothers if they wish to come.' He pushed her forward towards the village. 'Look!'

She saw that there were already men in uniform there, guiding children and their carers towards a cavern-like entrance. The uniforms were those of the national armed forces.

'You have to go to the mine entrance. But don't go down to the mine, take the green shaft. It will come out near the rim and there will be helicopters there.'

One of the soldiers turned and saw her and gestured that she should join the group.

'Come on, come on,' he said. 'We haven t got very long. They're about to take off.'

She still didn't understand. Somehow things had changed and the army was in control. She stood for a moment undecided.

'Come on, come on, hurry. They'll be taking off any minute.'

She looked to where he pointed and saw the helicopters in the sky above them heading to the far side of the ziggurat. Somebody else was tugging at her arm, screaming at her.

It was Rafa.

'Rosalita,' he shouted. 'Where is Rosalita? She's not with the others.'

It took a moment for her to register what he meant.

'Rosalita? She's not with the other mothers? Isn't she in the hospital then? In her room?'

'I try there'.

Of course, of course, he would have tried the hospital and Rosalita's room. But she'd been worried about Esteban's cough. She thought feverishly.

'The baby might have needed medicine. She might have gone to the pharmacy. We should try there.'

Even as she said it the thought hit her consciousness. Perhaps Rosalita had somehow got mixed up with the wrong group. The army was in the Valley. What did they intend to do with the rebels? They knew, it seemed that all the leaders were in the Chamber. She heard again the voice of the guard who had dragged her from the ceremony, his voice rough with fear.

'Come, stupid *Inglesa*. Do you wish to die with the others?' Would the army just kill the ones in the Chamber? Would Rosalita end up in prison or even worse. They just appeared to be moving the children and mothers out.

She tried to ignore her fears, concentrating instead on where Rosalita might be.

'When I was there the baby had a little cough so they could have put her in the special room, the one that is set apart at the end, for babies with infections.'

'I did not know about that. She was not with the other mothers and when I saw that I went to her room and then to the hospital but there was no one there. All the nurses, doctors, everybody gone. All the beds empty.'

'We must try the pharmacy,' she said, 'and that room,' unable to tell Rafa her greatest fear, that Rosalita and her baby had been swept up in the group which had gone to the Chamber. Should she send Rafa to look there?

'You try the pharmacy,' she said. 'I'll go to the special room. I know the way. I'll cut through the office block.'

She turned but the young soldier was barring her route.

'You can't go back now,' he said. 'There isn't time.'

'They've left someone behind. We've got to go back.'

'They won't be able to wait. It's too dangerous.'

She was already brushing past him, ignoring him, racing towards a skilfully concealed lower entrance which she imagined must lead to the office area, Rafa heading in the opposite direction.

She heard the soldier's voice behind her. 'You'll die if you don't come soon.'

Driven by fear for Rosalita she pounded onwards. Up the steps. Up another flight. Through the big double doors, blood coursing through her veins, breath coming in gasps. Her headlong rush stopped only as she came into the office area.

She knew something was wrong even before she went through the door. She could see that the main office within, leading to where she'd seen the Condor, had been completely trashed; papers, holocoms, routers and discs strewn everywhere, files wrenched out and thrown on the floor, computers gutted. Printers and monitors disembowelled. Sharp banging and crashing sounds came from the room where she'd seen Dr Chavez.

Brusca was there, red-eyed, furious, hurling files, headsets, handfuls of discs, at the wall. A refrigerator door hung open, revealing smashed vials, some lying in a pile of gloopy stuff on the floor. Dr Chavez was seated at the table, her head lying on the strewn papers, almost as if asleep except for the slowly congealing pool of red spreading from under her face.

Brusca was violent, raving, the weal still plain on his neck, his face puffy with the venom which had spread into the surrounding flesh. It made the bruise on the side of his head where the oxygen tank had hit him, stand out even more.

'What has she done with them?' The voice ratcheted up several levels in rage. 'The notes, the samples, the hard drives?'

He turned on Allie.

'It's all your fault. If you hadn't come she would have told me. She said you opened her eyes. She said she'd destroyed the notes. Stupid, stupid.'

'You shouldn't have killed her, Brusca. Now you'll never know.'

'She wouldn't tell me.' He was like a child, furious that his toy has been taken away. 'She wouldn't tell me.'

Poor Dr Chavez with her dreams of a return to a communal paradise. Even if Brusca hadn't killed her the others couldn't afford to have her survive. She knew too much about them and of course they'd be able to blame all the genetic modification on her. They thought they didn't need her anymore. Brusca had known better.

His eyes flickering with fury he came towards her. 'Why did you come here? It's all your fault! You destroyed my experiments.' He was waving a heavy paper weight. 'You talked to Dr Chavez. She listened to you. I should have killed you when I had the chance.'

Allie was backing away, a pulse pounding in her temple. He was swinging the paperweight. The clump of heavy boots outside in the main office caused his attention to waver and his arm to slacken. The military were here, no doubt to check for the notes as well.

He halted, undecided, and she rushed towards him, feinted and slipped under the arm wielding the paperweight and then through the side door in the direction of the hospital. He made no attempt to follow her.

Martin Carvajal and the rebel leaders had got Chavez to continue her father's genetic work without telling her what they really intended to do. Somebody else, perhaps even Martin, had thought up the amnesia, and it was Brusca who was clearly the driving force behind the chimera creatures. No doubt the Condor and Atahualpa had played along with her ideas of a return to the old ways but they'd never have implemented them. They'd just wanted the research, how to do it, so that they could use it for their own ends. They were playing for power. Once she'd realised how she and the Guardian Indians had been used, did they think she would leave her findings to them? What was it her father had said about Martin? That he was too much into politics? Had Lieberhart seen the danger even then?

Allie pounded through the research suite, her chest heaving. It would be quicker than going through the school corridor. She had to find Rosalita.

All the animals were dead in their cages. The Pig, lying on its side, could almost have been sleeping in its little bed of hay, its voice box tilted at a crazy angle.

Wulfi's cage was empty. She wondered with horror if some of the abominations in Brusca's lab had escaped like Wulfi. Would they come back to haunt humanity?

There was Rafa, dragging in great gulps of breath.

'Have you seen her?'

'No.' They raced through the hospital block.

'This way. This way.'

She couldn't believe it when she saw Rosalita, dressed and ready to go, seated on the bed in the quarantine room with the baby in her arms.

The girl was bewildered. 'They tell me to get ready, that somebody comes for me but nobody come.'

'They must have forgotten you.' Rafa grabbed her cloak and threw it over her and the baby. 'We must go quickly, Rosalita. The soldier told me that we must get out of the Valley.'

They scuttled out into the corridor.

Rosalita stopped. 'The clothes, the beautiful clothes, they are on the bed.'

'We can't wait,' said Allie, in an agony of impatience, but Rafa had turned and rushed back to the room, grabbing the bag from the bed.

He'd returned in seconds, looking at Allie. 'Through the schoolroom corridor?'

'No, it leads past the office and the military are there.' They could hear the distant sound of angry voices, shouted commands.

'Bring it all. Just bag it and bring it as fast as you can. We haven't got time to sort it out now. Not much time left.'

Somebody had clearly set off an explosive of some kind behind the office area and a blast of dust enveloped them.

'This way then.' Rafa was already running down a new corridor. 'We must go outside. There's another way to the mine entrance.'

Night was falling and Allie shivered as they emerged into the outside world, thunder rolling between the peaks and mingling with the series of explosions which shook the mountain. But the stones of the façade held firm. They scrambled down the pyramid on a path winding between the great stone blocks, Rosalita clasping the baby to her. In the chilly green light draining away behind the crater's edge they could just see a few soldiers below them, running for what must be a lower entrance. Even at this distance their heads looked a little odd. Were they wearing masks of some kind as well?

'Come on, come on,' said Rafa, choosing a shorter route. 'We go down here.'

Allie went first and Rafa was about to put Rosalita and little Esteban between them when stones rattled and a man thrust them violently aside, unheeding of the baby.

'Get out of my way. Get out of my way!'

Rafa was shouting an angry reply as Allie turned to find out what was going on and saw Velasquez, his eyes burning black, his face distorted with fear.

'Out of my way,' he snarled. 'Out of my way.'

He shoved Allie back hard against the rock wall, smashing her arm against the granite surface, tearing the skin. She clutched her elbow in agony. She would have fended him off, but Velasquez had no interest in them, leaping past her onto the track and clattering down the slope in great leaps and bounds.

Gradually the throbbing subsided and ignoring it she pressed on with Rafa and Rosalita behind her. They were almost down, a short distance to go only, seeing in the moonlight that nearly all of the soldiers had disappeared, when a grey shape flowed past them, following Velasquez. The wolf glanced in her direction as it went by but did not stop. In the yellow eyes there was no longer any trace of humanity, of compassion, of anger even, nothing human left.

At the entry to the mine shaft a young soldier, holding what looked like a gas mask in one hand, pointed to one of the tunnels. 'Through there,' he said. 'It joins the main shaft higher up. And be careful. Some kind of animal went in there a minute ago. I don't think it's in the main shaft but watch out for it anyway. And get a move on. You're the last.'

The soldier spun away, heading for the jeep which waited for him, engine running. They started into the shaft, eyes slowly adjusting to the change in light, realising that they were heading upwards, when they heard the shrill terrified screams from another tunnel. They were accompanied by guttural worrying noises, the two seeming to go on forever.

Velasquez!

The shrieks were scarcely human. Scrabbling and crunching noises. Then, in one abrupt moment, silence.

Allie felt sick and Rafa looked at her.

'He deserve,' he said.

She would have replied that nobody deserved to die that way no matter what terrible deeds they might have committed, when she felt a vibration at her waist. At first, such was her confusion and the horror of the moment, she couldn't work out what it was and then realised it was the moby, the moby with Stick's sim, hidden in the buckle of her belt. They must be close enough still to the outside for reception and it must somehow have been remotely reactivated. She fumbled as she thrust in the earpiece and pressed the button.

'Get out, Allie,' Stick was screaming, 'Get out! They've changed the gas. It'll kill all the people in the Chamber and probably poison the whole Valley. You must get away from there or you will die.'

Chapter 20
Betrayal

Alaina and Stick struggled up the slope to the crater's rim. Sergeant Willis had dropped them as close as he dared. It was all wildly confused; the great beat of the helicopter blades above their heads and army personnel running back and forth. They could see small groups of people struggling over the rim, mostly women and children.

A young sentry tried to hold the two of them back but they were in no mood to wait. Alaina drew herself to her full height, an imposing figure.

'I am the daughter of the ambassador. Take me to the UN commander immediately. I have a message from His Excellency, Señor Guevara, at the Ministry of the Interior.' Large drones wheeled past overhead carrying who knew what.

Bewildered the young man asked them to follow him, stepping over cables, around heaps of ammunition, past excited groups of soldiers.

'What's happening?' said Alaina.

'Not sure I rightly know, ma'am,' the young man said. 'We just have to get all those families into the helicopters and then we're gonna beat it outta here. I guess something real nasty is going to happen down there because my sergeant's freaking out.'

He stopped next to a tall thin man, talking urgently into a holocom.

'Here's the Commander.'

The man looked up surprised, piercing grey eyes flashing irritation as he registered Alaina and Stick's presence.

'What the hell…?'

'Message from Señor Guevara at the Ministry, S-ssir,' the young man said, his haste making him stammer. 'Ms Hamilton, daughter of the Ambassador.'

'God in heaven, don't they think we've got enough on?' The man swivelled, roared an instruction to a group of soldiers behind him, and then swung back to Stick and Alaina.

'All right, soldier. Carry on.'

The grey eyes sparked cold anger, every muscle of the lean body tense.

'What's this all about then?'

Alaina's voice was cool but urgent. 'Commander, we've discovered that a British national is still in the crater. You must stop your actions until everybody is out.'

The voice was a knife. 'With all due respect, it's not my actions, young lady. It's whoever's down there, bent on murdering everyone for miles around. I have no control over them. We're helping the military here and just trying to get everyone out that we can, but they've told me we're on a tight timeline.'

The trenched lines of his face showed the strain. 'I'm afraid I must ask you to wait over there, Ms Hamilton, well out of the way, so you don't hinder operations. Sergeant,' he beckoned over another soldier, 'Accompany Ms Hamilton and her friend to the secure zone. Find out the name of the British national and see if they've come out already. Then go and assist the lieutenant.'

He turned to Alaina. 'It's much too dangerous, Ms Hamilton. As soon as we've established whether your friend is here or not you should leave immediately.'

Stick tried Allie's moby again, accessing the reactivate button to call up its battery reserves as he had done before, but they were long gone. This time it really was dead.

At first Allie had not been able to take in the message. It was the closest she'd ever heard Stick come to losing his cool. They'd been cut off almost immediately and that had been it – no loving message, no personal touch, just the harsh command. And as she began to process what he'd said she realised with horror that all those in the Punchao Chamber, including Yupanqui, were doomed.

She must go back. She must warn them.

She'd pivoted, turned on her heel, when the gut-wrenching reality hit her. Time had run out. The Priest had been preparing to release the poison when she'd been dragged from the cave. According to Velasquez they had only had twenty minutes after its release, if that. It was already too late.

A shard of ice slid into her chest. She shivered. How had Stick known? The fact that he was on the far side of the world meant nothing to a gifted hacker like Stick. The web was an open path to wherever he chose to visit.

Rafa had gone ahead and was beckoning her on. Her legs leaden she went to catch up with him and found that they'd joined one of the main tunnels heading upwards, out of the mine area. Small groups of people mostly carers and children were ahead of them. Some of the teenage changed ones went past in orderly file, young, happy and proud, the swish of the cloaks accompanying the reedy wail of the panpipes. She wondered briefly what life would be like for these children, formidably intelligent, handsome and beautiful, able to breathe without the assistance of oxygen packs or masks, but all strangely similar. And lacking true human emotion.

The government were letting the Seven die. They wanted only the children. They hoped to use them for their own ends, she was sure, thinking they could mould them to their will. Perhaps. She heard again the contempt in Brusca's voice. 'Atahualpa and I have plans.'

The thought that the Seven would die was agonising. Not just Yupanqui, but Cusi, Asiri and the others from the mine were in the chamber as well. Rafa and Rosalita waited with her as she stopped, undecided, paralysed by the knowledge of what was going to happen. As the last group flowed past them a younger child who had attached herself to their little group relinquished her hand and ran to catch up with the others heading along the escape shaft.

And then, from out of one of the many subterranean tunnels, Yupanqui, carrying a small child.

Yupanqui!

He looked at her and frowned. 'Allee! What's happened? Why are you here? Asiri told me she'd delivered the message.'

For an instant she wondered if it really was Yupanqui as he put the little boy on the ground and then saw that it was Paquito. Hope fought with terror in her chest.

'I thought you'd have been well away by now,' he said.

'You're not in the Chamber.' Her voice sounded high and stupid.

His voice was harsh. 'I want no part in the slaughter.'

He was wearing the magnificent garb of the Inca warrior, all gold thread with the golden cloak. He must have put it on, she thought, for the ceremony and then his revulsion at the approaching massacre had held him back.

He patted the little boy on the head. 'This little one is mine but he said his carer went this way. I don't know why.' His brow creased. 'How are you here? Asiri delivered the message. I thought…'

Looking up he must have seen her face.

'What! What's wrong?' He grabbed her arm, noticing for the first time the last few mothers, carers and children ahead, and Rafa and Rosalita with the baby waiting for her.

His eyes burned. 'What's happening? What's wrong? Why are you here?'

Her brain refused to function. She stammered incoherently. 'Your people have been betrayed. The government knows. They've come to take away the children. You must get out.'

He was still puzzled, then saw the look on her face.

She told him baldly, without attempting to soften the blow. 'Stick, my friend, told me that they've exchanged the product,' she said. 'The gas. He's a hacker and he warned me. It will be released in the Chamber, not in the water. It will poison everyone in the Chamber and probably anyone in this valley. I don't know how he knows. But the military are taking all the children away. They told me we have only a short time to get out.'

She saw it strike him like a blow, the antique face turn to stone.

'My brothers.' The voice was a whisper of pain. 'They are all in the Chamber.'

'They chose,' she said. 'They chose to be there. You did not.'

The image of the long and agonising death of the small animal, whiskers twitching, the horrible contortions, came to them both.

'I must warn them.'

'It's too late.' She could feel her own heart turn to stone. 'They were about to release the poison when I was in the cave. It's too late.'

All those people she thought, closing her eyes. All dying in agony.

Yupanqui stood, immovable, calculating, and then seemed to reach a clear decision.

'There are better ways of dying. And I can perhaps get some out.'

'But the time's run out.'

He looked down at her unseeing. 'Perhaps not. I heard there was to be a delay, that some message had reached them. That they were to leave a runner at *Intihuatana* until the light reaches the Scorpion. Then he was to run to the Chamber and they were only to release the gas when he got there. A few extra minutes, I don't know why. Something to do with the units in the campamento in Avila.'

'But the army is here. Even if your people leave the Chamber they'll be under attack.' She was babbling. 'Stick, my friend, says that the poison will kill everyone left in the Valley, not just those in the cave.' She looked at him seeing the resolve on his face. 'You can't help them now,' she said in terror. 'You mustn't.'

He gave an odd grunt of pain and then leaned over and tapped her cheek.

'Don't look so worried, Allee. I might be able to get some out. I'm just wondering how to convince them, to warn them. The other *Panacas*, even my brothers, won't want to believe it.'

Rafa, his face screwed with concentration said, 'The control room?'

Yupanqui's face lightened. 'Lieberhart!'

Allie wanted to scream at him. 'Lieberhart's dead. How can he possibly help?'

But Yupanqui was gripped with enthusiasm. 'You're right, Rafa. Perhaps I can't stop them using the poison but at least we can get some to leave.'

He was spinning on his heel, wrenching a coil of rope from its fixture on the corridor wall. 'I'll need you two.' He looked at Rafa. 'Tupac can go and try and stop the runner and you can use the transmitter and tell them what's going to happen. You must be Lieberhart. Tell them that we've been betrayed. What the gas will do. That they must follow me and Huascar. I'll get down there.'

'What will be the good if they kill you all when you come out?' She thought of the Indians, the miners, their flushed and exultant faces as they thought they would triumph. She saw Cusi and Asiri in the throng, felt their excitement. Even if they tried to leave they'd be mown down by the military.

'No, there's another exit. It leads to the other side of the mountain to another valley. Only Huascar and I know about it. We found it when we were children.' He smiled at the memory. 'We know those tunnels like no one else. Once people are out it can be blocked off so that the army doesn't realise where it goes.'

He threw the rope over his shoulder and then picked up Paquito and rested his forehead gently against that of the child. 'Paquito, *mi caro*, I must leave you. Look after Rosalita for me and remember me.'

He stood him down and ruffled the beautiful blue-black hair as Paquito looked up at him with big eyes. He'd not named him after the Inca kings like the others, Allie thought wonderingly.

Yupanqui turned to Rosalita, now intent and organised. 'You must wait here with Paquito, Rosalita. Rafa and Allee will come for you soon and then you must run to the exit point. Rafa, Allee, follow me.'

He was away, running, and after a moment's hesitation they followed him. Along another corridor, up a huge flight of steps, scaling them two at a time, arriving breathless at the top.

Yet another rock door which at Yupanqui's voice command swung wide. Inside banks of monitors, command modules, transmitters, a fully equipped recording studio. The young Indian seated at the desk swung round.

Allie was surprised although, on reflection, she should have realised that they had something like this. Behind the young man was a large monitor showing the Punchao Chamber with its seething mass of excited humanity. At the far end you could see the dais, with the six brothers, the rebel leaders and the Priest. The huge glass box with the mummified Lieberhart. She looked desperately for the smaller box containing the poison and to her relief saw it still sitting on the stone table.

The young man turned, surprised, and stood. 'Lord Yupanqui!' His brow wrinkled in puzzlement. He spoke rapidly in Quechua, gazing at Allie and Rafa, clearly asking if something was wrong.

Yupanqui replied. It appeared he was explaining what had happened and asking him to do something. The young man looked shocked. He was still clearly protesting when Yupanqui wrenched off his seal ring and gave it to him. 'As fast as the wind, Tupac. Remember. Tunnel 88.'

'*Si*, my Lord.'

Protest halted, the young man spun round and raced back down the corridor, disappearing from view.

Allie looked after him.

'What's he going to do?

'He's going to *Intihuatana*. It's only halfway to the Chamber so perhaps he'll get there before the light hits the Scorpion. He has my seal so that the runner will listen to him. I've said that they must not under any circumstances go to the Chamber but that they must both leave by the exit from Tunnel 88.' He saw Allie's enquiring look. 'A secret one, known only to a few. This place is provided with a hundred escape routes and 88 is the closest and will lead them to safety.'

As he spoke Yupanqui was slotting into the desk console another memory stick.

'This will connect you to my wristcom, so I can contact you if needed when I get down to the Chamber. Rafa, you must take Tupac's place. You must be Lieberhart.'

'How can a mummy help?' Allie was confused. 'He didn't know anything about the poison so even if we had the time we couldn't cobble together enough of his speech from the recordings to make any sense.'

'Martin had hundreds of Lieberhart's tapes. He recorded all his experiments. He's installed a deepfake app which has retrieved that data and can convert any speech into one that sounds like Lieberhart. It always appears to be him if you transmit from here.'

He paused. 'I hope they'll listen.' He turned to Rafa. 'Remember, they have been betrayed. They must follow Huascar.'

'What happens if they release the gas anyway?' Allie was distraught.

Yupanqui was pulling out drawers and opening cupboards, clearly looking for something. His voice was grim.

'The Chamber is mined. It was to protect the Punchao.' He was spinning his wristcom to a series of numbers. 'The explosive is set in the Chamber roof, just below this room. It's actually quite thin. If the worst comes to the worst I can detonate the explosive and it will collapse the roof of the chamber completely. I told Tupac that he and the runner must leave immediately by a tunnel which should take them well clear of any collapse. But you two will have to leave long before then as well.'

'But you'll be in the Chamber too.'

He looked at her, his eyes blank for a moment, and then shook himself. 'Better to be killed by the rock than the gas. But we must hope that it doesn't come to that.'

To Rafa he said, 'You know what you must say. That you've found out that we've been betrayed. That the poison will kill them. That the army is outside so they must follow Huascar.'

The stress showed in the lines of his face. He'd found what he was looking for, a small remote. 'Rafa, brother, look after Allee and Paquito for me. It will take me maybe twenty minutes. There are helicopters on the rim. I thought they were ours but it appears they belong to the government. Make sure you get them there by then. If you take the service shaft further up it might be quicker.'

It looked as if Rafa also would protest but Yupanqui stopped him with a flow of Quechua. Rafa was frowning, protesting, but was silenced by the urgency in Yupanqui's voice.

'Please, Rafa, be careful. Don't let the soldiers get the children.'

'Anything, my lord.'

Yupanqui looked as if he would have said more but then, clearly conscious of the time passing, said rapidly, 'When you see me in the chamber you must go immediately.'

Rafa embraced him quickly and slid into the seat at the console, lifting the headset. 'We will do our best.' He looked up. 'Go with God, my Lord.'

'Thank you, Rafa. You too. Allee, follow me.'

In seconds they were out in the corridor. A few yards along Yupanqui halted in front of what looked like a cupboard door.

'It will take too long to get from here to the Chamber by the tunnels. From above it's much quicker.' They were in a small room, really little more than a cupboard. Yupanqui was hauling aside some old sacking which camouflaged a hole in the floor. As she peered fearfully in, looking into a tunnel of darkness, he swung round and began to fasten the rope to a stanchion on the wall.

He grinned at her. 'Another little route that Huascar and I found. A rock chute!' He tugged on the rope to make sure the knot would hold.

The hole didn't look big enough for a grown man to get through. They'd been children.'

'You'll get stuck.'

'No. It opens out a lot lower down. But there's a gap that I must cross halfway, a break in the chute. I'll need you to hold the rope for me while I get from one side to the other.' He was throwing the rope into the hole, feeding it down feverishly. 'And then I'll need you to throw me down the rope for the next section.'

Allie peered over the edge and saw only the blackness. And then she could hear the voices, echoing up from the chamber, the shouting and stamping of the

Indians rising above the noise of the river, the chanting as they rehearsed their coming victory. She could imagine the sconces flaring, the gold and silver statues beside the great Punchao, the boiling water flecked with madness.

He was searching for something desperately on a shelf above the stanchion.

'What do you need?'

'The chute lock.'

He'd found a small, metal object, little more than a two-pronged nail, which he thrust into her hand, pointing at a large block of stone on a nearby ledge. A smaller stone was set to the right below it in the wall. 'When I've gone push the key into those two small holes in the lower stone. The big stone above is finely balanced and will slide into place, into the chute, and seal it. It was intended as a protection from any enemy but it will keep the gas out of the corridor for a little while.'

He paid out the rope. 'I think the government will try to take the children so I told Rafa to say that Esteban and Paquito are his, that Rosalita is his wife. As a family group they're more likely to be believed. The minute they're away from the army they should disappear. He says he has an uncle in the mountains where they can hide.'

The strain showed on his face at the thought of his small son but he carried on paying out the rope. 'Once I'm across the break in the chute I want you to send me the rope down for the last bit. One tug means hang on. Two tugs means let it go.'

He looked up at her from where he knelt beside the hole, the blue eyes intent. 'The minute you throw me the rope you must close the chute. That will stop any gas escaping if there is any. Then go straight to Rafa, collect Rosalita and get out of this place. You must be nowhere near here if they release it.'

'But what about you? You don't need to do this. The mothers and children are out. How do you know the chute's not blocked at the bottom? You'll be stuck down there.'

He was at the edge of the chute, preparing to lower himself in.

'Your brothers chose this way.' She was desperate, grabbing his arm. 'Yupanqui you must not.'

He turned to her and she saw the rueful look in his eyes. 'Eh, Allee, you came into my life too late – but anyway –' he raised his head, 'I must try. I'll need your help but then you must release the stone and go.' The blue eyes burned. 'Fast.'

She turned to the stone she would have to unlock.

When she looked back Yupanqui had dropped into the chute.

Chapter 21
Destruction

A voice boomed up from the chute. Lieberhart's voice.

'Listen, my children, my brothers. Listen. We have been betrayed.'

Her throat was dry and her eyes prickled.

Down in the Chamber where the crowd stamped and chanted there was sudden confusion.

'We have been betrayed. The army is here. I, Doctor Lieberhart, am warning you!'

Most appeared to have stopped moving. Voices yelled back and forth in the Chamber. Were they listening?

Now the voice echoed around the Chamber again. 'My people you must flee. Your father who loves you tells you.'

She heard the screech, 'It's a lie. It's a lie,' and knew it was the Condor.

Looking down she could only see the top of Yupanqui's head, wishing that she had her wristcom and its light. He had turned his on and the rough flinty wall of the chute showed in odd flashes as he slid swiftly down the rope, the light catching the hint of gold from his tunic. Soon she could no longer see his head. And then he was swinging wildly on the rope, banging against the walls. Allie felt it burn though her fingers as she desperately tried to halt its crazy twisting, bracing it when she could with her feet as well. A flash of movement as he swung into her line of vision and then cannoned back into the darkness.

A sudden jolt.

She peered over the edge. He was now visible in the light of his wristcom but looked tiny he was so far down. The chute must have opened out and she could see one side of it quite plainly across a crevasse, a huge crack in the chute floor.

Yupanqui had landed on the edge of the fissure. He teetered a moment and then regained his balance, hanging on to the rope. Allie drew in her breath. The continuation of the chute on the other side of the crevasse was just a hole in the rock wall, an abyss of darkness.

He had to get across the crack. Into a chute at almost right-angles to the level he was on.

She hung on grimly to the rope as Yupanqui swung himself back and forth. In the light from his wristcom the walls showed jagged and rough and she could see the bloodied arm where he'd bounced off the rock. Twice he got almost to the edge of the chute but failed to make contact. And then the rope went slack. He was hanging on to the lower edge of the shaft, legs dangling into the void. For one heart-stopping moment he had to struggle one handed above the crevasse as he tried to hang on to the rope. Then he was heaving himself up into the dark hole.

Two tugs.

Fingers shaking she struggled to undo the knots which held the rope to the stanchion. Eventually she had it and called down. 'Hang on to the rope. I'm letting it go now.' Her voice echoed down into the darkness, ringing round the rock walls.

The echo returned to her. 'Let it go, Allee.'

It slithered through her fingers burning them. Gold flashed again, the light catching his tunic as he fixed the rope to an outcrop. For just a second she saw his face as he looked up from the chute, distraught. He was yelling, 'Go! Go now, Allee. You must run.'

Then he was gone.

She spun round and with trembling fingers pushed the two-pronged key into the holes in the smaller stone. Nothing seemed to happen and, beginning to panic, she pushed again. A loud grinding noise echoed round the tiny room and the large block of stone above began to move. For one hair-raising moment it teetered on the edge, unstable, grit trickling from one corner. She was going to be crushed. Leaping back she heard the loud grating of stone on stone, as the huge block toppled forward with a final crunch into the chute, cutting off any sound from below, sealing the shaft.

She didn't even know if Yupanqui had made it down safely or not. He could be imprisoned in the chute forever. As the stone rocked into its final resting place she turned on her heel and raced for the control room. Bursting in the door she had eyes only for the monitor. People in the Chamber were looking round. Looking at the dais. Swivelling round, trying to see where the voice had come from, clearly wondering if what it said was true.

The box with the poison gas was still there. The Priest was looking at the Condor.

'It's a trick!' she shouted. 'A trick. They are trying to prevent our attack. That's not Lieberhart. It's an impostor.'

Hoist on your own petard, thought Allie grimly.

Rafa bent to the headset again and again Lieberhart's voice boomed around the cavern.

'You must leave. A traitor has changed the gas. It will not dissolve in the water but in the air. It will poison everyone in the Chamber. The army is outside. Yupanqui and Huascar will show you the safe way out. My children you must flee.'

The warriors and the animal headed leaders were in total confusion. She could no longer see what was happening. Someone called out and one of the six turned.

'Huascar!'

The voice coming over the sound system in the booth was Yupanqui's. Tall as he was she could see him plainly as he fought his way through the bewildered and frightened groups of people, limping up onto the platform, blood dripping from the damaged arm, one leg dragging. Seeing him on the dais the milling crowd swirled. He was speaking directly to one of the warriors who had turned.

'I've seen the army, Huascar. They are here. We must go.'

Huascar had stiffened at Lieberhart's voice but when he saw his brother his body seemed to relax. 'Yupanqui!'

'You know the escape tunnel. You know how to get them out.'

Huascar was answering in a flood of Quechua but was interrupted.

'You lie!' One of the brothers had stepped forward, gesturing wildly and there was a temporary silence, broken by a rush of angry speech.

'Atahualpa!', said Rafa. He's asking what Yupanqui's up to. He says he's trying to sabotage the action. That he's a coward. A traitor.'

Atahualpa's face was contorted with hatred. He was yelling at the crowd. 'That is not Lieberhart.'

Yupanqui ignored him. 'We must get them out, Huascar.'

Huascar hesitated, looking at Atahualpa. The members of the elite on the platform were in as much confusion as the people below, turning from one to the other amongst themselves, clearly in a panic. Rumiñaui was hauling himself onto the dais and the Condor was throwing herself across the platform towards the box but was restrained by one of the Seven.

Yupanqui turned back to the group. 'My brothers, look at me! I have seen the army. We must leave.'

Huascar and the others stood for one long moment looking at Yupanqui and then they turned as one.

Was it some form of mental telepathy? Could they see in the mind's eye what Yupanqui had seen?

Only Atahualpa did not turn, his body rigid with hatred and anger. 'He's a weakling,' he yelled. 'A traitor. Too cowardly to fight.'

He sees his route to power draining away, Allie thought.

And then Atahualpa had grabbed the ceremonial knife from the stone table and was hurling himself across the dais towards Yupanqui, slashing towards his throat. Huascar was between them, blocking the blow, a thin red line pearling on the skin of his forearm, and then the blood spreading and running over his hand. Two of the other brothers got hold of Atahualpa and held him but he wrestled frantically, freeing himself, leaping back, swinging the knife before him. The others formed a cordon around Yupanqui and Atahualpa, eyes rolling, his face almost inhuman with rage, screamed 'You lie, you lie!' He turned to the left and right – but none of the brothers nor the *LIBJU* elite attempted to support him and in a sudden violent gesture he drew the knife across his own throat.

Aghast Allie saw the blood spurting, Atahualpa stagger and fall and Yupanqui leap forward to catch him. Dropping to his knees Yupanqui folded him in his arms, lowering him to the floor while the others tried unsuccessfully to staunch the flow. Yupanqui groaned.

He is saying, 'My brother, my brother,' said Rafa. The body sagged, the huge pool of red spreading. Yupanqui lowered his head.

The crowd below watched in horrified silence.

Huascar touched Yupanqui on the shoulder and said something and Yupanqui settled the body carefully on the floor, closing the eyes, and then rose slowly, swinging round to look at the upturned, puzzled faces below him.

He raised his head and stood, his voice echoing round the chamber, carried by the superb acoustics of the cave, Rafa translating.

'My people, my brother was overwrought and distressed for you. Later we will have time to grieve for him, but what I said was true. I have seen the army. They wait outside. They have taken our children – do you see them here? We must leave now but know that we will fight another day as Atahualpa would have wished. Follow Huascar now.'

His voice rose, magnificent, calling the people to follow him, promising to lead them to safety. He was a commander before his troops, resplendent in the warrior robes splashed with his brother's blood, inspiring, a leader like no other.

'He says they must leave now so that they may live; that they have been misled but they can regroup.' Rafa was translating as fast as he could. 'Today is not

339

the time to fight but they are strong and valiant and tomorrow they will succeed.'

Huascar was shouting something at the crowd below. He leapt from the platform and ran towards the great Punchao, hitting the wall at its side. Once, twice, three times. A grinding sound and a rock door swung forward into a narrow tunnel beyond. The others called instructions and the crowd began to separate into groups.

Yupanqui said, 'Quickly, quickly! Follow your lords. You know them.'

Topa, Viracocha and the others were marshalling their people into what was clearly a prearranged order while Yupanqui wrenched something from its case on the wall behind the group of leaders. A flare gun. He looked down at Huascar, tossing it to him.

'Get them out, Huascar, then close off the tunnel.'

The scene erupted into chaos as people closest to the corridor began to swarm into it – the warriors shouting instructions to them as Yupanqui spoke urgently to Huascar.

Rafa translated. 'Tupac and the runner have gone to Tunnel 88. They will bring all the people they find with them but Tunnel 88 comes out in the next valley a long way from this exit. Huascar must use the flare once they've got the people from the Chamber out. Then the others will know that they've escaped and where to find them.'

The Condor was screeching above him. 'He is lying. He is weak. He cannot face a war. We will win.'

Nobody was listening to her as the people rallied together. They must have been organised under one or other of the brothers in preparation for the coming war and as the brothers called to their groups they began to stream out of the Chamber in order.

Yupanqui was saying, 'Women and children first.'

The Condor was still screeching, 'I always knew you were a weakling. You have betrayed your father.'

In amongst the faces of those crowding towards the exit Allie saw Asiri and Cusi heading into the escape corridor along with others from the mine.

The Puma was at one of the niches, grabbing one of the golden figures, but as he turned found his way blocked by Topa who felled him with one blow.

'Women and children first,' Yupanqui yelled.

Rumiñaui, was shouting something, his face contorted with rage, and on the monitor they could see the man turn. He was running across the dais and grabbing the box. The brothers who were marshalling their people towards the exit tunnel were too far away to stop him.

Yupanqui turned as Huascar shouted a warning.

Rumiñaui had the box and it was clear that it was taking all of his immense strength to lift and carry it. But he had it in his arms, treading heavily down the steps of the dais, staggering towards the water. The Condor was shouting something in Quechua as, with the box clasped to his chest, Rumiñaui ploughed through the crowd that fell back before him.

Rafa, as mesmerised as Allie, watched as Stony Eye headed for the Granverde. The Condor's voice rose again.

'Now let them see,' she is saying. 'This will show them. We will triumph.'

Yupanqui had turned at Huascar's shout and was heading for Rumiñaui but he was hampered by the damaged leg.

Rumiñaui stumbled, almost fell, and then lurched forward again, hurling the box with all his force towards the Granverde. Despite his great strength he was not quite strong enough and the box sailed through the air and landed just short of the river. There was an ominous crack as it broke.

Allie couldn't move, was transfixed, as she saw Yupanqui run and pick up the broken box and carry it the last few metres to the river, throw it into one of the deeper basins at the edge and then watch as it sank just below the surface. He turned back to his people.

'Oh no,' said Rafa. 'The powder is spilled. The gas is out. We must go.'

Half of the people in the chamber were clustered at the entrance to the escape tunnel.

'Quickly! We must go'.

She dragged her eyes unwillingly from the screen. Her last sight of Yupanqui was of him picking a small child from the floor and handing him to his mother and then she began to run, following Rafa, hot salt blinding her eyes.

'Why did he pick the box up?'

'Maybe he think the water will hold the gas down.' They were leaping down the stairs they had climbed just a short time before, taking two or three at a time. 'Only tiny bit come out. Most still in the box. It cannot mix with the air underwater, so it might stop it. Box will stay in the rock pool, not go down the river.'

They were at the bottom of the stone stairs and there were Rosalita and her baby, waiting patiently with Paquito.

Rafa hardly broke stride, picking up Paquito and racing on down the corridor. They followed him, Rosalita with Esteban clasped to her, running surprisingly quickly. They soon reached the point where they had been before, still heading upwards.

A low rumble came from far behind them, and puffs of dust blew past. The military must have set explosives in the walls of the escape shaft, hoping no doubt to block off the creeping gas.

Clasping Paquito to him Rafa ran with greater urgency as they came to a narrower section. They were ahead of Allie as she ran forward, shale skittering away under her feet, when the ankle which had betrayed her on the bridge turned agonisingly on a stone and she was forced to stop.

Rafa came back to her. 'We wait, we go with you.' He stood Paquito down and held out his hand. 'I help.'

She tried her weight on the ankle and achieved only a hobble.

'No. You must go on, Rafa. Look after Rosalita. I can't go as quickly as you but there's still time.'

'No we wait.'

'No, no.' Her heart began to pound. They would die because of her. 'You must go on.' She looked wildly at Rafa. 'Save Rosalita, Rafa. The baby. Paquito. Yupanqui expects it.'

His face agonised, Rafa hesitated and as he did so one of the explosives detonated just to one side of them, releasing some fault in the rock which split beneath Allie's feet. Chunks of granite split away from the wall with a grinding roar and the cavern ahead of her disappeared in clouds of dust, a boiling cloud of air she couldn't breathe. She couldn't see the end of tunnel, only the crack which had opened in the floor at her feet, and Rafa, Rosalita and Paquito on the other side. Amazingly she was unharmed apart from a bruise on her shoulder where a piece of rock had caught it.

She waved.

'Go on, go on. I will find the service shaft. Yupanqui said it would be quicker.'

They hesitated again, Rafa's distress clear on his face, and she gestured violently. 'Go on! Keep moving! I'll join you.'

Rafa said something to Rosalita and the little group slowly turned, gradually speeding up as they hurried up the main shaft. Allie hid herself back against the cavern wall, as small pieces of rock and gravel trickled down, waiting for the rock to settle, feeling the uneasy earth moving beneath her feet.

She stumbled back as quickly as she could, looking for the service shaft.

Thinking she must have missed it her heart beat faster as she thought of the time running out. Twenty minutes from the release of the gas. But then, there it was, only a narrow corridor but heading in the right direction. She limped upwards as quickly as she could, trying to ignore the pain in her shoulder and ankle. Even with the blocking of the corridors the gas would eventually seep up towards her. She must hurry.

As she stumbled on, tears blinding her route, she was tormented by the thought that this suffering was all her fault. When she'd had the chance to warn those in the Chamber she'd failed. She'd been too frightened, too cowardly, too scared of the garrotte to shout out at the right time – and so she'd failed.

Banging her damaged arm on the rock wall as she limped onward her sense of misery increased. She'd interfered as she'd been warned not to. She'd just rushed in without thinking it through, finding out all the facts, discovering who the real leaders of the rebellion were. Perhaps if she'd made sure the briefcase had got back to the Ministry none of this would have happened. She'd taken sides, only she hadn't really known what the sides were. She'd believed the rebels to be in the right, but their leaders had been more interested in power for themselves than in protecting the people following them, the Condor poisoned with resentment at being passed over, interested only in her own advancement rather than the good of the ordinary people. Amongst the gods only Yupanqui had cared. Freedom and Justice were weasel words. She had indeed, as he'd said, been naïve.

Another explosion sounded behind her and she was galvanised into movement, limping ever more painfully onward. Was that the military's explosive or was it Yupanqui collapsing the roof?

She thought of the great Punchao chamber, the golden animals and flowers, the statues in their niches, all buried. The Punchao itself. All that artistry gone. Dr Chavez's research, the work of a lifetime, gone too. Had Yupanqui or any of his brothers got out, the gods?

He'd thrown the box into the water so that the powder wouldn't be able to react with the air. But he'd touched it himself. He was doomed. Her tears ran faster as she stumbled on. As she did so she heard, from far back in the tunnel, a faint noise, at first a thin unearthly wailing, the keening sounds gradually rising in pitch to something inhuman, as an underground pipe system linking the tunnels carried the sounds of agony upwards.

Her muscles tensed and she stopped dead. The poison was working. Not all had got out.

And then the knowledge struck her as a blow. The pipes would be carrying, not only the sound, but the gas itself. In terror she began to run, ignoring the searing pain in her damaged shoulder, in the ankle. At first it was little more than a hobble but soon her muscles took over, momentum carrying her onward, fending off the rough walls as she cannoned from side to side, breathing in great gasps, lurching, stumbling but driving onward. The gas was coming. She had to keep moving.

She could still hear the thin, eerie keening but then, obliterating it, a huge rumble as the ground began to buckle under her flying feet.

Stick tried the moby one last time, going as close to the crater's edge as he could.

'Don't get any closer or you'll be shot,' said the young soldier with them.

The bursts of gunfire below and crump of mortar shells appeared to be slackening and only a few final stragglers were making it over the rim, but Allie was not amongst them. Stick tasted bile in his throat, feeling the terror rise. The government didn't care how many died. They'd known about the plot all along. They'd just used Chavez and the other conspirators to do their dirty work and now they no longer needed them. They had the children.

'Please,' Stick prayed, 'Please let me not be too late. Please let her get out.'

He was full of raging self-contempt.

How stupid he'd been. How selfish. It was as if he'd just wanted to own her to satisfy his own insecurity. All the missed opportunities he'd had to let her know how much she meant to him, his pride not allowing him to say it.

If only she was all right.

A flare roared into the sky on the other side of the mountain, beyond the far edge of the crater, its violent orange flame penetrating even the smoke and dust-filled air. The ground suddenly heaved and rocked under his feet and the sergeant turned alarmed to his post.

Somebody screamed, 'Get those kids to the helicopters. This whole thing's gonna blow.'

Alaina said, 'Jeez, they're destroying the ziggurat.' But she was talking to thin air.

As the stones and earth beneath her feet moved and more dust began to rise she knew that Stick was heading down into the crater.

Running for the helicopter and Sergeant Willis, Alaina was praying.

'Come on, come on,' she said. 'Whoever's up there, hear me. I need some favours.' The elegant face was wet with tears. 'Allie is down there.'

Allie knew that the time had run out but drove on anyway, breath coming in short gasps, suddenly feeling the thin, cold air of the crater. She was almost there. She couldn't allow herself to think about what was happening in the chamber. Perhaps Rafa could get one of the helicopters to wait for her. She threw herself forward, ignoring the pain, eyes fixed on the end of the cleft showing the flare of searchlights on the distant escarpment.

She saw through the dust and smoke the helicopters on the rim, several in the process of taking off, and just on the brow of the hill, staggering some distance behind a file of carers and children, Rosalita, with the baby clasped to her and Rafa, with the little bag of clothes, holding Paquito's hand. At least they would be saved. Her efforts had not been entirely in vain.

Then, flying down the slope, alternately leaping and sliding on the shale, a tall thin angular creature, red hair turned dark by the moonlight, careering down the mountainside in huge bounding jumps, taking no account of the perilous terrain, plunging towards the cavern's mouth. She did not see his distraught face as he hurtled down the crater wall, jacket flying, skidding down rocky inclines, with the scree sliding away from under his feet, registering only the hectic impetus of his flight. Her heart leapt even though she knew, her reason told her, that it couldn't be Stick. That he was on the other side of the world.

She hurled herself forward through the rubble and dust, the ground rocking under her feet, further ominous rumbles and cracking noises behind her, no longer aware of the excruciating pain in her ankle and arm. She was heading out of the cavern, paying no heed to the beat of helicopter blades above her, her eyes riveted on the tall gangly figure leaping down the slope.

It was Stick, how or why she couldn't tell, couldn't begin to imagine, but it was him. He was waving wildly, pointing to the helicopter above her, his jacket swinging open to reveal a patch of blue shirt just about where the heart should be.

Straight as a laser line she sped to the small patch of blue.

If you have enjoyed *The Green Enclave* and *Keepers of the Sun* why not try the third book in the Runa series
ENCELADEAN

Due to be published in 2024

ENCELADEAN

Chapter 1

The director walked round the top gallery accompanied by the rather pretty holiday job student. They looked down on the labs below. Not that there was much to see as most of the lab technicians had gone home. Only one remained, fetching the various pieces of equipment to Lab Five and setting up for his final test of the day.

'That's Jerome,' said the director. 'He's a good man is Jerome. He's meticulous in his alignments and measurements. You never have to worry that things can go wrong or that life will be endangered with him. He's much too cautious an old bird for that.'

Not that you could actually see Jerome, dressed in his hazmat suit and helmet, the standard protective gear for this particular job. He had a large glass box on the bench and inside through a porthole on the side he was arranging a variety of flasks, clearly labelled, in the flask-holders which kept them stable.

The director smiled at the student to show that he meant no disrespect to Jerome. 'He'll be sadly missed when he retires at the end of this year. He's what we call a safe pair of hands.'

'So this is the final test is it?' said the student. 'It must be quite exciting testing for Enceladean life forms.'

The director grinned. 'Well, it would be if there were any. I think I can say now without too much fear of contradiction that there are none. Originally, when they found these complex carbon-based molecules in the waters under the ice on Enceladus they thought a strong chance existed that it had been capable of supporting life in the past. Compounds like this have only previously been found on earth.'

'And in some meteorites?'

'True, but where those compounds come from we have no idea.'

The student, he decided, was really very pretty. And bright too. She'd come warmly recommended by her college. Her name was Allie, if he remembered right.

'They think that the molecules on Enceladus were formed by reactions between the water and the warm rock at the bottom of its subsurface ocean.'

'So would that mean that there had been life at one time?'

'Well, though they're not life in themselves their presence suggested that Enceladus *could* have hosted living organisms once. But alas, as with Mars, no genuine lifeforms have been found. Only the simpler forms of amino acid usually associated with life. This final test will probably confirm that.'

He pulled a face. 'At least we'll be able to report that every avenue has been explored, every stone upturned, so to speak, but really there's nothing.' He looked rueful. 'Rather disappointing. After all the trouble they went to to get it.'

Jerome disappeared into the back store and returned pushing the large, refrigerated unit in which the Enceladean ice was stored.

'Get Freddy to do that,' the director called down.

Jerome looked up and made a face but rubbed his arm and yelled for Freddy.

'There should always be two on the floor anyway if there's the remotest risk of contamination.'

Jerome said something to someone out of their sight and a young man, also dressed in protective gear, appeared on the floor and began to push the refrigerated unit to Lab Five. Jerome meanwhile was writing something on a slate and fixing it to the side of the glass box. Once Freddy had got the unit to within a few inches of the box on the bench Jerome inserted his hands into the heavy-duty gloves let into the wall of the unit and began to align the clamp over the flask holding the ice. When he was satisfied that all was stable and the clamp held the flask securely he nodded at Freddy who pushed the unit forward the last few inches to the glass encased section in front of them and began to line up the two portholes. Jerome moved him aside and double checked that the fit was perfect, then slid in the bar which sealed the two together and prepared to drop the second one to ensure the vacuum lock.

Freddy stood back and Jerome went to the console, ready to press the button which would send the clamp with its flask on its way. Instead he just stood there, waiting for a second, still rubbing his upper arm, the second bar ready on the ledge next to him.

'I told him to get Freddy to do the heavy work. That's what he's there for.'

It happened so suddenly that neither the student nor the director had the chance to see what was going on. Jerome must have somehow pressed the button, as the flask began to move on its way into the glass case. But Jerome was clutching his chest and stumbling forward against the case, grabbing vainly at the bar to hold himself upright. And then he was crashing to the floor with the bar in his hand, the portholes swung apart and the flask, halfway through, smashed against one side of the glass cabinet.

'Oh my God!'

The director began to sprint for the lift. An alarm sounded. He looked back towards the student running after him and screamed, 'Stay there! Don't move!' and banged the button for the lift to the labs.

The student, peering over the balcony at the glass roof below saw Freddy on his knees next to Jerome, frantically performing CPR on his chest.

The director appeared out of the lifts and ran towards Lab Five but the door did not respond to his entry card. Automatic lock-down had already started.

He was banging on the glass and yelling at Freddy but the young man ignored him and continued working on Jerome, tearing off Jerome's protective headgear as well as his own and trying mouth-to-mouth resuscitation.

The director was on his wristcom and then hammering on the glass again. Bells seemed to be shrilling all over the building as Freddy looked up, his face ecstatic. Jerome twitched and Freddy folded him into his arms.

The student saw on the huge display screen on the opposite side of the gallery

QUARANTINE SITUATION LAB FIVE.

Acknowledgments

My thanks first of all to Nancy Pugh in Chile who has been extraordinarily patient in reading various drafts, suggesting changes and correcting my Spanish.

Amongst all those others who helped improve this book my thanks also go to:

Nicola Mostyn *The Love Delusion*
Cressida Downing, *The Book Analyst*
Bev Allen, *The Solemn Curfew and Other Tales*
Harry Bingham, Polly and all at Jericho Writers, who dealt with my anguished questions,
Jim Sheasby who helped with the first chapter
The Happy Scribblers Writing Group , in particular Sally Hart (*Out of her Mind*) and Roger Webster (Vikings) for being greatly encouraging and a Source of helpful suggestions
Nisal Wijesinghe – a beta reader *par excellence*
My long-suffering extended family, including Jon, Mike, Dominic, Pam and Michelle who ploughed through all the various drafts and made any number of sage suggestions

And last but not least much loved friend Rachel Yates who has been an unfailingly encouraging beta reader, copyeditor and advisor.